THE DEADLANDS
HUNTED

THE DEADLANDS
HUNTED

SKYE MELKI-WEGNER

SCHOLASTIC INC.

ISBN 978-1-339-03310-5

12 11 10 9 8 7 6 5 4 3 2 1   23 24 25 26 27 28

Printed in the U.S.A.   40

First Scholastic printing, September 2023

Book design by Michelle Gengaro-Kokmen

To Jason
who supported this story
from my earliest babbling about ankylosaur battles
all the way to publication

DINOSAURS OF CRETACEA

THE MOUNTAIN KINGDOM

Iguanodon
Name in the Old Stories: Spikegrip
Notable Territory: The King's Domain, the Tumbling Stream

Iguanodons are large herbivores. They possess spiked thumbs to wield in combat and to strip foliage from trees.

Oryctodromeus
Name in the Old Stories: Earthsinger
Notable Territory: The Broken Ridge, the Twilight Vale

Oryctodromeus are small, speedy herbivores that dig underground burrows. In the Cretacean war, they serve as soldiers, trench diggers, and crafters.

Stegoceras
Name in the Old Stories: Ridgebone
Notable Territory: The Sunless Meadow, the Flowering Crest

Stegoceras are relatively small herbivores that use their domed heads to ram their enemies in combat. They fight in large squadrons, overwhelming mightier foes by sheer force of numbers.

THE PRAIRIE ALLIANCE

Ankylosaur
Name in the Old Stories: Bristler
Notable Territory: The Fern Lea, the Scrub Plains
Ankylosaurs are large herbivores with armored bone-plates protruding from their backs. They use their vicious clubbed tails to strike down enemies.

Triceratops
Name in the Old Stories: Moonchaser
Notable Territory: The Lowland Marsh, the Graystone Dale
Triceratops are large herbivores with a distinctive trio of horns on their faces. They use their great size and strength to engage in battle.

NEUTRAL SPECIES

Anurognathid
Name in the Old Stories: Windwhisper
Notable Territory: Lightning Peak
Anurognathids are tiny bird-sized pterosaurs that

consume a mixture of plants and insects. They take no side in the war, preferring to serve their own interests as crafters or mercenary spies.

Sauropod
Name in the Old Stories: Starsweeper
Notable Territory: The Cold Canyon

Sauropods are the largest dinosaurs alive, with extremely long necks and tails. They belong to no kingdom, but travel along the Cold Canyon collecting myths and stories.

CARNIVORES OF THE DEADLANDS

Carnotaurus
Name in the Old Stories: Thorneyes

Carnotaurus resemble tyrannosaurs at a glance, although they are stockier and sprout horns above their eyes.

Pterosaur
Name in the Old Stories: Skyprowler

Pterosaurs are massive winged predators. They soar above Cretacea and swoop down to pluck their prey from the earth below.

Raptor
Name in the Old Stories: Nightslicer

Raptors are small, vicious carnivores that roam the Deadlands in search of prey. To compensate for their stature, raptors tend to hunt in packs.

Tyrannosaur

Name in the Old Stories: Coldclaw

Tyrannosaurs are the largest carnivores in the Deadlands. They use their massive jaws and fearsome bite strength to tear apart their prey.

CHAPTER ONE

THE STARSWEEPERS

Nightfall leaked into the warren, cold and gray. Eleri tensed in the gloom, his long tail curled around his body. Lichen crinkled as other dinosaurs nestled into neighboring burrows. How long would it take his herd to fall asleep?

As Eleri drew a sharp breath, nerves tingled from his gray face to his speckled legs. His feathers prickled down his spine. His herd lived in the complex web of tunnels they'd dug, sheltered from enemy troops—and wild carnivores. But right now, the last place Eleri wanted to be stuck was underground. He had plans for tonight.

Be still. Be silent.

Eleri repeated the mantra in his head, counting the minutes.

Around the corner, his father gave a muffled snort. A snore, or was that just wishful thinking?

If Eleri couldn't sneak out tonight, he wouldn't get another chance. His homeland, the Mountain Kingdom, was at war with the Prairie Alliance. The enemy's triceratops army was on the march—and there were rumors of an ankylosaur siege at the edge of the kingdom. Whenever the war flared up, young oryctodromeus like Eleri were confined to the warren, all the entrances guarded. If he didn't go tonight, it would be too late.

Now or never.

Eleri rose, muscles clenching as he struggled not to crunch his lichen nest. He tiptoed on his hind legs, balanced by his sweeping tail. His claws were tools for digging tunnels . . . or tonight, for sneaking out of them.

He crept forward, throat tight as he passed each sleeping nook. His herdmates curled in their nests, feathers rustling as they dreamed. A carved stone marked the Heir's Cavern, where his brother Agostron slept. Agostron was the perfect soldier: strong, sensible, and fiercely patriotic to the Mountain Kingdom.

Beside him, Eleri was . . . nothing.

A disappointment.

That was the word his father had used. He'd spoken it in hushed whispers, when he thought that Eleri was out of earshot. *Nothing like his brother, I'm afraid. A disappointment, that one . . .*

Eleri's throat clenched. He didn't care. He didn't need approval. Who cared about the Wise Ones, anyway? All they did was dig holes, obsessing about tunnel width and burrow depth. Eleri had other plans for his life. One day he would journey beyond the warren. He would explore faraway lands, collecting the tales of their herds. He would venture where the clouds swelled and ebbed, teasing him toward the horizon . . .

Where the sky wasn't dirt, but starlight.

Outside, the air was tangy: a stark contrast to the cool damp of the warren. The breeze bristled, sharp with grit. Ash storms were rare nowadays, fifty years after the Fallen Star had struck, but they did sometimes occur.

Just dirt, Eleri told himself. The Deadlands weren't burning tonight, and the distant Fire Peak wasn't ablaze.

His family's warren lay deep within the Mountain Kingdom. Even if the Prairie Alliance sent a scouting party, it would be easy to hear a gang of ankylosaurs or triceratops smashing through the undergrowth. Horn heads weren't exactly known for their subtlety.

Instead, he feared the carnivores.

The carnivores held no allegiances. They belonged to no kingdoms or armies. They lived alone—and they killed alone. Like the pterosaur that had snatched Eleri's mother, plucking her from the Broken Ridge when Eleri and Agostron were still in their eggshells. And so Eleri crept in silence, his claws scrabbling in time with the patter of his heart.

Crunch.

Eleri froze. He whipped around, scanning the undergrowth for signs of movement. *Crunch.* There it was again: a clawstep in the dark . . .

If a raptor lunged from the brush, Eleri wouldn't stand a chance. Carnivores didn't care that he was a sworn citizen of the Mountain Kingdom. To them, he was just a snack—a trifle to crush between their teeth.

He couldn't move.

He couldn't breathe . . .

"Eleri?" a voice whispered.

Relief roiled through him, wild and giddy. Then came exasperation as the speaker prowled into a patch of moonlight and Eleri recognized his brother. Agostron clutched a precious starfleck in his claw, using its crystalline shine to cast a path between the trees.

Eleri forced a cool smirk, concealing his moment of panic. "Good evening, Brother Dearest. Nice night for a stroll."

"You're a fool!" Agostron hissed, scurrying forward. He loomed above Eleri, making the most of his height and heft. "Do you have any idea how much trouble you're in?"

"Only if you tattle on me."

"Flaming feathers!" Agostron swore.

"Watch it, Princeling." Eleri threw him a grin. "The Wise Ones don't approve of cursing. What would they say if they heard their future leader using such language?"

4

Agostron's tail gave an unhappy flick. "You've got to come back— it's too dangerous to be out at night."

Eleri stood his ground. "I can't miss tonight, you know that! It'll be a whole year before they're back again."

Agostron groaned. "By the stars, you've got less brains than a stegoceras. I should've known this'd be about *them* . . ."

"Hey, I've known some perfectly nice stegoceras."

"That's not the point!"

Eleri turned from his brother, resuming his trek through the undergrowth. "You're welcome to tag along, if you like."

"Tag along?" Agostron hurried after him. "I'm not going to 'tag along,' Eleri. I'm going to fulfill my duties as heir. The safety of this herd is my responsibility."

Was Eleri imagining it, or was there a cold undercurrent in Agostron's tone? His voice stiffened on the word "heir"—as if to remind Eleri of his superior rank.

"I'm your brother," Eleri pointed out. "Not just a herd member."

"I won't show favor to relatives."

"You keep telling yourself that, but we all know the truth. Deep down, you want to see the show too."

"Your skull is overstuffed with daydreams," Agostron snapped. "It's time to take your responsibilities seriously."

"I do," Eleri said. "Doesn't mean I can't take my daydreams seriously too."

Agostron gave an irritable huff.

As the brothers padded toward the Broken Ridge, the

breeze grew stronger. It blew from the Deadlands—and even now, it carried the reek of decay.

Fifty years ago, the Fallen Star had brought death and despair, ash and toxic rain. Thousands of dinosaurs had died on impact. Millions had starved as forests withered and seas boiled. A strange mist had encircled the world, staining its victims with starlight.

But some survived. A few rare herds dwelled in sheltered ravines or found hidden canyons where the forests still grew.

When the dust settled, the true impact of the Fallen Star had emerged. Although the starmist had faded, the surviving dinosaurs had . . . *changed*. Their minds grew alert, rich with songs and thoughts and language. They learned to speak. To dream. To share their stories. To trade resources and form alliances.

To wage war.

Agostron was a born warrior, intensely loyal to his herd and kingdom. But from the day he'd hatched, Eleri had been weaker than his peers. As the runt of the herd, he barely reached his brother's shoulders.

Eleri was no warrior. He dreamed of becoming a storyteller—of traveling the world and collecting legends of distant lands. Of bringing those stories back to the Mountain Kingdom. He would share breathtaking tales of trickery and bravery, cleverness and heroism, while his herdmates listened in awe . . .

But in wartime, such dreams cracked like eggshells.

Eleri was doomed to be a digger: a disposable soldier who scrabbled at the dirt to aid the war effort. Unless he ran away, he would spend his life gouging trenches on the battlefield, his hopes and feathers stained with mud.

Just a *disappointment*.

But tonight, Eleri took the lead. He scurried along the Broken Ridge, which capped the peak of a narrow crag. When the trail plunged into darkness on either side, Eleri used his tail for balance. Scraggly trees rose from the edges, painting creases in the night sky.

"No need to run!" Agostron huffed, bustling after him. "And I should go first—I'm the one with the starfleck."

Eleri glanced at the light in his brother's claw. Starflecks were precious fragments of the Fallen Star. When they burned, they increased the strength and speed of their bearer. It was wasteful to burn a fleck tonight, but Agostron could afford to fritter away its power. As future Prince of the Broken Ridge, he had a steady supply from those hoping to win his favor.

Beside him, Eleri walked in shadow.

Beyond the ridge, they climbed a gravel slope. Pebbles skittered, but their claws gave them grip and leverage. One at a time, the brothers scrambled up to the Southern Lookout.

"We made it!" Eleri puffed. "Just in time for the show."

He hurried to the edge of the Lookout, eyes widening as he drank in the view. From here, the whole of Cretacea seemed his to claim. Rangy cliffs protruded beneath him, like the teeth of a long-dead carnivore.

Eleri drew a deep breath, tasting the night. This was his home. His world. The open sky, littered with stars, and the endless plains beyond. Not the damp, stuffy old warren.

"I don't like this." Agostron's voice was a growl. He clenched his claw around the starfleck, cutting off its light. "We're too exposed here. It's too open."

Eleri ignored him, focusing on the sweep of the landscape below. The Mountain Kingdom trailed down from cliffs into foothills. The kingdom was a knot of peaks and vales, home to herds of iguanodons, stegoceras, and orycto-dromeus. Far below, the Cold Canyon split the landscape in half, slithering away to the southern horizon.

West of the canyon, foothills melted into a patchwork of scrub and gorges, home to the Prairie Alliance. Out on the plains, triceratops and ankylosaurs banded together, waging war against the Mountain Kingdom in an attempt to claim its fertile land.

On the prairie, a dark mass was gathering. Eleri couldn't make out any details, but it wasn't hard to recognize the shape of a mustering army. His insides tightened. It was true, then. The Prairie Alliance planned a fresh attack. Every siege, the Alliance claimed more land. Every battle, their onslaught pushed farther.

One by one, the foothills fell into enemy claws.

But the war was reaching a tipping point. Day by day, the number of soldiers dwindled. No one admitted it aloud, but Eleri had heard the rumors. The elders spoke of it in hushed tones, whispering their worries in the dark of the warren.

Sooner or later, the war must end. One kingdom would win—and the other would lose. And when that happened, King Torive of the Prairie was determined to claim these peaks as his own.

In the silence, Eleri refocused on the canyon's east side. There, the view held something far more sinister than an army.

"The Deadlands," he whispered. "Hey, do you think—"

"The migration's starting," Agostron cut in. "Since you went to all the effort of sneaking out, I assume you'd like to actually see it?" His mouth curled. "Or has your attention span shrunk to match your height?"

Eleri whirled back, stung by the jab. Growing up, he had always liked to think of Agostron's insults as brotherly teasing—but recently, the heir's words had . . . sharpened. As if something acidic had seeped into the mockery.

Then he heard them. Footsteps. Dozens of footsteps, creaking like mountains. With a rush of anticipation, Eleri pushed Agostron's insult from his mind. He gazed into the Cold Canyon, searching for the source of the noise.

The starsweepers were coming.

Clouds shifted, spilling moonlight into the canyon. Eleri's insides flipped as light fell across their bodies: huge and heaving, their necks as tall as trees and their tails as long as rivers . . .

"It's them!" He leaned forward in excitement. "Flaming feathers, it's really them . . ."

"Now *you* watch your language," Agostron muttered.

The final herd of sauropods—the largest dinosaurs left alive—lumbered along in the night. These bards and poets traveled up and down the canyon each year, spreading tales from the farthest corners of Cretacea.

Wise and ancient, the giant sauropods didn't care for petty wars or border squabbles. They simply traveled, year after year, decade after decade. They were living, walking stories. According to legend, they had swept the stars across the skies, using their elongated necks to scatter specks of light across Cretacea.

In Eleri's wildest dreams, he made the journey with them.

"How long do you reckon they'll stay this year?" Eleri breathed.

"Not long," Agostron said. "Not with another battle brewing."

"But no one would dare attack them! They've got the favor of the stars on their side."

"Doesn't matter. They don't like violence."

Eleri nodded. His brother was right, of course. Sometimes, the sauropods stayed in the lower foothills for a few days, grazing in preparation for their journey north. But this year, they wouldn't linger. The giants would continue their migration, passing through the Mountain Kingdom into the Unknown North.

By tomorrow, they'd likely be gone.

"Well, we saw them," Agostron said dismissively. "One last time, at least. Time to head home."

Eleri threw him a sharp look. "Don't talk like that."

"Like what?"

"'One last time'—like they're about to die out or something."

Agostron shrugged. "Their herd shrinks every year. And I don't see any hatchlings, do you?"

"But—"

"You're too softhearted, Eleri. Grow up and face reality."

Eleri glared, preparing a retort. Of course, countless herds and species had died since the Fallen Star, but this was different. These were the *starsweepers*. They couldn't just . . . die. It would be like a story dying.

Before he could speak, a sharp cry stabbed the night. Eleri flinched, tossing his head skyward to spot the source of the screech.

Dark wings blotted the stars.

"Run!" Agostron screamed. "Run, Eleri!"

For a moment, Eleri stared. Then he tore after his brother, skittering down the slope in a churn of grime and gravel. Dust flew into his face, and he spluttered as his claws scrabbled for purchase.

High above, the pterosaur dove.

CHAPTER TWO

WINGS AND HORNS

Psssrhieeeek!

The pterosaur screeched, a whirlwind of claws and hunger. Agostron spun toward the Broken Ridge, but Eleri yanked him back with a cry. "Not that way, it'll just pick us off!"

"Then where . . . ?"

"Follow me!"

Oryctodromeus were fast on their feet, and Eleri was the quickest youngster in the herd. He vaulted onto a stack of boulders below and hurtled down another gravel slope.

Agostron skidded after him, cursing as talons flashed overhead. Eleri ducked, raising his foreclaws in a futile attempt to ward off the attack, but the pterosaur missed them in the darkness. It wheeled away, arcing in a tight circle, as it prepared to swoop back for a fresh assault.

Psssrhieeeeeek!

Eleri leaped behind a boulder, helpless as a hatchling. His breath rasped as Agostron thudded behind him. The pterosaur whistled above their heads—and this time, its claws raked the top of Agostron's brow. The heir screeched in pain, his voice half a sob of shock.

"Come on!" Eleri shoved him, urging him down the slope. "Those trees!"

Agostron gave a shaky nod, blood dripping into his eyes. They plunged into the undergrowth, zigging and zagging for cover. Each breath stung, hot and ragged. But the foliage was sparse—and with a sharp jolt, Eleri reached an open clearing. No, not open. Someone else had claimed this clearing. He wrenched to a halt, body stiffening as his gaze fixed in horror . . .

A trio of scouts from the Prairie Alliance.

Two grizzled ankylosaurs stood beside a young triceratops. Like all ankylosaurs, these massive beasts had bristling armored backplates—and vicious tail clubs that could kill with a blow. The lead ankylosaur wore a starfleck on his brow, marking his status as a commander.

Eleri froze, torn between fear and confusion. What were they doing here, so close to the Broken Ridge?

The scouts hadn't seen Eleri, but they'd heard the ruckus.

14

They spun, searching for the source. In the foliage behind Eleri, Agostron quavered.

Dark wings flared overhead.

Eleri's blood ran cold. In a wild flash, he pictured another pterosaur—and another victim. Although he hadn't seen it happen, he had dreamed the scene over and over. His mother screaming as talons raked her spine and a monster swept her from the Broken Ridge into the night . . .

"Run!" Eleri cried, stumbling forward. "Pterosaur!"

It took a moment for his warning to register. At first, he didn't realize that he'd shouted it. But then the young triceratops bellowed, rearing on her hind legs and snarling at the carnivore as it skimmed above her head.

Startled, the pterosaur banked away, and again, it barely missed its prey. As the Prairie soldiers roared at it, the carnivore skimmed the canopy, disappearing into darkness.

Silence.

Eleri stood, frozen and exposed. In his panic, he'd made a terrible mistake. He'd shouted a warning to save the *enemy*—and stumbled into their grasp.

Stupid. So stupid . . .

The Prairie scouts lumbered toward him, huge and menacing. The young female triceratops was double his height and at least ten times his weight. And as for the ankylosaurs . . .

Eleri was going to die. But he refused to go down without

a fight. He was faster, wasn't he? Nimbler. What he lacked in strength, he owned in speed.

He raised his foreclaws.

"Tortha!" The first ankylosaur's voice was a creaking boom. "It's high time you made your first kill."

The young triceratops blinked, staring at Eleri with an odd intensity. Eleri returned her gaze, claws raised and heart pounding. He couldn't reach her eyes—not with those horns in the way. Where else was she vulnerable? Her throat? Her heart? Nowhere he could easily reach, not without being crushed . . .

But the young soldier didn't move.

"Tortha of the Lowland Marsh!" the second ankylosaur barked. "You face an enemy combatant. Do your duty, soldier."

The triceratops hesitated. She glanced at her commanders, her expression tight behind her horn. When she spoke, her voice hitched with the sharp Rs of an outer prairie twang. "But sir, the Laws of Noble Combat say you can't—"

"Do. Your. Duty."

Tortha turned.

Eleri fled.

His body exploded into action with all the force of an unleashed strand of lightning. Muscles tensed and released. Claws flashed. He dashed into the undergrowth, careening under ferns and over tangled roots. He reached the gravel slope—and then Agostron was beside him, hurtling through the dark . . .

"The ridge!" Eleri rasped.

He ran and ran, panting and heaving, scrambling up the gravel slope.

At the top, he dashed out onto the Broken Ridge. Agostron followed—and together, the brothers bolted along the narrow trail of stone. Darkness fell away to either side, each abyss a hungry maw. Halfway across, Eleri hurtled to a halt. Whirling, he scanned the landscape for their pursuers.

Nothing.

The Prairie scouts had stopped, muscles tight with fury. Their enormous bodies were too heavy to risk crossing the Broken Ridge.

Eleri remembered the Tale of Astrilar the Wise, ancient queen of the Fire Peak, who had saved her herd by leading them across a narrow path between two gurgling pits of lava. The Broken Ridge wasn't quite so dramatic, but this echo of his favorite story made Eleri's heart race.

Still fighting for breath, he turned to Agostron with a hysterical laugh. "We made it! We got away . . ."

But his brother wasn't smiling.

Agostron stared at him, dark eyes cold in his pale gray face. Blood dripped from the wound on his forehead. When he finally spoke, his word sliced the night like a raptor's claws.

"Traitor," he said.

CHAPTER THREE

THE MOUNTAIN COURT

The warren thrummed, as hectic as a hive of insects. Oryc-todromeus soldiers poured into the night, fast and fran-tic, claws raised and eyes darting.

Clearly, the absence of the heir had been noted.

Twenty yards from the entrance, Eleri's insides tangled. "Agostron, please . . . I didn't mean . . . I couldn't just watch that thing swoop down and—"

"You could have. You *should* have." Agostron's voice was raw. "Those soldiers are our enemies. They might have died tonight if you hadn't warned them."

"But they—"

"And in the battle tomorrow? If they slay our soldiers, whose fault will that be? You know what's at stake, Eleri.

Every season, the Prairie hordes claim more of our land. With every siege, they move closer to our homes."

Eleri blinked. "I . . ."

"If those Prairie soldiers kill our comrades, the blood of the Mountain Kingdom will be on your claws." Agostron's voice tightened. "I can't show favor to my brother. I just . . . I can't. You must face justice, like any traitor."

"But they'll send me to the Deadlands!"

"I serve my kingdom." Agostron's claws clenched on the final word. After a long moment he straightened, drawing a deep breath. "One day I will lead this herd, Eleri. I have a duty to defend it."

Eleri opened his mouth to retort, but it was too late. The crowd jostled across the clearing, figures flicking between shadow and moonlight.

They'll send me to the Deadlands . . .

According to legend, the Deadlands had once been magnificent forest. But the Fallen Star had obliterated the land, burning it to ash and poison. Now it was an endless sea of charred bones and barren wastes.

Eleri inhaled, his tail tight and feathers bristling. Apart from wild carnivores, the only inhabitants of the Deadlands were exiles. These were dinosaurs who had committed crimes beyond forgiveness: killing an ally, stealing an egg . . . or betraying their kingdom.

Agostron refused to meet his gaze. He focused on the

rest of the herd and drew another deep breath, as if steeling himself for the task ahead. Then he waved a foreclaw, demanding the Wise Ones' attention.

The elders burst into a flurry of questions.

"Where have you been?"

"Are you hurt?"

"Agostron, you're wounded! How . . . ?"

Agostron cut them off, rising high on his hindquarters. In that moment, as he reared in the moonlight, he wasn't a youngster. He was a prince in waiting, with a crown of blood on his brow. For the first time, Eleri saw his brother as he truly was. Cold, regal, majestic . . .

. . . and pitiless.

"I have news," Agostron said.

The crowd fell silent.

"Earlier tonight, my brother defied protocol. He snuck out alone from the warren. He refused to return to safety, despite my *express* instructions as heir."

There were mutterings of disapproval.

"I followed to keep him safe—every member of this herd is my responsibility, no matter how foolish. But what I witnessed can barely be described."

Agostron paused.

As the tension stretched, Eleri clenched his claws. More than anything, he had yearned for his herdmates to hear his stories. For their eyes to widen and their breath to quicken, enraptured by his words as a storyteller.

But now Agostron's story was all that mattered. If Eleri dared to contradict their beloved heir, he would only make things worse. The elders loved Agostron. They tolerated Eleri. In the elders' eyes, any protest would prove that Agostron was right—that Eleri was too rebellious. Disrespectful.

Traitorous.

"A pterosaur swooped toward us." Agostron gestured at the bleeding cut above his eyes. "While I used my training to camouflage in the foliage, my brother blundered into an enemy scouting party."

A sharp sting filled Eleri's throat.

"Before I could intervene, the pterosaur dove to attack our foes." Agostron raised a claw. "I thought that a great victory was upon us—a chance to watch the blood of the Prairie Alliance be spilled! An omen of the stars, foretelling our victory on the battlefield tomorrow."

The elders stared, tense with anticipation.

"And yet my brother shouted a warning."

Silence.

For the first time since beginning his tale, Agostron met Eleri's gaze. The sharpness was back: the cold curl of his mouth, a glint of disdain in his eyes. But this time, Agostron wasn't just delivering an insult.

He was delivering an accusation.

"Treachery." Agostron bowed his head in regret. "It was an act of treachery, Wise Ones. My brother saved our enemies' lives."

21

The herd broke into murmurs.

Eleri stood still, numb with fear. His throat clenched, just as it had when the pterosaur had swooped—but this time, it was a different terror. That fear had been hot and fast. This was cold, slow, and toxic. This couldn't be happening.

Could it?

The largest oryctodromeus stepped forward. The Prince of Broken Ridge wore a crown of thorns threaded loosely into his dark blue feathers. His craggy face was as coarse as the cliffs, and his dark eyes stared from a nest of wrinkles.

Eleri's heart sank. "Father . . ."

The prince of the herd didn't speak. He stared at his youngest son, his disappointment raw. Eleri scuffed his hind claws in the dirt, unable to face his father's stare. In the Old Stories, oryctodromeus were called "earthsingers"—but right now, their most powerful weapon was silence.

Across the clearing, quiet fell.

"My little Eleri . . ."

His father's voice was hoarse, almost a rasp. He shook his head slowly, as if struggling to find a way out of this. A way to avoid the proclamation he must make. "Sometimes, Eleri, you are so like your mother . . . ," he whispered. "I see her dreams in you."

But Agostron stepped forward, eyes tight and claws raised.

"Eleri has betrayed us, Father," Agostron repeated, loud enough for the others to hear. "We all know what must be done, for the good of the Mountain Kingdom."

22

The herd murmured. Several of the elders nodded, eyes sharp and heads raised.

Eleri's father stared at them, his own expression trapped. Then his face hardened—and he stepped in front of Agostron, as if to reestablish his rank. The herd watched: a sea of wide eyes and expectation.

"Eleri of the Broken Ridge," he said heavily, "you have not only betrayed our herd. You have betrayed our entire kingdom."

The wind tripped across the rocks, sharp with grit. Eleri caught the stink of sulfur in the air—an errant gust from the Deadlands.

"And for that," his father said, voice cracking, "you must face the Mountain Court."

The Mountain Court met at dawn.

It was a gathering of the kingdom's most important dinosaurs: the rulers of every herd and King Nylius himself. Stegoceras, iguanodons, and oryctodromeus met atop the highest peak. Messengers had been sent across the crests and valleys, forewarning the lords of each herd that a defendant would be tried today.

Just before dawn, Eleri climbed the mountain. Alone.

His father was already at the summit, awaiting his arrival. Again, Eleri remembered those overheard whispers. *Nothing like his brother, I'm afraid. A disappointment, that one . . .*

Eighty yards below the court, Eleri paused next to a cliff-side plateau. It jutted into the frigid sky, wide and imposing. Behind the plateau, a cavern punctured the mountainside. The King's Domain was home to King Nylius and his herd of royal iguanodons. In that cavern, the king was likely preparing to hold court. Right now, his assistant might even be placing the Crown of Judgment on his brow.

Eleri's stomach flipped.

He hurried up the path, mouth dry and shoulders tight. But at the next bend, Eleri jolted to a halt. Ahead, the path curved around a stack of boulders. Between the rocks, a narrow crack threaded into the cliff, a back entrance to the king's private chambers.

And there, two figures lurked in the shadows.

Eleri shrank behind the boulders, heart racing. The first figure was King Nylius: a muscular iguanodon, his authority writ from his sharply ridged head to his sweeping tail and vicious spiked thumbs.

But it wasn't the king who drew Eleri's attention. It was the second figure, lurking in the shadows: a beady-eyed stranger, with razor-sharp teeth and grasping foreclaws, ready to impale the throats of its prey.

It was a raptor.

Eleri's muscles tightened, every instinct jerking him backward. Ever since the Fallen Star, carnivores had dwelled in the Deadlands. This raptor was a wild beast, a predator.

24

It would happily feast on the bones of every dinosaur in the Mountain Kingdom.

So why was it here?

And why was King Nylius *talking* to it?

Eleri's breath quickened as the conversation continued. He couldn't make out any words, but King Nylius looked agitated, waving a spiked foreclaw. Then the king turned back to his royal cavern, slipping away into the dark.

The raptor glanced around, its beady eyes flashing, before it scuttled into a patch of brush. It avoided the main path, picking its own way down the slope to avoid prying eyes.

Five seconds. Ten seconds. Twenty . . .

The raptor was gone. Still, Eleri forced himself to count to sixty before he moved again, drawing a deep breath to propel himself up the path. His body pulsed with nerves. It didn't make sense. The king should have summoned the guards, or sounded an alert . . .

Something wasn't right.

Was it a diplomatic envoy? No, that made no sense. The carnivores were a disorganized rabble. They couldn't even form an army, let alone a kingdom of their own.

Was this a trade deal? No, the predators had nothing to trade. They lurked in the Deadlands, where the sky was choked with ash and the Fire Peak snarled. No natural resources, apart from broken stone. Perhaps . . .

But as Eleri climbed higher, rounding the final bend, all thoughts of the raptor were wiped from his mind.

The Mountain Court lay waiting.

It was a vast, cold expanse of rock. Eleri had seen it before, of course, but never as a defendant. In the past, it had seemed a grand monument to the kingdom: a stony crown at the nation's peak.

Today it lay stark and bare.

His legs quavered, threatening to buckle. What had he been thinking, crying out to save his enemies? He had been so reckless. So foolish. One shout in the dark—and now his future hung in the balance. Again he thought of his mother, snatched by a pterosaur while Eleri was still in his eggshell. If someone had shouted a warning cry, perhaps she . . .

Don't think it, Eleri ordered himself.

Should he have let the Prairie soldiers die? The question had two answers, battling like armies: the instinct in Eleri's gut . . . and the contempt in Agostron's eyes. *You're too soft-hearted, Eleri. Grow up and face reality.*

The court had already assembled, composed of the rulers of each Mountain herd. They stood in a solemn circle, waiting for Eleri to take his place in their center. His throat tingled as he took his position by the Rock of Judgment.

To his left stood the Prince of the Tumbling Stream. He led a prominent herd of iguanodons, who dwelled in fields and caves by a waterfall. His crown of waterweeds twitched, its fronds prickling in the gritty breeze.

The Prince of the Tumbling Stream held a high position in the court, thanks to his status as an Eye of the Forgotten. In some rare cases, the mist of the Fallen Star had brought strange dreams. These were visions of the distant past—and of ancient tales that the dreamer shouldn't know. In their sleep, they saw shadowy flashes of the world before the star had fallen.

A world lost forever.

According to legend, Astrilar the Wise had been the first Eye of the Forgotten. She had used her visions to guide her herd to the Fire Peak, saving them while the world burned. These powers were rare, but they still existed. Such dinosaurs were held in high regard, and their visions of the past were always trusted.

Beside him stood the Princess of the Sunless Meadow, the Prince of the Dappled Stones, the Lord of the Ferns, the rulers of half a dozen other Mountain herds . . .

And finally, Eleri's father.

The Prince of the Broken Ridge was stiff-backed and stone-faced. His thorn crown looked as sharp as his eyes, which fixed on the horizon.

The Deadlands.

Be still, Eleri told himself. *Be silent.*

It took all his courage not to run. He felt like a hatchling again, crawling from his egg into a world full of dangers.

To calm himself, Eleri silently recited the Tale of Astrilar the Wise. He had always clung to old stories: tales from the

Time of the Fallen Star, when dinosaurs had faced unspeakable horrors and survived. If Astrilar could be brave, Eleri could too.

Couldn't he?

"The king approaches!" a guard called.

King Nylius's crown was a glorious tangle of thorns, starflecks, and flowers, woven by the oryctodromeus. With their dexterous claws, the members of Eleri's herd were the designated craftsmen of the Mountain Kingdom. The king had a fresh crown woven every two days—and in a bitter twist of fate, Eleri had helped weave this one himself.

Now it would seal his doom.

King Nylius took his place at the front of the court, as the princes and lords rearranged themselves behind him. "State your name, rank, and offense," he ordered, not quite meeting Eleri's eyes.

Eleri strained to hide his fear. "Eleri of the Broken Ridge, Your Majesty. I don't have a rank yet, sir. I'm not old enough. But I'd like to be our herd's storyteller one day."

There were a few murmurings of interest, but no one protested. The king gave a slow nod and then waved a spiked claw. "And your offense?"

"Last night, I saw a scouting party from the Prairie Alliance." Eleri tripped over his own words, scrambling to share his story before the king formed his judgment. "A pterosaur swooped overhead, Your Majesty, so I . . . I shouted out a warning cry."

The murmurings became angry mutterings.

Eleri's insides sank. "It was just instinct, Your Majesty. I wasn't trying to help them—I mean, I was, but I wasn't thinking that they were enemy scouts. I just saw some herbivores about to be attacked, and I . . ."

"You saved them?"

"I don't know," Eleri said. "They were quite big, they might have survived an attack anyway."

"But you *tried* to save them." No pity sparked in Nylius's eyes. "A group of enemy soldiers, who may well kill our own soldiers on the battlefield later today. And what of the land they might claim? Year after year, those Prairie beasts are stealing what is ours."

Eleri's breath caught in his throat. "Your Majesty, I . . ."

"Silence!" King Nylius turned to his court, his expression grim. "This is an act of treachery as bleak as any that I have seen in my time as ruler. Do any disagree?"

None of the rulers of the herds spoke up—but for a moment, Eleri's father wavered on his feet. A glint of wild hope kindled in Eleri, fierce and fragile. His father blinked, tight eyes crinkled in the glare of the rising sun.

Would his father speak for him? Would he declare that Eleri was innocent, that he deserved a second chance?

Silence.

Eleri's hope flickered out.

"Very well," King Nylius said. "The defendant has confessed to his crime. This is not a question of guilt, but of sentencing. Those in favor of leniency, step backward. Those in favor of exile, step forward."

One by one, the dinosaurs stepped forward. Each claw-step echoed on the hard stone, slicing Eleri's nerves with a rhythmic beat. He could hear their judgment in the weight of their steps. *Guilty, guilty, guilty* . . . It was the horror of Agostron's verdict again, the heir's voice sharp with that single word.

Traitor.

But one figure didn't move. His father remained in place, refusing to step forward. For one brief moment, their eyes met. Was he wavering? Would he . . . ?

With a raw breath, his father stepped backward.

Eleri jerked, biting back a cry of emotion. In that moment, he didn't care that the court had ruled against him. He didn't care that he was going to be exiled, that he would likely die before the day was out.

His father had voted to save him. His father had voted *against* Agostron's wishes. And in his moment of despair, Eleri found a single spark of hope to cling to. It wasn't much, but it was enough.

Enough to keep him on his feet.

Enough to keep his head held high.

"Eleri of the Broken Ridge," King Nylius said, "you are sentenced to exile. Your herd is responsible for carrying out your sentence. May the Deadlands show mercy and end your suffering quickly."

Eleri stumbled backward, as if the sky itself had shoved him. As the court broke into whispers again, a southern wind curled across the mountaintop. It sent leaves skittering and pulled Eleri's feathers into ruffles.

The desert wind was hot. Harsh. Hungry.

It was the wind of the Deadlands.

And this time, it had found its prey.

CHAPTER FOUR

THE SPY

Zyre lay cocooned in her wings.

Her roosting tree sprouted on a high peak, beyond the reach of most predators. Not that flightless carnivores could catch her, but better safe than sorry. After all, there was always the risk of larger pterosaurs.

Zyre unfurled her wings and forced herself onto her hindclaws. Dawn dripped over the prairie, signaling time to start the day's work. Since she'd been kicked out of her parents' nest, she had no one to boss her around.

Life or death, Zyre was responsible for herself.

As an anurognathid, Zyre was barely the size of a warmblood bird. In the Old Stories, her kind were known as "windwhispers." Though omnivores, they didn't prey on other dinosaurs, but ate a mixture of plants and insects. In wartime, they took no side but their own.

The wealthiest of her kind lived at Lightning Peak—but Zyre could never afford a nesting spot there. The highly exclusive flock demanded ten starflecks in payment, and Zyre had yet to earn a decent haul.

Like the wind, she flew alone.

Zyre examined her food supply, feeling glum. A pitiful stash, really. All she had were a few dead beetles from the forest and the dried-up husks of water greens from the Lowland Marsh. Her starfleck pouch was even sadder: an empty scrap of fabric, woven from dried weeds. It had been weeks since she'd earned a single fleck.

Still, no point moping. Zyre would find some larger dinosaurs today, and hopefully they'd be keen for a trade. They could provide better food—or even a precious starfleck—and she would pay them with information.

Most anurognathids worked as crafters, using their dexterous claws to build objects for wealthy triceratops or ankylosaurs. They wove thorny crowns, plaited pouches, or twined delicate blankets of fern fronds. But like the most ambitious of her kind, Zyre had found a more interesting role to play in the war.

Spying.

Zyre liked going unnoticed. Being forgettable. It allowed her to overhear things . . . things that certain dinosaurs might not want their enemies to learn. And if those enemies paid handsomely for the information, who was Zyre to complain?

The Prairie Alliance gathered in the distance, its squadrons resembling stains on the landscape.

Time to fly.

Zyre launched herself into the sky. The wind buffeted her sideways, so she flapped harder to keep her featherlight body on track. Cretacea stretched out like a secret below, belonging only to her. What had her parents always said? *You are a windwhisper, Zyre. A master of the sky—and all those fools who crawl beneath it.*

With a twist, Zyre streamlined her wings and dipped into a descent. She plummeted so fast that the world blurred. Twenty seconds to impact with the fern prairie, then nineteen, eighteen, seventeen . . .

She wrenched herself upward and flared her wings. Her gnarled claws brushed the ferns as she skimmed the surface. A joyous laugh rose inside her: the bubbling thrill that only a decent flight could provide.

But where to fly today? Zyre was overdue for a lucrative trade. She held some information for the Mountain Kingdom regarding the Prairie's new general. On the other hand, the Prairie Alliance had promised a starfleck for details of King Nylius's latest plan . . .

Then again, why not both?

If Zyre visited the Mountain Kingdom first, she could

sell King Nylius her information about the new enemy general. At the same time, she could gather fresh intelligence on Nylius's plans and sell *that* to King Torive of the Prairie Alliance.

She flapped faster, buoyed by an invisible smirk. If Zyre played this right, she could end the day with a full belly and a starfleck in her claws.

It wasn't a bad life, being a windwhisper.

Approaching the Mountain Kingdom, Zyre rode a gust of wind skyward. Her beady eyes searched the land below for anything of interest.

Her heart skipped a beat.

The Mountain Court was in session—and by the looks of it, a defendant was on trial. Zyre circled high above, wary of descending into view of the dinosaurs below, but her curiosity won out.

As a compromise, Zyre descended into the canopy just beneath the peak. It was always a gamble, shooting into a forest from a height. Each branch threatened to slash her wings—and a broken wing was a death sentence.

Still, Zyre was an agile flier. She slipped into the foliage and landed on a branch. Her empty starfleck pouch hung from her leg, slapping down with barely a whisper. The cover of trees dappled the undergrowth with light and darkness. Zyre felt a faint twinge of unease. She never knew what might be hiding in such shadows—and for Zyre, knowledge was currency. If there was one thing she hated, it was *not knowing* something.

Breath tight, she edged toward the leafless crest of the kingdom, sidling behind a pile of rocks to stay unseen.

This was no ordinary day in court. A young oryctodromeus stood on trial, alone by the Rock of Judgment—and from the fear in his eyes, it wasn't going well.

Zyre watched, silent in the shadows.

"This is an act of treachery," King Nylius bellowed, "as bleak as any that I have seen in my time as ruler. Do any disagree?"

No one did.

The only herd leader who voted for leniency was an oryctodromeus who shared the dark sapphire feathers of the defendant. They were probably related—perhaps the elder was an uncle, or even his father?

Either way, his vote stood alone.

Before the court could disperse, Zyre scurried back down the path. In the forest, she paused for a moment. Slivers of sunlight danced like insects between the leaves. There was an opportunity here. There had to be, didn't there?

A young oryctodromeus had shouted a warning to save a Prairie scouting party—and apparently, the traitor was related to the Prince of the Broken Ridge. Why would he risk it? And more importantly, why had enemy scouts been lurking so high in the mountains? They had no reason to venture so far from the battlefield . . .

The scouts hadn't even been sneaking near the king's quarters. Instead, they had been creeping around near a warren of oryctodromeus. But why? What was so important about the Broken Ridge herd?

In the right set of claws, the truth might be quite valuable.

CHAPTER FIVE

INTO THE DEADLANDS

The Exile Cliffs sliced a jagged scowl between the Mountain Kingdom and the Deadlands.

All his life, Eleri had dreamed of leaving home to collect the world's tales—but not like this. He had imagined crossing Cretacea, exploring its forests and plains, rivers and ravines . . . and then returning home with a hundred stories to share.

He had never dreamed of the Deadlands.

At noon, Eleri's herd gathered on the clifftops, stern and solemn. Eleri stumbled in the middle of the pack, a runt in a sea of full-grown oryctodromeus. Fear curdled in his belly, twisting like a murkthorn vine. He would die alone, starving and dehydrated in the desert—unless a carnivore grabbed him first. The idea of setting out into the Deadlands, with its scorching sun and ravenous beasts . . .

It couldn't be happening. It couldn't be real.

And yet it was.

His herdmates formed a tight ring around him, as if he might try to run for it. But where could he run? Behind lay the kingdom that had exiled him. To curve back around toward the mountains, he would have to cross the Land of Falling Sky: a vast, shallow gully prone to rockslides from the slopes above. Ahead, the Deadlands sprawled to the horizon: an endless stretch of sand and rock. No trees or meadows. No rivers or woodlands.

Just . . . death.

Out there, the only remnant of life was the Forest of Smoke: a labyrinth of petrified trees, obliterated when the Fallen Star had crashed to earth. The forest stood bitter and twisted, as inedible as charcoal. According to stories, smoke poured through cracks in the forest floor, and fireblast stones exploded at the slightest hint of a spark.

But there was still hope, wasn't there? The stories also told of oases, far out in the desert. Pools of water, patches of surviving foliage. If Eleri could find an oasis, he might survive . . .

For a while, at least.

His herd clustered at the edge of the cliff, where a sharp bluff dropped away into the desert below. Only his father wasn't present. Despite his vote for leniency, the Prince of the Broken Ridge hadn't attended his own son's exile. He claimed that he needed to prepare for the coming battle— but perhaps he was simply too ashamed.

Disappointment . . .

Nothing like his brother . . .

Agostron had volunteered to take their father's place as the Deliverer of Justice. As future prince of the herd, he claimed it was his duty to lead his first real ceremony.

Of course, Eleri knew the real reason. Agostron was desperate to prove himself a worthy ruler, with no hint of weakness. A wartime prince could spare no mercy.

Not even for his own brother.

"Eleri of the Broken Ridge," Agostron announced, his tone cold, "you have been found guilty of treachery. Go. And never again darken the borders of our fair Mountain Kingdom."

Eleri turned to face the Deadlands. Every gaze in the herd weighed on his back, silently urging him onward. They had always tolerated Eleri, but they had never loved him. Not as they loved Agostron.

Eleri's insides cracked.

Secretly, he had dreamed that one day they might look at him as they looked at Agostron: as a valued member of the herd. He would grow old and wise, telling tales to eager hatchlings. One day, his herdmates would love his stories. Perhaps they would even love—

Don't think it! Eleri told himself, cutting off the sting.

It would never happen now.

With a sharp breath, Eleri descended.

Crack. Crack. Crack. Thorns snapped under his claws, keeping time with the snapping of his nerves. Burntflecks slipped under his weight. These gritty stones had once been starflecks, but their power had long ago winked out. Eleri lost his footing and skidded, crying out in alarm, but caught himself with a jolt.

Trembling, he pressed on.

Step by step, Eleri pushed through a sea of bristling thorns. He used his tail to steady himself, trusting its weight for balance. His skin stung, dashed by countless tiny scratches.

Just like a story, he told himself. He tried to remember Astrilar the Wise, the first Eye of the Forgotten, who had saved her herd in the Time of the Fallen Star. Or there was Yari the Strong, an old iguanodon who had battled an entire pack of raptors to save a nest of hatchlings . . .

If this were a story, what would Eleri's name be? He was no Eye of the Forgotten. He had no visions, no magical powers. He was just a runt. Eleri the Weak? Eleri the Coward? No, he refused to allow it. He would be strong, like the heroes in his favorite tales. He would face the Deadlands with his head held high.

At the base of the slope, Eleri looked back. His herd was gone. Only one figure remained, silhouetted against the clouds. *Agostron.* The heir stood alone, staring. Was it a silent farewell? A brotherly salute?

No. Eleri knew the truth in his gut.

Agostron was waiting to watch him fall.

Eleri walked on. The slope gave way to hot, fractured earth. *Earthsinger.* That was the name for oryctodromeus in the Old Stories—but even so, Eleri found no songs in this landscape. No living earth, ripe with soil and moss and fungus. No worms or beetles. Just scorched rock, cracked and crumbling.

Wasn't this what he'd wished for? An endless horizon, without elders to decide his path. No dirt. No burrows. No rules. He remembered Agostron's furious words: *Your skull is overstuffed with daydreams . . .*

His own wish slapped him in the face.

The sun burned. Eleri walked faster, his head down, trying to shield his eyes from the glare. His scratches throbbed, but he refused to buckle. This was his story, wasn't it? One day, he would tell it. All he had to do was survive . . .

Enormous craters pockmarked the landscape. It would be cooler down there, in the shade. But if Eleri slipped into a crater, he would never come back up. He was too broken. Too exhausted from a night without sleep. He had to keep going.

He wouldn't let Agostron see him fall.

And so he walked on, farther and farther across the sunscorched terrain. Blood dried on his scratches, forming an ugly crust. Every time he looked back, Agostron was smaller and smaller. A dwindling figure, alone on a clifftop. Then he was a smear, a dot, and . . . nothing.

Eleri was alone.

High in the mountains, a stream gurgled.

It lay in the darkest crook of the Mountain Kingdom, tangling between two jagged peaks. No sunlight touched this ravine—and the only trees were stunted and twisted.

Zyre perched on the Stone of Secrets, making herself as visible as possible. If any high-ranking member of the Mountain Kingdom wished to engage a spy, they would come here to hire an anurognathid for the job.

The day they kicked her out of their nest, her parents had brought her here. Their voices had been cold, laced with disappointment. In their eyes, Zyre had always been too soft. Too spoiled. To grow up, she must prove herself.

To survive, she must be merciless.

"This is a place to trade," her father had said. "To trade truths—and sometimes, to barter lies. Learn the worth of both, or you will not live for long."

Today, the valley lay silent. Zyre perched high, straining for the slightest sound of movement. Her starfleck pouch hung from her claw, empty as ever.

The trees whispered. The breeze curled . . .

Crunch.

A clawstep. She whipped around, trying to hide the jolt of excitement. "Is someone there?"

As her eyes focused, she made out a slight glint in the trees. Someone was sticking to the shadows, concealing their face—and even their species. In the darkness, the figure might be an iguanodon, an oryctodromeus, or a stegoceras. It might even be King Nylius himself.

Of course, Zyre didn't particularly care. Most of her clients valued their privacy and kept their identities secret. It didn't bother her, so long as they paid for her services.

"Is someone there?" she asked again. "For a price, the wind may carry whispers."

A long pause.

"I am here," said the stranger.

Zyre didn't recognize his voice—but that didn't mean much. The speaker might be disguising his tone. All she could discern was that the speaker was male, presumably a citizen of the Mountain Kingdom.

"I am Zyre of Lightning Peak," she lied, feeling bold. Of course, she could never afford to buy a valuable nesting place on the peak—but as a windwhisper spy, she added some heft to her reputation. "Who are you?"

Another pause.

"You may call me . . . Shadow."

Zyre laughed. "Very original."

But when the stranger replied, there was no joke in his tone. "I'm not here for a grand show of creativity, Zyre of

Lightning Peak. I am here to negotiate a business deal." He paused. "An urgent deal."

Zyre perked up. Urgency meant she held negotiating power. If she played this right, she might fly away with a hefty payout.

"Go on," she said. "What's your offer, then?"

In response, Shadow tossed an object into the clearing. Zyre glanced down—and with a start, she recognized it. A shining fragment of crystal, the size of a piece of gravel.

It was a starfleck.

"What . . . ?"

"Twenty starflecks." Shadow's voice was a quiet hiss. "One upfront, as a gesture of goodwill. Nineteen later, if you bring what I ask for."

Zyre stared at the tiny stone, her insides churning. *Twenty starflecks.* More than she had seen in her life—enough to thread the crown of a monarch. Each fragment of the Fallen Star was worth a week of decadent meals.

If she owned *twenty* starflecks, she could trade them for months of feasting. No, even better—she could buy a prime nesting spot. She could join the flock at Lightning Peak: the most revered anurognathids in Cretacea . . .

Of course, it wasn't just about the prestige.

When Zyre was a hatchling, she had briefly stayed at Lightning Peak with her grandmother. While Zyre's parents were cold and ruthless, her grandmother was . . . different. For three short weeks, the old windwhisper had made Zyre feel safe. Wanted. Protected. Her world was a soft nest, built of moss and mauve-berry leaves. She had told Zyre tales of faraway places: of the Salted Scorch, of secret pathways, and of the Brother Peak that lay beyond the wastes. Zyre had listened, enthralled by tales of a life not her own.

Then Zyre's parents had returned to collect her, and the world's edges had sharpened once more.

Zyre would never admit it aloud, but the memory made her insides twist. Her grandmother was too old to travel—and now that Zyre was almost grown, she could no longer visit the peak for free. To see her grandmother again, she had to buy a nesting spot of her own.

Twenty starflecks . . .

Focus, Zyre told herself. Time for business, not daydreams.

"Today at noon, an oryctodromeus was exiled into the Deadlands," Shadow said. "His name is Eleri of the Broken Ridge, and he betrayed his kingdom. I want you to track him down—and make sure he never returns."

Zyre stiffened. "What?"

"It won't be difficult. The Deadlands are rife with peril—and of course, there are always the carnivores." Shadow's voice curled. "Follow the exile and tell a pack of raptors where to find him."

Zyre's skin crawled. "I'm a spy. Not an assassin."

"You're a windwhisper. All you need to do is whisper into a few raptors' ears. For twenty starflecks, surely it's worth it?"

A long pause.

"How will you know I've done it?" Zyre asked. "I could just come back here and say, 'Oh hurrah, the exile is dead!' and you'd have no way to know if it was true."

"When Eleri was a hatchling, one of his rear claws was broken," Shadow said. "When the predators are done with the rest of him, bring me that broken bone, to prove that he is dead."

"But I . . ."

"Each night for the next week, I will wait here at midnight. Once you have the claw, you will meet me here— and give it to me. Then, and only then, will I pay the remainder of your fee."

Zyre did not speak.

"I'm not asking you to kill him," Shadow said. "He will die regardless, out in that desert. All I want is proof that the job is done. It will . . . put my mind at ease." He paused. "Consider it an act of mercy, if you like. To end his suffering quickly."

Silence.

Zyre stared into the trees—but when those cold eyes met her own, she quickly looked away. The exile had seemed her own age, barely more than a hatchling. Why should anyone want him dead?

Perhaps Eleri knew a secret. A deadly secret. Perhaps he had seen something he shouldn't have or held some vital information to ransom. It wouldn't be the first time that she was hired to suppress a whisper rather than to spread it. But Zyre was a trader of secrets, not of flesh . . .

She fluttered down and seized the starfleck, examining it carefully. It was genuine. She could tell from the glint inside the stone and the way that it tingled in her claws. With a squeeze and a thought, she could set its power ablaze.

Gently, she slipped it into the pouch around her leg. Then she glanced into the gloom of the trees, her insides tight. "You've got a deal."

Shadow didn't respond.

Zyre refused to speak again. She didn't want the stranger to glimpse her uncertainty. If Shadow decided that she was too young, or too cowardly, he would choose another spy for the job.

Her parents' words rang in her ears, lessons drummed into Zyre over and over again. A great windwhisper spy was ruthless. Relentless. *Master of the sky* . . .

Either way, the exile would die. The Deadlands would kill him: the burning dust, the carnivores, or simply starvation.

Why shouldn't Zyre profit from it?

She took to the sky: wings flapping, mind buzzing. Her mind tingled with memories of sweet moths and mauveberries, of mossy nests beneath the stars . . .

Of her grandmother.

As Zyre wheeled toward the Deadlands, the breeze tossed her higher. Who cared about the exile's life, anyway? The herbivore armies were lumps on the ground: filthy puddles of scales and muscle. Earth crawlers, the lot of them. They thought they were better than anurognathids because they were larger, stronger, faster.

But Zyre could fly. She was free. Her kind were the real rulers of Cretacea. Not the triceratops, not the iguanodons, but the windwhisper spies. Those who traded their secrets— and ultimately, who soared above them all.

With twenty starflecks, Zyre could earn a place in their greatest flock. And for the first time since she was a hatchling, she could rejoin the only windwhisper who had made her feel worthy.

CHAPTER SIX

ENEMIES

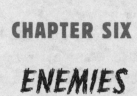

Eleri was running out of time.

As each hour crept by, his limbs grew heavier. His tail dragged, a dead weight pulling him back. No sign of water. Just scorched stone and crumbling craters.

Had the battle started yet? Surely the Prairie Alliance had struck by now. He could picture it: hordes of ankylosaurs, barreling forth to steal another scrap of the Mountain Kingdom. Squadrons of triceratops, all horns and spikes and bloodshed . . . Would the Alliance expand their territory? Would they claim another tract of foothills? Eleri's father might already be on the front lines, leading the Broken Ridge herd into the fray.

His father might be—

Don't think it! Eleri clenched his claws. To distract himself, he counted his steps. *One, two, three* . . . The number slipped into the dozens, the hundreds, the thousands. When Eleri finally lost count, he recited the Tale of the Old World under his breath. *Once upon a time, the sky was dark and the earth was cold. Then the starsweepers came, with their mighty necks, to paint a trail of lights across the dark . . .*

Eleri gave a weak laugh. The starsweepers? Right now, he'd pay a thousand starflecks to have never heard of them.

He trudged on. In the distance, the craggy bulk of the Fire Peak scarred the horizon. According to legend, the earth near the volcanic peak was more fertile. In a few rare places, it was even rich enough to grow plants. To find an oasis, Eleri must head toward the Fire Peak.

Long ago, Astrilar the Wise had built her enormous warren in that mountain, shielding her herd from the Fallen Star. She had used explosive fireblast stones to carve out caves and tunnels, creating the largest warren in history. As an Eye of the Forgotten, her shadowy visions had led her to the mountain—and to safety.

It was Eleri's only hope.

After several hours, he spotted a wavering shape in the distance. Something rose above the flat expanse: a bristling thicket of shadows. Eleri picked up the pace, his throat stinging. Was it an oasis?

Step by step, the shapes solidified. Trees! They were thin and scraggly, but alive. An embankment sheltered this tiny oasis from the elements. Their leaves were sharp prickles, nowhere near as tasty as ferns or moss. Back home, Eleri would have turned up his nose at them—but here, they seemed a miraculous feast. And if there were trees, there must be water.

There was faint movement among the trees. Was it just the sway of foliage in the wind? Eleri was too exhausted to make sense of it. He scrambled forward, driven by thirst and desperate hope. In that moment, all that mattered was the promise of water. His tongue ached as his gaze fixed on that wavering promise of life ahead . . .

As he struggled on, something itched at the back of Eleri's mind. Something was wrong. It took him a moment to realize that the air clung to his skin, dead and dry as bone. The wind had stopped.

But the trees were still moving.

Eleri jerked to a halt. His breath caught and he dropped to his belly, suddenly desperate not to be seen. The movement wasn't just foliage—it was living figures. Someone was moving around the trees. Other dinosaurs! But who could survive out here?

The answer wasn't good.

Keeping low, Eleri wriggled along the dry earth. He crawled to a craggy boulder, fifty yards from the meager oasis. His breath heaved and his scratched skin stung as he peered around the rock. His eyes widened.

Carnivores.

A pair of raptors circled the oasis, marching like soldiers

on patrol. Even at a distance, they moved like killers. If they saw him . . .

A cry pierced the sky.

Heart thudding, Eleri dropped into the shadow of the boulder. Above, two enormous wings blotted the sun. Pterosaur! But it passed, wheeling down to the oasis, and sunlight flashed back so sharply that Eleri's eyes stung.

The enormous beast landed at the edge of the oasis, depositing a carcass from its claws. Eleri flinched. The carcass was a stegoceras: a small, speedy dinosaur with a hard-ridged head. It was likely a soldier of the Sunless Meadow herd. Eleri remembered the Princess of the Sunless Meadow, standing high in the Mountain Court as she sentenced him to exile. Was this dead soldier a friend of hers? A relative?

In a cold flash, Eleri thought of his mother. His father's voice echoed in his memory. *Sometimes, Eleri, you are so like your mother . . . I see her dreams in you.*

Had a pterosaur carried her out here too? Had she hung limp and lifeless in its grip, like this stegoceras? Or worse, had she still lived as she soared above the Deadlands?

Eleri felt sick.

One of the raptors scuttled forward, quivering with hunger and excitement. "How goes the battle, sir?"

The pterosaur laughed. "Superbly for us, Yirian, as always. Our larders will be well stocked after this one."

The battle. Eleri's breath caught in his throat. The Prairie Alliance must have moved against the Mountain Kingdom, fighting to steal another scrap of land. Their invasion would leave countless soldiers strewn across the battlefield . . .

For these carrion eaters, the battle was a feast.

Eagerly, the raptor called Yirian hurried over to the fallen stegoceras. His teeth gleamed, preparing to slice into the carcass. But the pterosaur gave a furious cry, batting the raptor back with a swoop of his wings.

"How dare you?" the pterosaur cried. "You know the protocol! General Korvia gets the first pick of the fresh meat. Take it to the larder."

Yirian scraped his claws in the dirt, frustrated. "But sir, the general won't be back until tonight! Are we to starve until then?"

"There are older kills in there." The pterosaur jerked his head toward a rocky cave. "Take what is starting to rot."

Eleri's heart pounded. The pterosaur spoke as if they were part of an army—as if they had rules to follow and officers to obey. But that wasn't right! Everyone knew that the carrion eaters were a disorganized rabble. They could never form a kingdom. They could never form an army.

If carnivores were capable of unifying, they would have conquered Cretacea years ago. A carnivorous army could destroy the Mountain Kingdom—and the Prairie Alliance too. It would mean death. Despair. An endless feast for predators who preyed on Eleri's kin.

It wasn't possible. And yet . . .

Furious, Yirian nodded. Clearly, he didn't dare to disobey

a superior officer. Looking bitter, he gestured for his companion to help. Together, the raptors dragged the carcass toward the cave in the embankment.

The pterosaur bent to the earth and then raised his beak to swallow, as if he were drinking. Water! There must be a stream or pond in the oasis, too low for Eleri to see. He licked his own parched lips, more desperate than ever.

If only he could steal a sip . . .

Heart pounding, Eleri waited for a chance to make his move.

Zyre flew.

The Deadlands stretched below her: a tangled knot of tan and gold, restless as lava. The starfleck pouch hung from her claw, its single precious fleck tucked safely inside. *Nineteen more*, she told herself. As long as the exile died.

And finally, Zyre could earn a nest on Lightning Peak.

Her wings hung heavy with heat, but she struggled on, squinting for movement below. It didn't take long to spot the exile. He was the lone living figure: a dark speck, his feathers glinting in the afternoon sun.

"Got you," Zyre whispered.

She followed from above, watching as Eleri staggered across the desert. He was approaching a pockmarked stretch of landscape, where enormous craters riddled the earth. Zyre watched with a vague sense of unease.

He looked . . . weak. Exhausted. If Zyre was lucky, the exile might keel over himself—and she could claim Shadow's bounty without a lick of effort.

But for some reason, the idea made her insides knot.

Profit isn't personal, she told herself sharply. It was another of her parents' mottos, and the creed of every wealthy anurognathid. Zyre had chosen to work as a spy, not a weaver of crowns or trinkets. Spying was more lucrative, of course—but what it earned in profit, it cost in conscience.

Spies survived by selling secrets. They betrayed soldiers' plans and army movements, which often led to deaths. A master of the sky was never sentimental. But even so, as the exile struggled through the Deadlands, an odd anxiety twisted Zyre's belly.

He was trying so hard. Part of her wished that he would fall. But a larger part, a foolish part, silently urged him onward. What was wrong with her? Even *thinking* such weak thoughts would have earned her parents' scorn. But her gaze fixed on an oasis ahead, alive with the promise of plants and water . . .

A cry pierced the sky.

Zyre glanced up—and to her horror, an enormous pair of wings flashed overhead. A pterosaur. The full-grown monster could snatch her in a single talon . . . or devour her in a gulp.

Had it seen her?

Zyre dove, all thoughts of Eleri forgotten. For a wild moment, her mind and body spun like a broken leaf. She tumbled madly, wings pinned to her sides, begging gravity to yank her away from the beast . . .

It soared past her.

Zyre flared her wings, catching herself with a violent yank. Rasping, she watched as the pterosaur raced toward the oasis—but it wasn't scouring for prey.

Its claws were already full.

Zyre glanced around in a sudden panic, realizing that she'd lost track of Eleri—but then she spotted him, crouching behind a boulder. She jerked her head up in surprise. The exile hadn't retreated from the oasis, but crept even closer to the predators' lair. It made no sense, unless . . .

Was he *spying* on them?

Zyre almost fell from the sky in astonishment.

"Keep it together," Zyre muttered to herself. This was her chance to earn her reward. If she revealed Eleri's hiding place, the carnivores would take care of him—and later, she could retrieve his broken claw to trade to Shadow.

Zyre flew forward, steeling her nerves. She skimmed the desert below as she drew closer to the oasis. One shout and it would be over.

She drew a breath, prepared to doom the young oryctodromeus.

Her stomach flipped.

Something felt . . . off. Usually, a mission filled her with a sense of purpose. Complete the task, earn the reward. But this time, unanswered questions tangled like vines.

What was wrong with her?

Zyre glanced toward the boulder where Eleri hid. She found herself paralyzed, flitting back and forth at a distance.

It was too early, wasn't it? As a spy, she should gather more information. Why had the exile saved an enemy scout? And why had those Alliance scouts trespassed so close to the Broken Ridge in the first place?

If the exile died too soon, Zyre might miss out on valuable information. Information she could trade to the Prairie Alliance, in addition to her payment from Shadow . . .

Yes, it was far more sensible to wait. It was only the first afternoon, and Shadow had given her a week. Watch and wait, watch and learn, and squeeze as much profit as possible from the situation. After all, she wasn't sparing the exile's life; she was merely delaying his execution.

Eleri stared at the oasis, waiting for a chance to make his move. If the carnivores were distracted, perhaps he could sneak a little closer and—

No. No point thinking about it. He couldn't steal a sip of that water—not without joining the stegoceras in the larder. Ignoring the burn of his throat, Eleri dropped to his belly and retreated. He wriggled away for several hundred yards, beyond the view of the oasis, before he risked clambering back to his feet.

His body aching, Eleri pressed on. He had to find

another oasis, that was all. An oasis that wasn't under carnivore control . . .

The sun glared. The horizon glinted.

All he found was desert.

Dry and desperate, Eleri fought to form a plan. A story tingled in his mind, mingling with panic: the Tale of Scyliara the Lost. Scyliara had been lost in a dark forest, separated from her herd. She had almost died of thirst. But she knew that water ran downhill—and so when her path forked, she always chose the lower path. Finally, she had found a gully stream . . . and her herd waiting on its banks.

Eleri's chest felt heavy. He would never find his herd out here, but perhaps he could find water. In one direction, the horizon seemed slightly lower—or was that just the shimmer of heat, blurring his vision? Either way, he swiveled to face it. If nothing else, heading downhill might save a few dregs of strength.

All the while, he kept stealing glances behind his back. If the carnivores headed in this direction, Eleri would be exposed in the open space. Easy prey.

"Just a little farther . . . ," Eleri rasped. "Got to . . . keep . . . going . . ."

As he staggered on, a bitter wind kicked up. Eleri's steps turned to stumbles, dizzy with thirst. Was he speaking aloud? He felt delirious, unable to tell the difference between thoughts and words. The heat was all-consuming. But if there was one oasis out here, there *must* be others.

"Just . . . a little . . ."

The horizon gave an odd shimmer, almost a twitch. Eleri stared, blinking through the glare. His mind felt hazy, refusing to focus. What was happening? The horizon was moving. It was drawing closer, erasing the sky. No, that couldn't be right . . .

With a roar, the Burning Dust swept in.

CHAPTER SEVEN

THE BURNING DUST

Zyre started—and for a moment of shock, her wings stopped beating. Why was the air dancing?

The stink hit. A whiff of sulfur, thick and rotten . . .

The Burning Dust. She'd heard of it, of course. Terrible storms sometimes swept across the Deadlands, so thick with dust that you couldn't see a foot ahead. Sometimes the storms burned, carrying flecks of acid in their blast.

Zyre dove, zipping like a hailstone to find cover. The Dust roared toward her as she raced downward. Her wings strained. Her lungs burned. If she was airborne when that tumult hit, she would be shredded.

Once, when she was a fresh hatchling, an older anurognathid had come to her family's nest for aid. His wings had been eviscerated in a storm, leaving him flightless. He had crawled to their nest, begging for scraps.

Instead, Zyre's mother had put him out of his misery.

The memory seared as Zyre dove. Her mother's cold face swept in, sharp and pitiless. *We are windwhispers, Zyre. We do not crawl.*

She had to make it. She had to . . .

A crevasse opened below: an open vein in the desert's flesh. Her breath caught. A chance of shelter—if she could only make it below the surface! The Dust rolled toward Zyre like a carnivore, spitting, snarling, scorching . . .

The Dust hit.

It slammed Zyre like a wall, smashing the breath from her lungs. She spun out of control, crashing down in a tangle of rasps. She couldn't fly. Couldn't think. The world was violent wind, burning specks, the whiff of rotten eggs, and the whiplash of—

Zyre tumbled.

Down, down, down . . . Below the lip of the crevasse, the air stilled. Dust spilled across her, but it was a sprinkling waterfall, not a slashing wind. She thrust out her wings in desperation, ignoring the stab in her joints. Her wings flared, yanking her to a violent halt just above the base of the ravine. Zyre skimmed above the gravel, choking for breath. Ahead, darkness loomed. Her heart leaped.

Sanctuary.

A crack splintered the crevasse wall: a slit of shadow,

tucked out of harm's way. Her body burned with the bite of the Dust, but she pumped her wings and blasted faster, aiming straight for that tantalizing slice of shelter . . .

She slipped inside.

Instantly, the world stilled. With no space to beat her wings, Zyre pinned them back and let herself fall. She braced for bruises before she even hit the stones.

Pain. Shock.

And a new surge of fear.

As Zyre's heart pounded, one claw closed around her starfleck pouch. Barely conscious, her thoughts dissolved like dust. Where was Eleri? If the Burning Dust killed him, would she even find his body? It might be buried, lost to the sands of the Deadlands. Without his claw as proof of death, Shadow wouldn't pay her fee.

Stay awake, Zyre ordered herself. Somehow, she had to find him—before it was too late. She had to . . .

Her body throbbed. Her thoughts blurred.

Her eyes closed.

Fighting for breath, Eleri scrambled down into a ravine. A few dried-up trees sprouted at the bottom, all long dead. When he touched one, its trunk crumbled into dust. Coughing, Eleri hurried forward. His mouth was clogged with tree crumbs, hot flecks scratching his tongue.

The Burning Dust roared.

Eleri charged along the path, keeping his head low. Rock walls rose to either side of him, obscuring his view of the world outside—but soon enough, it made no difference. The sky above was burnished brown, choked by dust.

Most of the Dust blustered across the ravine, carried by wild churns of wind. But a few stray clawfuls spilled into the dark, and Eleri yelped as the stinging specks burned his wounds. The dust stank of sulfur, like a broken egg left to rot.

If only he had a starfleck! Burning a fleck would give him light—and more importantly, it would lend him strength and endurance. But Eleri was not Agostron. He had no hordes of admirers, no pouch of gifted starflecks. He had only desperation to drive him.

The ravine forked, splitting into multiple paths. Eleri chose the left path, scurrying with narrowed eyes. When the path forked again, he realized too late where he must be.

"The Tangled Pits!" he rasped.

It was an infamous maze of ravines, raveling across the Deadlands. Eleri turned and twisted—but soon, he was hopelessly lost. Should he turn left? Right? Dust and darkness clenched around him. Even if Eleri *wanted* to retreat, he'd forgotten half the turns he'd made.

He was trapped.

The Burning Dust continued to fall, pricking sores across his body. The stink was physical now: a muffled fuzz on his tongue that left him gagging. "No, no . . ."

But the worst pain was in his throat.

Thirst clawed at his flesh. Every breath was a blister of dry sand. His tongue had doubled in size: a swollen lump that clung to the back of his teeth. When he breathed, dry air scraped inside his mouth. At this point, even a starfleck wouldn't save him. Eleri needed a fireblast stone, like the ones used by Astrilar the Wise, to blow a cave into the ravine wall. Some hope of shelter, a chance to escape from the churn of the Dust . . .

When the path forked once more, Eleri tested the slope with his claws and chose the slightly lower path. He repeated this process again and again, stumbling blindly through dust and pain . . . One turn, two, three, four . . . Left, right, ever downward . . .

"Please . . . ," he whispered.

As Eleri moved lower, the air grew cooler. The dust felt sparser—or was that just wishful thinking?

Eleri collided with a pile of boulders, splintered from the ravine wall above. Throat tight, he crammed himself beneath them. He barely fit into the cavity—and for the first time, he was grateful for his status as a runt.

High above, the wind howled. It whistled down the ravines, blowing an eerie melody through the Tangled Pits.

His thigh brushed something cold and wet. Startled, he drew back—and gave a gasp of wild relief that was half a sob. *Water.* A thin trickle of liquid, infusing the dirt beneath him. It welled below the surface, seeping beneath Eleri's weight.

Eleri bent and licked, desperately sucking the moisture from the grit. His tongue grew raw, scraping like a dried leaf, but he didn't stop until the inside of his mouth was coated with filthy liquid.

Eleri wrapped his tail around his body, curling into a tight ball. He squeezed his eyes shut. In the space beneath the rocks, he pretended he was back in the warren. Safe and warm, in a soft bed of lichen . . .

The wind screamed. The dust swirled. In the dark, Eleri waited for the storm to pass. And finally, as the Burning Dust raged outside, he slipped into the numb relief of sleep.

Eleri woke.

It wasn't the wind that woke him. The Burning Dust had faded, its stormfront sweeping past into the desert. All that remained was eerie quiet, punctuated by a sound before his face.

A hot, rasping sound . . .

Almost like breathing.

Eleri's eyes snapped open. A huge horned face loomed right in front of him, glaring into his hiding hole as if ready to rip him limb from limb.

"You!" the triceratops snarled, raw with fury. "Flamin' feathers . . . I'm gonna kill you!"

CHAPTER EIGHT

AN UNLIKELY PACT

Eleri burst from beneath the boulders, scrambling to his feet. The triceratops snarled. She shook her skull, a flurry of horns and hatred.

"Wait!" he protested. "I don't . . ."

When he met her gaze, he felt a surge of adrenaline. It was Tortha: the young scout from the Prairie Alliance. Last night, her commanders had ordered her to kill him—but Tortha had hesitated, sparing Eleri's life.

Apparently, she regretted it.

"I'm gonna kill you!" Tortha's accent was a broil of *R*s, her prairie twang as sharp as her fury. "This here's all your fault, you piddlin' little—"

Eleri gaped. "You were exiled too?"

The word "exile" seemed to strike Tortha like lightning. She barreled forward, tossing her head with a growl. Eleri forgot his scrapes and bruises, his burnt skin and aching feet. All he remembered was to *flee*.

The ravine was narrow, and Tortha's bulky frame was slow to turn. Eleri darted and twisted, fast as a fish, while she snapped in his wake. When she finally completed her turn, she scuffed the dirt, preparing to stampede.

"Where's your honor?" she spat. "Filthy little dirt muncher—try facin' your death with dignity!"

"Well, I'd rather not face my death at all . . ."

She charged.

Eleri considered her for a fraction of a second. Then, deciding that he was *not* a trained soldier and had no intention of fighting fair, he bounded onto the stack of boulders. Scrambling up their side, he whipped his tail out of reach, just as Tortha charged past like a living rockslide.

Roaring in frustration, the triceratops whirled back toward Eleri. Hot air spurted from her nostrils as she prepared to charge once more. "Fight me! You've gotta fight me—accordin' to the Laws of Noble Combat, you—"

"Um . . . I'd rather not, thanks."

"You ruined my life! You took me from my home, my squadron, my family . . ."

Eleri stared at her, heart racing. Triceratops were called "moonchasers" in the Old Stories, named for their three great horns that arched like crescent moons. The creatures chased these moons with every step, though they could never catch them.

But right now, Tortha was about to catch *him*.

As she charged toward the rock pile, Eleri leaped. For a long moment he flew, limbs pinwheeling, scrambling for balance . . .

He landed on her back.

Tortha yowled. Eleri's claws dug in, grasping in desperation. Her hide felt as thick as stone—all he needed was a weak spot, a chance to seize control and make her see . . .

In a rush, he knew what to do.

Eleri scrambled up to Tortha's neck, reaching over the hefty ridge of bone that she wore like a crown. With a sharp cry of warning, he thrust his foreclaws at her eyes, halting barely half an inch from her pupils.

The triceratops slammed to a halt, her breath heaving in fear and fury. Eleri held his claws as close to Tortha's eyes as he dared, allowing her to fully register the threat.

"Flaming feathers . . ." Eleri rasped a breath. "Now, will you stop trying to kill me and *listen* for a minute? My name is Eleri of the Broken Ridge, and I—"

"You're a cheat, that's what you are—and you fight as filthy as a carrion muncher. It's our duty to follow the rules of battle."

"I've never been the best at rules."

Tortha growled in disgust. "You ain't got a smidge of honor."

"Maybe not," Eleri said. "But to be honest with you, horn head, I'd rather be dishonorable than dead."

"Horn head?" Tortha spluttered. "Soon as you hop down from there, you'll be the one with horns stuck through your—"

"Not going to play nice, are you?" Eleri said. "Think I'll stay up here for now."

"You can't stay there forever, dirt muncher!"

"Tell you what." Eleri fought to sound confident, but a crack in his voice betrayed his desperation. "Just listen to what I've got to say. If you don't like my deal, I'll hop right down and you can trample me, all right? It'll be a quicker death than the one we'll both face if we can't make this deal."

"Deal? What deal?"

"The one where we wind up with bellies full of leaves."

A long pause. Eleri held back a ragged breath, hoping against hope that he'd judged her correctly. She might be trained as a brutish soldier—but last night, she had hesitated. When the ankylosaur had ordered her to kill Eleri, she'd allowed him to escape. The young triceratops might be all bluster on the surface, but she had an honorable heart.

At least, he hoped so.

"Go on," she said finally.

Eleri exhaled, raw with relief. "Look, if we're gonna survive out here, we've both gotta play to our strengths."

She gave a sharp laugh. "And you reckon you've got strengths, do you? A piddly dirt-munchin' raptor snack?"

70

Eleri bristled. "I've got skills to offer, you know. I've got dexterous claws. I can grab things—and I'm quick on my feet."

"Ain't that a shame," Tortha muttered.

"And you've got size and horns," he went on. "You can intimidate our enemies."

Tortha tensed. "Enemies? You're a citizen of the Mountain Kingdom, you are! *You're* my dang enemy."

Eleri shook his head, although she couldn't see him. "Out here, there's only one kingdom that matters . . . and neither of us are part of it. Not unless we're being served for dinner, at least."

"The carrion eaters?"

"Exactly."

"They ain't got a kingdom! They're just a bunch of wild beasts."

"That's what I thought," Eleri said. "But earlier, I passed an oasis. A pterosaur gave orders to a raptor, like a commanding officer in an army. And it sounded like they had a general, someone in charge of their unit . . ."

Tortha's muscles clenched. "Impossible!"

"It's what I saw."

For a long moment, she didn't respond. Then she sagged beneath him, the tension in her muscles slackening. "Fine," she said. "Let's figure you're tellin' the truth. Which I highly doubt. What's it got to do with this 'deal'?"

"The carnivores are hogging the oasis," Eleri said.

"They've got it set up like an army outpost, with a larder of food and fresh water."

"I don't want their food," Tortha said, disgusted.

"Of course not! But there are *trees* there—and there might be undergrowth too. We need those leaves, Tortha. If we can't find food, we'll be dead before the Night of Half Moon."

"Got yourself a plan, do you?"

Eleri paused. What he had was not exactly a plan—it was a story. The Tale of Jyrok the Cunning, a stegoceras who had tricked his way into his enemy's lair . . .

"I think so." Eleri hesitated. "Can I ask your full name, at least? If we're going to work together, I reckon we should be introduced."

It took her a long moment to respond. "Tortha of the Lowland Marsh," she said abruptly, as if admitting a deep personal secret. "And how are we supposed to scrap with a pack of predators?"

Eleri tried not to look too cocky. "We don't have to fight them. If you help me trick them, they'll carry me right into the heart of their camp."

When Zyre woke, the world was silent.

Her eyes were bleary. It took five long blinks to open them properly, struggling through the haze that smeared her pupils. Where was she?

Memories hit. Zyre scrambled upright, cursing her bruised limbs in the darkness. The air outside was still. All signs of the Burning Dust had passed, swept aside like embers.

Zyre staggered out into the daylight, opening her wings with a wince. She had pulled a few muscles, but her wings seemed intact. They were stippled with scorch-specks, which stung like salted cuts, but nothing was broken.

She exhaled, sagging in relief.

Then she remembered Eleri. Her breath caught. Where was he? If he had died in the Burning Dust, she had to find his body. If he had survived, she had to track him down. She could only hope that his body wasn't lost beneath the sands.

Her payment depended on it.

With a hoarse croak, Zyre flapped her wings and lifted skyward. Every wingbeat throbbed, but she snared an updraft as she rose above the crevasse. Higher and higher, faster and faster . . . She scanned the desert below, fast and frantic.

Where was he?

She felt the twenty starflecks slipping through her claws, spiraling away into the desert below. Her hope of a future, snatched away. Her chance to nest on Lightning Peak, to reunite with her grandmother, melted like a mirage . . .

She flew on.

Minutes stretched. An hour passed. Afternoon congealed into dusk, until Zyre could barely breathe with the ache of her wings. But she pressed on, her talons curling tightly. She had to find him. She *had* to. This was her chance at a better life. But if the Dust had buried the exile's body, she would never find the proof of death that Shadow demanded . . .

Zyre backtracked, wheeling across the desert skies. After a while, a familiar oasis came into view: the carnivores' larder, where Eleri had risked his life to spy before the storm. Zyre scanned the nearby landscape, wheeling lower to squint at the desert.

Eighty yards away, two dark figures brawled in the dying light. They were locked in vicious combat, their writhing bodies silhouetted on the sand.

An oryctodromeus. A triceratops.

And from the looks of it, they were aiming to kill.

CHAPTER NINE

THE OASIS

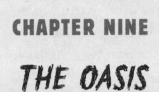

"**N**o!" Eleri cried, crumpling to the ground. "No, please . . ."

The triceratops reared, then brought her enormous forelimbs plummeting toward him. Eleri curled up tight, bracing himself for impact.

Tortha crashed down. She gave a ferocious bark, spitting curses into the air. "To the victor goes the honor!"

Her shout slapped across the rocks. Eighty yards away, the oasis shimmered like a mirage in the twilight.

The raptors' heads pricked up, swiveling toward the noise.

"By the Laws of Noble Combat," Tortha bellowed, her voice echoing across the plains, "you've robbed me of my dignity—and so I've robbed you of your life!"

Eleri lay still, playing dead. The triceratops had barely

missed him, her great legs crashing down inches from his skull. He fought to keep his breaths shallow. He'd painted his face with streaks of dark red dust, which crusted on his skin like blood. Would it fool the raptors?

"Good luck, dirt muncher," Tortha whispered. "I reckon you'll be needin' it."

She reared again, hollering a triumphant cry into the evening sky. Then she galloped away, leaving a trail of dust in her wake. Eleri waited, utterly alone and exposed. His body tingled. Now that Tortha had retreated, he realized the true risks of his scheme. It had all seemed so simple—and so far, it had all gone perfectly to plan.

Together, they had found a path out of the Tangled Pits. Under a clear sky, it wasn't hard to find the oasis again. With Tortha by his side, Eleri had felt invincible. A triceratops soldier could easily fight off two scraggly raptors. But now, alone and exhausted, Eleri's pulse fluttered. This could go very, very wrong. He assumed the raptors would carry him into their larder, but what if they disobeyed the pterosaur's orders?

He couldn't fight them off. He was too small. Tortha was supposed to hide behind some rocks nearby—but if a raptor lunged for Eleri, or Tortha decided to betray him . . .

Eleri fought to slow the thrumming of his heart. He had to be dead. If they suspected that Tortha hadn't finished the job, they'd be happy to do it for her.

Be still. Be silent.

Clawsteps approached, soft and scrabbling. The raptors were eerily light on their feet, claws scratching on the rocks as they approached. Their voices drew closer and closer: a torrent of furious hisses, as if they were arguing.

"But it's just been killed! It's been weeks since we had meat so fresh . . ."

"Didn't you hear our orders? It's for the general!"

The first voice gave an irritable whine, clicking its tongue in impatience. "What the general doesn't know won't hurt her. It's just a little runt, anyhow. I'm starving, Thystril . . ."

"If General Korvia finds out you stole her rightful rations, it'll be *you* who takes this runt's place for her supper."

"But I—"

"Don't be a fool, Yirian! Either this meat goes to the larder, or you do."

Eleri kept his eyes tightly shut, holding his breath as the raptors reached him. The one called Yirian bent lower, sniffing hungrily at his torso. "Just a little nibble . . ."

The raptor's hot breath brushed his limbs. Eleri's skin crawled—and it took every ounce of his determination not to shudder. Was Yirian about to strike? His teeth hovered above Eleri's skin, ready to take a bite. This plan was mad, completely mad. Eleri had just served himself up to a ravenous predator—and at any moment, it would tear him apart.

Eleri braced himself for the agony.

"No!" Thystril snapped. "If there's a single chunk missing, the general will have our scalps. Help me carry it back."

Eleri almost choked in relief.

Grumbling, Yirian bent to grasp at Eleri's tail. Thystril seized one of his hind legs, and together, they dragged him back across the stony desert soil. Eleri didn't dare open his eyes. As his wounds scraped across the rocks, he fought back yelps of pain.

The dirt beneath him grew gradually softer, shifting from sharp rock to gravelly sand. Then tiny fronds prickled at Eleri's torso, and a waft of damp leaves filled his nostrils. *The oasis.*

The earth changed texture beneath Eleri, shifting back to hard stone. Cold and damp, like the inside of a cave. Sensing darkness beyond his eyelids, he dared to flick them open for half a second.

Inside the larder, all was black. Still, he didn't need to see. The stench of rotting meat told him enough. Eleri shut his eyes again, fighting to suppress the nausea that rose in his belly. He tried to pretend that this was just a story, but the stink was overwhelming.

All he could do was hold back a retch.

"Right," Thystril said sharply. "Now, back to patrol. General Korvia will be pleased with our offering."

Yirian muttered something under his breath, but his grip released Eleri's tail. A moment later, a soft scuffle of claws suggested that the raptors were retreating.

Eleri forced himself to count to thirty under his breath.

Then he opened his eyes again, more cautiously. Dizziness spun inside his skull. The stench thickened, raw and musty on his tongue. How long must he hide here? He couldn't stand another minute, let alone the hour they had planned . . .

He crouched near the mouth of the cave, peering at the oasis outside. The plan was working, wasn't it? The raptors' attention was fixed on the darkening desert, not the cave behind them. If Eleri was quick, he could flee before they even noticed him.

At least, that was his hope.

But the raptors were too alert. After the excitement of witnessing a "lethal" fight on the plains, they circled the oasis with claws poised to strike and beady eyes watching, ready for intruders. Eleri hadn't planned for this. He'd assumed they'd be slow and lazy, like the sentries he'd met in the Mountain Kingdom's army.

He had to wait for them to grow bored again. When their enthusiasm dulled, he would seize his chance. He crouched in the shadows, watching and waiting. At least the air smelled fresher here, at the mouth of the cave. The sky outside was darkening, sharp with the chill of dusk.

Eventually, the decision was made for him. A heavy thudding echoed across the plains. It was rhythmic and steady, like clawsteps. But what could be huge enough to cause such a ruckus? The sauropod herd would never venture out into the Deadlands. But that only left . . .

Eleri froze. Too late, he remembered what the raptors had said earlier—that their general would visit at night. The sun was fading. The general was coming.

But General Korvia wasn't a raptor. She wasn't even a pterosaur.

She was a tyrannosaur.

The monstrous creature stormed toward the oasis, her great claws pounding dust into the air with every step. The last thing her prey would feel was the grip of those cold, vicious claws digging into their flesh. She was coming to inspect the outpost . . .

And to devour the meat that her soldiers had gathered.

The raptors dropped into respectful bows as the general approached. Eleri seized his chance to dart outside. At the edge of the stream, he uprooted fistfuls of ferns and moss with his foreclaws. He snapped a giant mouthful of bracken, no longer caring if he caused a racket.

All that mattered was speed.

The raptors turned, startled by the crunch of twigs—but Eleri was already sprinting, burning with adrenaline. Fragments of moss broke off, flying behind him as he zipped across the rocky terrain.

The tyrannosaur roared. She'd spotted him now, and her great body swiveled toward him. The pounding rhythm of her clawsteps increased, although her hefty frame could never compete with his speed.

But the raptors could.

Eleri put his head down and ran faster, heart pounding, breath straining. He hurtled across a patch of gravel, cursing the rocks as they slowed his claws, before vaulting up onto a stretch of eroded stone.

The stone was slippery, polished by decades of wind and Burning Dust—and with a shocking jolt, Eleri tripped. He cried out as he fell, rear claws skittering out beneath him on the stone. Bruised and winded, he fought to regain his balance. A chunk of foliage slipped from his grasp, but there was no time to retrieve it.

The raptors were just five yards behind him. He heard every detail clearly now: the scrape of their claws, the hunger in their snarls, the slobbering rasp as one of them licked his lips in anticipation . . .

With a shudder, Eleri remembered the touch of Yirian's breath on his skin. The memory curdled like nausea. He wouldn't let that happen again—he *couldn't* let that happen again.

Eleri ran.

He careened from the rock onto a stretch of dry sand, and heard a cry of panic as one of the raptors skidded behind him. Its companion yowled as they crashed into each other, upended by the same polished stone that had unbalanced Eleri.

This was his chance.

Ignoring the roars behind him, Eleri put ten yards between them, fifteen, twenty . . . The raptors yowled, crying out in fear and fury as they scrambled to their feet. Once the general interrogated them, they would suffer for their mistake.

They'd be lucky to survive the night.

Heart pounding, Eleri dodged and weaved. He ducked behind boulders and dashed around outcrops, trying to vanish into the landscape. He scrambled down into a crater, skittering gravel and leaves behind him as he fled. Without a starfleck to lend him strength, Eleri used sheer desperation to propel his body forward.

Eleri hurtled into the jaws of the Tangled Pits. As he'd arranged with Tortha, he always chose the lefthand path. To avoid getting lost in the labyrinth, consistency was key.

Left, left, left . . .

His body heaved. Froth gathered on his lips, and he licked it back, unable to lose the precious moisture. Finally he dropped to the ground, panting, as fistfuls of foliage tumbled from his claws and jaws.

The only sound was his own ragged breath. No booming footsteps or scrabbling claws. No sounds of pursuit at all. Just the quiet of the night and the sharp pain of exhaustion that tore at his lungs.

For now, at least, he had survived.

CHAPTER TEN

A SURPRISING STRANGER

Eleri clambered to his feet, utterly spent.

In the shadows, he gathered the stolen foliage. He was tempted to gobble the lot and disappear into the desert, but the branches were too bristly to gulp quickly—and with his parched throat, he seemed more likely to choke than swallow.

Besides, he'd made a deal, hadn't he? Half the food belonged to Tortha.

And so, body aching, he limped toward their meeting place. With her size and strength, Tortha was a valuable ally: a rare thing in the Deadlands. Eleri wasn't mad enough to steal her share of the food. And if he was honest with himself, he couldn't survive his exile alone.

He *needed* a herd. Although his mother had been killed

when he was just an egg, he'd always had his father. His brother. The herdmates who had fed him and given him a home in the Broken Ridge warren. All his life, Eleri had dreamed of earning their acceptance. Of finding his purpose, his role in the herd . . .

And now, he had Tortha.

Of course, he could never admit this to the triceratops. If he spoke of working together in the long term, she would probably demand another duel to the death. For Tortha, this was a one-time deal to survive their first night in exile.

Eleri had to change her mind.

Tortha paced anxiously around their meeting place: a massive rock formation resembling a cluster of eggs. Eleri had named it the Giant's Nest, and it glistened strangely beneath the rising moon. Eleri was oddly touched by her worry—but then again, perhaps she was just eager for dinner to arrive.

"Hungry?" he called.

Tortha jerked her head, startled. Then her face broke into a crooked expression that could almost be called a smile. It looked out of place on her great horned head. "Still breathin', dirt muncher?"

"Sorry to disappoint you."

Eleri dropped his loot at the foot of the Giant's Nest. Examining it now, it seemed quite a pitiable haul. It was barely a single meal for Tortha's massive frame, let alone for Eleri as well. He glanced at her, suddenly nervous that she might snap at his meager offering.

"Glad you're safe," she said.

A wave of relief swept across Eleri.

"I've been hankerin' for a feed," Tortha added. "Besides, it's *my* right to kill you in a duel of honor, soon as we go our separate ways. It'd contravene the Laws of Noble Combat if them corpse munchin' dolts nicked my victory."

"Oh," Eleri said. "Um . . . Well, how about we save that victory for another day?"

He divided the food, ensuring that Tortha had the larger share. As much as he longed to take half of it, he required far less food than the massive triceratops. To his surprise, Tortha pushed some of it back into his pile.

"Keep your fair share," she said. "I'd be stainin' my honor if I took that much."

Eleri studied her, frowning. These military notions of "honor" and "dignity" reminded him uncomfortably of Agostron, and he turned back to his pile with an odd curl in his belly. His brother's face swam in his mind, eyes tight and claws flexing as he spoke that lethal word.

Traitor.

Eleri drew a short breath. He shook his head, trying to refocus on the meal.

Tortha attacked her pile with gusto, gobbling the branches with a hunger that Eleri had only witnessed in carnivores. She crunched branches in her great jaws, her huge flat teeth grinding the foliage into mush. Suddenly, she froze.

Eleri dropped the fern frond in his claw. "What's wrong?"

85

"Shut your trap!" Tortha stared into the enormous pile of boulders. Her gaze was tight and ferocious, as if she'd scented danger.

"What is it?" Eleri whispered.

She glared at him. "If you make one more noise, dirt muncher, I'll drag you back to that oasis and feed them raptors for real. Got enough brains to try shuttin' up?"

Eleri considered this. He also considered her enormous horns. "Um . . . yes?"

"Good."

Inside the Giant's Nest, the shadows lay dormant. Now that Eleri focused, he glimpsed a deeper darkness in the pile of stones. Like the entrance to a cave, or a tunnel . . .

Inside the tunnel, the shadows moved.

Tortha barreled forward with a cry, her horns flashing in the dusk light. Something loomed. As it stepped closer, its true bulk became apparent. Eleri stumbled backward, tight with fear. Was it an ambush predator, lying in wait to attack them? As its steps scraped the tunnel floor, Eleri imagined a carnotaurus, with brutal horns and gnashing teeth. Or perhaps a tyrannosaur, which could crush Eleri in one snap of its jaws . . .

Step by step, the unseen beast drew closer. Its breath came loud and slow, as if it were tasting the air, drawing in the scent of their fear . . .

"Ooh, hello!" it said.

Eleri blinked.

A young ankylosaur bustled into view, bouncing a little on her enormous feet. Even partially grown, she could kill Eleri with a single swipe of her clubbed tail. Plates of bone and membrane sprouted from her spine, creating a shield of defensive armor.

"Lovely to meet you!" she said. "Oh my, it's been ever so lonely out here on my own."

Eleri eyed Tortha, who looked as flabbergasted as he felt. This wasn't the welcome he'd expected from a giant walking weapon who lurked in a mysterious tunnel in the Deadlands. He took a moment to catch his breath, processing the fact that he was *not* about to fight a ravenous tyrannosaur.

"Um . . . nice to meet you too," he said, after the silence had stretched past awkward and into uncomfortable. "I'm Eleri of the Broken Ridge, and this is Tortha of the Lowland Marsh."

Tortha scuffed an angry claw in the dust, as if he'd cheated her by trading away her name so lightly. He ignored her.

"Ooh, what stupendous names! You must have lived such exciting lives—gosh, I can hardly imagine the stories you must have to share! I'm Sorielle of the Grotto—well, that's my new name at least, since I live in the Grotto now—and I've been living out here all alone for weeks, since the last Night of Half Moon, so you can't imagine how pleased I am to make your acquaintance. Oh my, did you steal that food from the carnivores? Gosh, you must be very brave!"

Sorielle spoke so fast that the words tripped over one

another, creating a rhythmic jumble of blather. Her accent sounded soft and bulbous, pitched in contrast to Tortha's twang. She must have come from the inner prairie—perhaps the Scrub Plains or the Fern Lea—rather than the outer marshes.

"Were you *spyin'* on us?" Tortha demanded.

"Spying?" Sorielle's eyes widened. "Oh goodness, no! I heard some voices outside, so I came to see if I had visitors."

Eleri stared at her, bewildered. "This is the Deadlands, right? Pit of all despair, scorched stone and desert, home only to heinous criminals and hordes of vicious carnivores?"

"Oh yes, of course!"

"Just checking," he said weakly.

Tortha scraped back her pile of leaves, out of the ankylosaur's reach. "I've no inklin' of who you are, bristle-butt, but we *earned* this food. You can't share it."

Sorielle blinked. "Oh golly, I wouldn't dream of taking your food! I've got much more food than I need—and more scrumptious than this." She hesitated. "I'm so sorry, that was rude! I didn't mean to offend you, I'm sure your meal tastes lovely . . ."

"More food?" Tortha cut in. "Where?"

"Oh, down in the Grotto! Would you like me to show you? It's where I've been living, you know, and it's ever so lovely."

"Yeah, you mentioned that."

"Come along, then." Sorielle turned toward the Giant's

Nest, where a dark tunnel wound beneath the rocks. "Just follow me!"

Despite her enormous size, she bounced along like a hatchling. Eleri waited five seconds before he moved to follow, keeping well out of reach of her wagging tail.

"Wait!" Tortha hissed.

He turned to her, perplexed. "What?"

"I don't trust her. Ain't right to be so cheerful, especially out here. It's gotta be a trap."

Eleri tilted his head. "She's an ankylosaur, isn't she? That makes her part of the Prairie Alliance. If this was the war, she'd be on your side."

"Well, this ain't the war. This here's the Deadlands. And if you run around trustin' every numbskull you meet, you'll be lucky to survive a week."

Eleri frowned, staring toward the dark tunnel. Sorielle had already vanished, her clawsteps clattering down into the earth.

"Look," he said. "We need food, and we need shelter. If this is a trap, we're dead. But if we don't go, we're dead anyway. How long can we survive without supplies?"

"There ain't no 'we,' dirt muncher!" Tortha raised her chin in defiance. "There's gotta be other oases around here—and clearly, the corpse munchers ain't too hard to fool. I'll just come up with a plan to trick 'em again."

"Oh yeah? And how many times will that work? They're

an organized army, and they've got pterosaurs to spread word of any tricks. They'll figure it out, and then you'll die."

She looked ready to interrupt, but Eleri raised a claw. "I'm serious, Tortha! The carnivores control all the food and water in the Deadlands. Sorielle might be our only chance of survival."

They both stared into the tunnel. From inside, a merry voice echoed up toward them. "Are you two slowpokes coming? Oh, I've got such lovely things to show you!"

Tortha ground her teeth. "Flamin' feathers . . . If that brainless bunch of bristles says the word 'lovely' one more time, I'll be sellin' her to the corpse munchers."

"If she's really got a stockpile of food," Eleri said, "I reckon she can say whatever she wants."

CHAPTER ELEVEN

THE GROTTO

Step by step, Sorielle led them down the tunnel. Their claws crunched the gravel, lending a percussive beat to their descent.

Down, down, down . . .

The tunnel twisted, writhing like a snake. Forks branched from the main tunnel, spiralling away into unknown parts of the Deadlands. Eleri thought of Astrilar the Wise, who had used explosive fireblast stones to carve a labyrinth of tunnels beneath the Fire Peak. Her herd had sheltered there in the aftermath of the Fallen Star, allowing them to survive those first few weeks of devastation. Eleri tried to imagine that he was there, sheltering in Astrilar's care—but she had filled her warren with food and bedding.

By contrast, this tunnel was bare.

How could there be food here? The tunnel was dust and darkness. Unless Sorielle had invented a cuisine out of gravel, it seemed the young ankylosaur was out of her mind. But Eleri trekked on, winding through the tunnel. Where else could he go? Better to die with companions than to face his death alone.

Tortha looked oddly wary, twisting her head back and forth to scan the darkness. "I don't trust this place," she hissed.

"You don't trust anything," Eleri said. "And it's just a tunnel, nothing to be scared of."

He expected a cutting retort, but Tortha turned to face him with an odd look. She looked suddenly uncomfortable, as if on the verge of saying something that she shouldn't. "You'd be surprised, dirt muncher . . ."

She trailed off, shaking her horned head.

Curiosity sparked, Eleri was about to press her further—but the tunnel bottomed out and he glimpsed a glint ahead. He frowned, struggling to squint between the bodies of the larger dinosaurs. But he had no hope of seeing past a triceratops and an ankylosaur, even if they were only half grown.

Inhaling deeply, he sniffed a faint waft of sweet leaves—like the scent of his favorite ferns. His belly grumbled. Could it be? No, ferns couldn't grow down here. It was too dry, too dark . . .

Then he heard it: the gurgling whisper of running water.

Heart leaping, he scampered after Tortha into Sorielle's hideout.

An underground river gushed into the Grotto, bubbling out from a wide black tunnel. Water trickled down the back wall, dripping a constant rhythm on the rocks. In the damp, a riot of foliage sprouted across the wall: soft ferns and fuzzy moss, with a scent so sweet that Eleri's tongue ached.

The Grotto was alive with sound. Water drizzled. The river burbled, tickling its rocky banks. Faint chirrups echoed in the offshoot tunnels—the songs of small nocturnal creatures, dwelling in darkness.

But the Grotto wasn't dark. It was . . . dappled with light. Had they stepped into a treasure trove of starflecks? No, the glow was external. It streamed through cracks and crannies, painting specks of light across the stone. If Eleri squinted, it seemed a sky full of stars. Some of the plants even glowed, casting their shine across the cavern walls.

"Wow," he whispered. "You live here?"

"Oh yes!" Sorielle said. "Home sweet home. I've been here for three moons now, ever since I got exiled. Isn't it just splendid? When I first found this place, I said to myself, 'Oh golly gosh, whatever have I done to deserve such a treat?'"

"I'll bet you did," Tortha muttered.

"How did you find it?" Eleri asked.

"Oh, by accident! A huge pterosaur was patrolling overhead, and he seemed rather keen to take a bite out of me."

Sorielle beamed, as if being chased by a ravenous carnivore was a delightful adventure. "I noticed that my clawsteps created a slight reverberation, so I used the sound and frequency to estimate the size of the tunnel that must lie beneath me. I also noticed that the wind was hitting my backplates at an angle, as if slipping through a gap in that pile of boulders. My calculations led me to the tunnel, and here I am."

Eleri gaped. "You guessed all that from an echo and a bit of wind?"

"Oh, it was nothing! I've always liked numbers, you see. They're just so jolly reliable, even when the rest of the world isn't in a friendly mood."

"And why are you tellin' *us* about it?" Tortha demanded. "Ain't you worried we'll nick all your food?"

Sorielle laughed. "Don't be silly—there's enough here for an entire herd of sauropods. And besides, it wasn't quite so delightful here without anyone to share it. But now that you're here, it shall be perfectly jolly!"

She waved her tail, gesturing around the Grotto, and Eleri ducked to avoid being accidentally disemboweled by her tailspikes.

Tortha ground her teeth, clearly displeased to be called "silly" by the sort of dinosaur who said "golly gosh" and "jolly." But the temptation of food won out, and she dismissed her irritation long enough to crunch a mouthful of nearby ferns.

"Thanks, Sorielle," Eleri said.

She smiled at him. "No need for thanks, Eleri! Always a pleasure to help a friend in need."

Eleri paused, taken aback by her choice of words. He barely knew this ankylosaur—and she was a member of the Prairie Alliance, wasn't she? Perhaps they could be allies, at most . . . but friends?

Then he caught the warmth in her eyes. She was genuine. When was the last time someone had looked at him so fondly? Eleri couldn't remember. Suddenly nervous, he returned Sorielle's smile before turning his attention to the feast at hand.

The Grotto bristled with so much greenery that he didn't know where to start—but soon enough, his instincts led him to the back wall. The moss was sweet and tender, ripe with damp green shoots of ferns.

Beside him, Tortha picked at the waterweeds, which sloshed and jostled at the edge of the underground river. Eleri drank until his body was overflowing and gobbled moss until his belly ached. Finally, weariness engulfed him.

"Is it all right if we rest?" he asked Sorielle. He had a vague idea that it was rude to eat a host's food and immediately fall asleep on their floor, but right now Eleri was too exhausted to remember the elders' rules of etiquette.

Sorielle wriggled a little, bouncing on her toes. "Of course! I've estimated that eight hours' sleep provides the optimum balance between rest and performance, and by my calculations, I'm thirteen hours short of my sleep budget for the week. Golly, no wonder I'm tired! How about we all bed down for a kip?"

"Are you mad?" Tortha demanded. "All of us at once?"

Eleri and Sorielle blinked at her.

"We've got to post a sentry." Tortha enunciated slowly, as if speaking to fresh hatchlings. "We'll be takin' shifts, course, so everyone gets an equal chance to rest."

"A sentry?" Eleri said. "Oh, come on, Tortha, you're not a soldier anymore. You don't have to follow their protocols."

"That right, is it?" Tortha asked. "And who'll take the blame when a herd of carnivores rampages down that tunnel over yonder, all hankerin' for a midnight snack, and we're all curled up like a clutch of hatchlings?"

Eleri followed her gaze toward the underground river. Now that she mentioned it, the river tunnel *was* quite wide. Even a tyrannosaur might fit along it, if push came to shove.

"All right," he conceded. "Maybe we should have a sentry."

"Three hours each," Tortha said firmly. "I'll be takin' the first watch, of course. After all, I reckon I'm the only real soldier in this group?"

She looked at Eleri and Sorielle as if daring them to challenge her.

"I'm a storyteller," Eleri said. "Not a soldier."

Tortha gave a derisive snort. "Oh well, I'm sure *that'll* help us survive out here. Gonna tell a bedtime story to the

96

next raptor who sneaks in here for a nibble?" She turned to Sorielle. "And you?"

Sorielle's eyes were as wide as river stones, and she stared at the triceratops with an expression that was almost awe. "Oh, you're so clever! Of course we should have a sentry— and it's awfully kind of you to volunteer."

If possible, Tortha looked even more irritated by this attention. "I ain't kind, nor clever," she said coldly. "Unlike some folks, I've just got myself a lick of common sense."

Sorielle stumbled backward, visibly crushed. "I . . . I mean . . ."

"Ignore her," Eleri said to Sorielle. "She's cranky because you've helped us so much. I don't think she likes being in anyone's debt."

He met Tortha's gaze. In a flash, a memory passed between them: the clearing near the Broken Ridge, when Eleri had shouted a warning. A cry. A shriek. The flap of a pterosaur's wings . . .

Tortha huffed and turned away. She bustled to the river-bank, where she stood at utmost attention. Her gaze fixed on the river tunnel, squinting into the unknown dark.

"Come on," Eleri said. "Let's get some rest."

Sorielle's smile was slightly weaker. There was an odd fragility in her gaze—the whiplash of Tortha's rejection. But when Eleri pulled a face, imitating Tortha's grumpy expression, the ankylosaur broke into giggles.

Tortha whipped around, glaring, but could find no obvious

cause to complain. "This here's a military situation," she said. "Try showin' more respect for procedure, even if you're just a useless storyteller."

"Excellent point," Eleri said, as he fashioned a nest out of moss and bracken. "Have a good night, *sergeant*."

"Hmph," huffed Tortha.

Eleri curled in his nest. It reminded him of home: a cool bed of lichen in the dark of the warren. As he closed his eyes, he wondered what Agostron was doing. Was his brother already asleep? Did he care whether Eleri had survived the day?

But even as his imagination conjured an image of his warren, a fresh wave of weariness washed over him. Suddenly, Eleri was too tired to think. Too tired to feel.

All that mattered was sleep.

Outside, Zyre perched on the heap of boulders.

What had Eleri called this place? *The Giant's Nest.* A ridiculous name, but a useful landmark. She perched uneasily, shifting her weight from claw to claw. Should she follow the exiles underground?

No, not yet. Her instincts told her to wait. She had no idea what lay in that darkness—and if she clipped a wing on a tunnel wall, she might even break a delicate bone. For an anurognathid, a broken wing was more terrifying than a tyrannosaur.

Better to wait. They had to emerge sooner or later, right?

Zyre hated to admit it, but she was secretly impressed by Eleri. The oryctodromeus had shown great courage today—recklessness, yes, but courage as well. To lie still while the raptors dragged him to their larder . . . Zyre would never have risked it. She'd have fluttered away before the predators got within ten yards of her.

Then again, Zyre had an easier time finding food out here. She had raided a termite mound for supper, and as the evening wore on, a few flying bloodsuckers had zipped within reach.

Still, Eleri had been brave. The thought of selling him out to the carnivores made Zyre's insides flip. It didn't seem right, somehow. But a true spy lived without mercy, and to join her grandmother at Lightning Peak, she had to put aside her qualms. Again, her parents' faces swam before her: the disdain in their eyes—the bitter disappointment—when Zyre had shown a hint of empathy.

A hint of weakness.

Profit isn't personal. We do not crawl.

Tonight she would wait, watch, and learn. She would gather the facts of the situation. Tomorrow, she would find the carnivores—and tell them where to find their prey.

A clawstep cracked the night.

Zyre stiffened.

The triceratops emerged slowly, trying to keep silent.

What had Eleri called her again—Tortha? Well, clearly no one had trained her in hunting techniques. She was a soldier built for strength, not stealth. With every step, her claws crunched the gravel.

Zyre watched, curious. Why was the triceratops sneaking out alone? Was she abandoning her new companions in the night?

Tortha headed for an expanse of empty rock, not far from the Giant's Nest. As quietly as she could manage, Zyre flitted after Tortha. She stayed twenty yards behind the triceratops, darting between rocks like an insect herself.

The night was a breezy one, and Zyre's flutters were lost in the rustle of sand and grit. The air murmured, a sea of dark whispers. In other circumstances, this might have put her at a disadvantage—masking voices that Zyre wanted to hear—but tonight, she was quite happy to let the night's grumbling disguise her flight.

Tortha's pace slowed as she approached a ridge. Zyre perched behind a nearby stack of boulders, just out of sight.

Tortha stared skyward.

The triceratops didn't seem to be doing anything. She simply stood there, gazing at the stars—and to Zyre's befuddlement, the moonlight struck a strange glint of moisture on her horned face.

Was that . . . a *tear*?

Tortha scuffed the dirt, giving a low growl. She began to

circle, tracking around and around on the rocks, her body quivering with frustration.

No, not just frustration.

The vicious battle-trained soldier was grieving.

Zyre knew it in the depths of her bones, in the flutter of air within her lungs. In the privacy of the night, Tortha was mourning the life she had lost—and the future that had slipped between her claws. The warrior was . . . broken.

And Eleri was vulnerable.

As a breeze bustled across the plains, Zyre's skin tingled. This was her chance. The exiles were unguarded. Eleri and the ankylosaur—Sorielle, Zyre remembered from her introduction—were probably asleep, and their sentry was distracted by self-pity.

They were down there.

They were easy prey.

She should do it now. It would be so simple. Her parents would act with barely a blink. All she had to do was fly back to the oasis and tell the general where Eleri was hiding. When it was all over, she could take his broken claw back to the Mountain Kingdom—and twenty starflecks would be hers. Zyre had sold secrets before, hadn't she? What made this one so different?

Zyre perched, taut with indecision. Her starfleck pouch hung from her leg, taunting her with the promise of riches to come . . .

Her thoughts were interrupted as Tortha gave a weary sigh. With heavy steps, the triceratops trundled back toward the Giant's Nest. Zyre shrank into the shadows, watching her descend back into the mysterious tunnel.

Surely, Zyre had missed her opportunity now that the young triceratops was back on guard, right?

Yes. Better to wait. She needed more information. That was all. She had to assess the situation fully—after all, wasn't it her job to spy? It would be unprofessional to rush into action without all the facts.

"Right," she whispered. "That settles it."

Zyre drew a deep breath, gazing into the gloom of the Giant's Nest. She didn't dare fly inside the tunnel, but that didn't mean that she couldn't enter at all.

On the ground, she inched along. Her claws scraped on the tunnel floor as her precious starfleck pouch dragged behind her. A noise. A lure. A promise of the prize that awaited, if only she could find the nerve to strike . . .

Scratch, scratch, scratch . . .

Zyre crept into the dark.

CHAPTER TWELVE

DANGER IN THE DARK

Three hours later, a horn jabbed Eleri's chest.

"Get a wriggle on, dirt muncher," Tortha hissed. "Your turn for sentry duty."

"Hmpgh," Eleri managed, breathing into his bed of moss.

Tortha poked him again, harder this time. With a sigh, he hauled himself upright and gave a weary nod. "I'm awake, I'm awake . . ."

Eleri dragged himself into position by the river. Behind him, he heard the heavy thud of Tortha circling for a moment before collapsing onto a pile of bracken. With a long exhale, she let her tail curl around her and dropped her snout onto her forelimbs.

Eleri sighed. More than anything, he longed to curl up

back on his moss bed—but from the sounds of it, Tortha had just crushed it.

Oh well. Might as well make the most of it, then.

He tried to study the Grotto, memorizing its layout and features. If they *were* attacked here, it might help to have an escape route planned, but most of the tunnels were too small for Tortha and Sorielle to use to flee.

Of course, if an enemy came down the river, the three of them could run back up the main tunnel to the Giant's Nest. And if a predator prowled from the Giant's Nest, they could flee along the river tunnel. It must end up outside, mustn't it? Assuming, of course, that the river didn't conceal too many dangers of its own . . .

Even as he thought it, Eleri caught a flash of silver in the water. He stiffened, leaning forward, but it was gone. Had he imagined it? Maybe, maybe not. There were plenty of aquatic dinosaurs, and anything might lurk in those dark ripples . . .

Something skittered behind him.

Eleri whipped around, his heart racing. In the corner of his eye, he caught the tiniest flick of movement, somewhere in the shadows. But there was no sign of an intruder. Perhaps it was just a tiny warmblood: a cave bat or a rodent.

A guttural moan echoed down the tunnel.

Eleri stiffened. He glanced at the others—but they were both deep asleep. Sorielle gave gentle little snores, snuggling into her bedding as if enjoying a delightful dream about flowering meadows. Tortha twitched, tossing her horns as if fighting an imaginary battle.

If Eleri woke them, he'd likely get a startled claw in the guts for his trouble—and with the size of his companions, that could well be lethal. Besides, was he even certain about the noise? Perhaps he'd imagined it.

It came again. A low moan. Eleri's skin prickled—and again, he remembered the brush of the raptor's breath. His fear spiked. For the first time since his exile, he had felt safe in the Grotto. But if some unknown creature was lurking in the dark, or a predator was creeping along the river . . .

Eleri turned back to face the dark, his mind racing. Perhaps there was a natural explanation. Sometimes the earth creaked, didn't it? The soil of the Deadlands was quite unstable—perhaps it was just a natural groan of the tunnel.

Only one way to find out.

What would Astrilar the Wise do? Or Yari the Strong? Investigate, of course. If Eleri hoped to weave his own story, he had to be courageous too.

With a nervous breath, Eleri ventured toward the river tunnel. Narrow stone ridges ran along its sides like raised shorelines. If he kept to those ledges, he could avoid touching the water—or provoking any strange beasts that might lurk in the depths.

He sidled along a riverside ledge. As he moved from the Grotto into the tunnel, the world melted from dark gray to black. Eleri hesitated, then backtracked briefly to pluck a glowing mushroom from the cavern wall. He clutched it tightly in his right foreclaw and tiptoed deeper into the dark.

The tunnel wound and wiggled, twisting like an enormous warren. It was vast—almost cavernous—and his clawsteps echoed unnervingly in the gloom. He crept forward, breathing heavily. An occasional *plop!* or *splosh!* struck the water, and each time, Eleri almost dropped his light in shock.

Something was alive in that river.

But it wasn't the source of the moans. They came more frequently now, floating down the tunnel to coax him deeper. On and on he walked, winding through the gaping black. His skin prickled. His claws itched . . .

Rounding the corner, he saw it.

A beast. An enormous beast, the size of a hill, trapped and writhing in the water. Its neck was as long as a tree, and its great tail thrashed behind it, churning waterfalls in the dark.

"It can't be . . . ," Eleri whispered.

It was a sauropod.

Or, in the Old Words, a starsweeper.

The beast was young—perhaps a quarter of its eventual size. But to Eleri, it was still too enormous to fathom. After years of sneaking out to watch the sauropods' annual migration, he'd never seen one so close.

The creature moaned: a low, shaking creak strangled with fear and pain.

"Hey!" Eleri called. "Are you hurt?" His own voice startled him, the vast tunnel warping the sound.

But the young sauropod was too distressed to listen. It groaned again, its great tail sweeping waves along the river. It strained at its foreleg, which seemed to be trapped underwater. Perhaps its foot was tangled in waterweeds, or crushed beneath a subaquatic ledge . . .

"Hey!" Eleri shouted again, louder. He waved his foreclaws, jumping up and down to catch the beast's attention. "Hey, down here!"

Even in the darkness, this wild movement caught the sauropod's attention. Its great legs stiffened and its tail hung limp. A final wave crashed with a slurp before the river water rippled into stillness.

The sauropod's long neck swiveled, arching around to bring its face closer. Eleri fell still, his throat tight. The sauropod's eyes were dark and enormous: pools of liquid shadow in the night.

"Hi," Eleri said, taut with nerves. "I'm Eleri of the Broken Ridge. I can try to free your foot, but you've gotta stay still."

The sauropod stared at him. Eleri glanced at the river. It frothed around those enormous legs, churning up frenzied waves as the sauropod bucked in pain.

"Are you hurt?" Eleri asked.

For the first time, the sauropod spoke. His voice was a strange, deep boom. His accent was melodic, but there was something haunting about that tone—an otherworldly quality, just as Eleri had always imagined the starsweepers would sound. They were not mere dinosaurs, but pilgrims of the night sky.

"Thank you, Eleri," he said, in that great slow voice. Each word echoed down the tunnel. "I am Lerithon of the Cold Canyon."

Eleri pinched himself with a foreclaw, not entirely convinced that this was happening. "I'll try to help you," he promised.

Lerithon blinked, his expression oddly distant. He seemed to look *through* Eleri—as if he could see the tunnels beyond, or the night sky that glinted far above them. His reply was slow, each word chosen with great thought. "Here beneath the earth I fall, adrift at the mercy of an earthsinger. Is life itself but a song? The stars have led me into your care."

Eleri paused. He had no idea how to respond, so he settled for focusing on the task at hand. Beneath his stony ridge, the river rippled, roiling slowly in its great journey beneath the earth. He remembered that flash of silver and the pain on Lerithon's face . . .

Eleri stared into the dark ripples. What was lurking beneath the surface? The thought made his skin crawl. Anything might skulk in that black liquid, waiting to sink its teeth into fresh prey.

But he had no choice. With a deep breath, Eleri plunged into the water.

Cold shock exploded along his limbs, engulfing him in jaws of froth. Eleri flicked his tail and kicked his legs, diving into the murk. He clutched the luminescent mushroom in a foreclaw, squeezing hard. It cast an eerie circle of light, wavering in the black water. He fought down a surge of fear and pressed on.

Lerithon's leg sprouted ahead, as gnarled as a tree trunk. Following it down, Eleri descended into a foaming forest of waterweeds. He dropped the mushroom, letting it settle on the riverbed, a flickering beacon in the algae.

Throat aching, Eleri tugged at the weeds. They tangled so tightly that they sliced Lerithon's flesh, scratching bloody lines.

No, it wasn't the weeds that had sliced him . . . As the light shifted with the mushroom tumbling in the churned riverbed, Eleri caught a better glimpse of the wounds.

They were bite marks.

With fresh urgency, Eleri clawed at the weeds. He quit yanking and tried to cut them, wielding his claws like blades. He hacked and sawed, but the weeds were too stringy to yield. He was running out of air. His lungs burned, he had to surface . . .

The water shifted.

Eleri spun, claws outstretched—and that reflex saved his life. Teeth flashed, claws slashed, and the water foamed with fresh blood.

It was a slicerfin.

These predators weren't dinosaurs, but fish. They couldn't think or reason, let alone speak. When the Fallen Star had gifted thoughts and dreams to the dinosaurs, it had left these primitive beasts unchanged. They roamed rivers and streams, preying on unlucky fools who slipped below the surface.

Most slicerfins were small, hunting in packs to attack their prey. Judging by the tiny wounds on Lerithon's leg, he'd already fought off a school of tiny slicers. But this one had lived long enough to grow . . . and now the monster was two yards long. It could never bring down Lerithon, but Eleri would be easy prey.

He flailed, ducking aside. The slicerfin shot past him, gnashing its teeth. Eleri surfaced with a gasp, sucking a panicky lungful of air, before the predator was on him. Its teeth pierced his tail, and Eleri cried out, losing half his air in a string of bubbles.

Blood frothed. Water churned. The slicerfin pulled him down, hungry and eager. Eleri shouted into the darkness.

A huge leg kicked out, smashing the slicerfin backward.

The beast released Eleri, falling back in a torrent of writhing fins. He lurched aside, barely escaping Lerithon's leg as it crashed back down to the riverbed. It crushed the luminescent mushroom, plunging the water into blackness.

It was a race against time now. The slicerfin was too injured to attack again, but the scent of blood in the water would draw other predators . . .

Eleri surfaced, gasping for air. "Stay still!" he cried, struggling to choke out each word. "I'll . . . have . . . to . . . feel . . ."

"The stoic stars do not fall," Lerithon said.

Eleri took this as a "yes." He dove again, running a claw lightly down Lerithon's tangled leg to keep his bearings. He followed it blindly into the murk, like a warmblood scrambling down a tree trunk in the forest.

At the leg's base, Eleri sank into the tangle of weeds. All was black. Relying on touch, he hacked at the weeds, straining against the rubbery strands with all the strength in his claws.

Come on, Eleri begged silently. *Come on, just break . . .*

With a final yank, the weeds snapped free.

Eleri kicked to the surface, gasping and spluttering. He dragged himself onto the rocky shore, ignoring the agony in his tail. The creature hadn't bitten deep, but its teeth had punctured the skin.

"Lerithon?" he gasped. "I think you're free. Try to walk . . ."

In the darkness, water sloshed. A great wave crashed over the ridge, as if the giant sauropod had displaced half the river. But Lerithon made a little sound of pleasure, deep and melodic in the echoing tunnel.

"With the aid of a friend, I may travel once more," he said.

His great voice boomed, echoing down the tunnel. Dizziness pierced Eleri as he scrambled for purchase on the slippery rocks. He took a moment to catch his breath before he turned back in the direction of the Grotto.

"Lerithon?" he said. "If you follow my voice, I'll take you somewhere safe. Does that sound all right to you?"

Lerithon considered this. When he spoke again, the faintest hint of a smile laced his slow words. "I will follow, Eleri of the Broken Ridge. Only the Fallen Star must trace her path alone."

CHAPTER THIRTEEN

FOUR FIGURES

The Grotto was in a state of uproar.

When Eleri emerged from the river tunnel, dripping and exhausted, it took five long minutes to calm the others. After waking to find him missing, Sorielle and Tortha had trampled half the cave in a mad attempt to find him.

"Are you hurt? Where did you go? Were you abducted?"

"I'm fine!" Eleri said, waving off Sorielle's ministrations. Since the ankylosaur's idea of helping involved flailing around her lethal spiked tail, it seemed wise to change the subject. "I'm fine, really! But I've got something big to show you before—"

Tortha scraped her claws on a rock, seething. "You abandoned your post! Don't you know it's a capital offense to skedaddle durin' sentry duty? Useless little dirt munchin' . . ."

She faltered.

A wave slurped from the tunnel mouth into the Grotto. The rush of water was followed by Lerithon, who ducked his long neck as he splashed into view. He blinked shyly, as if taken aback to see so many startled eyes on him.

"The stars have led our trails to cross," he said. "I am Lerithon of the Cold Canyon, and I walk this world alone no longer."

Tortha and Sorielle gaped. Neither could form words as Lerithon hauled himself from the river, gasping with effort at the weight of his own enormous frame. Half the river poured from his body as he rose, gushing waterfalls along his legs and tail.

"You're so big!" Sorielle breathed, her shock morphing into awed delight. "Golly gosh, you can't be older than the rest of us—if you continue at such a rate, you'll be thirty feet tall by the time you're grown!"

"Big as a hill," Eleri said. "That's what my elders always said, when they told us stories about the starsweepers."

"The hills are ageless and see all," Lerithon said.

They stared.

"Flamin' feathers!" Tortha swore. She threw a sidelong glance at Eleri. "Gonna tell us where this half-drowned lump of lunacy washed up from?"

"He . . ." Eleri faltered. Where *had* Lerithon come from? The sauropod herd had passed along the Cold Canyon, of course, but there had been no sign of youngsters with them.

Hadn't Agostron even remarked that the herd was dying of old age?

"No idea," he said. "Just fished him out of the river."

"And you dragged him back *here*?" Tortha demanded. "A complete stranger? What if he's an enemy combatant?"

Helpfully, Lerithon chose this moment to nibble at a crop of flowering ferns by the riverbank. "Sweet are the flowers that know not the kiss of daylight," he said. "Without the light, one cannot see one's own fears."

Glancing at Tortha, Eleri bit back a laugh. "Uh-huh. Such a terrifying enemy combatant."

Lerithon chewed the flowers. His great teeth ground the petals, filling the silence with echoes of each chomp.

"All right, so perhaps he ain't an enemy," Tortha conceded. "But he ain't no ally neither, is he? How are we supposed to know if he's on our side?"

"What is it with you and *sides*?" Eleri asked. "This isn't a war anymore, Tortha. Out here, there's no Prairie Alliance or Mountain Kingdom. No generals or soldiers or princes or kings. There's just us and the Deadlands—and if we want to survive, we've got to trust one another."

Lerithon crunched another mouthful of flowers.

"Ooh!" Sorielle perked up, flushing in excitement. "Golly, I just thought of something!"

"Will wonders never cease?" Tortha muttered.

"Well, my mother always said that four dinosaurs were the minimum for a herd!" Sorielle blinked around the group.

"Five is best, but four will do in a pinch. Don't you see? There are four of us now! That means we could form a herd, all our own. *The Grotto Herd*. Doesn't that sound lovely?"

Eleri sucked a sharp breath, stepping backward. He already had a herd. The Broken Ridge herd had rejected him, yes, but they were still his herd. His brother. His father. His elders.

His family.

Eleri knew they had never truly loved him. But they were all he had—and the Broken Ridge was his home. It was where his mother had died. Where Eleri had hatched. Where he had learned to run, to speak, to dream.

Where he had learned to tell stories.

He couldn't just throw all that away, could he? Not yet. Not with his exile so raw in his mind. All his life, Eleri had dreamed of earning their respect. He would roam the world collecting stories and bring them back to share with his herd. Finally, the elders would see his worth.

Finally, he would have a purpose.

Logically, he knew that dream was likely over now. But even so, he wasn't ready to throw his past aside. He was Eleri of the Broken Ridge, not Eleri of the Grotto.

He settled for silence.

Tortha's eyes narrowed. "*This?* This piddlin' little group of misfits? You reckon *this* is a herd?"

"Well," Sorielle said, "I don't see why not. We've already got a warrior, and a storyteller, and—"

116

Tortha cut her off. "I belong to the Lowland Marsh herd! The most victorious herd in the Prairie Alliance. You wait and see, I'm gonna . . ." Her voice grew higher and faster. "I'm gonna go back, and I'm gonna prove myself, and I'll be a hero. A real hero. Folks'll be beggin' to have me back . . ."

Her voice cracked. Tortha recovered quickly, hiding the pang of exile behind her anger. She stormed off across the Grotto, choosing a nest against the far wall. There, she circled three times with furious stomps and dropped into a curled-up ball, wrapping her tail around herself defensively.

In the darkness, something moved.

Eleri whipped around, searching the shadows. It had been a tiny movement: the scratch of a rodent's claws or the flap of bat wings. A warmblood, perhaps, lurking somewhere in the dark. Some tiny creature, dwelling in the gloom . . .

No, there was nothing there. He was jumping at shadows, wasn't he? Perhaps the shock of exile was making him paranoid.

Eleri hesitated before creeping cautiously toward Tortha. Luminous mushrooms shone on her, painting her horned face in light and shadow. *Moonchaser*. In the shine, her horns resembled the name of her kin in the Old Stories.

Eleri broke the silence. "Tortha . . . I'm not finding this any easier than you. But maybe Sorielle is right. Exile is forever. I know it's hard to accept, but—"

"Hard?" Tortha looked up, sharp with incredulity. "You've

117

got no idea, *storyteller*. No darn idea of what I lost. Of what you cost me."

"I know you had a military career lined up, but—"

"I was the *heir* to my herd."

The shock hit Eleri like a physical blow—as if he'd plunged back into that foaming river. Suddenly all he could see was Agostron: a proud figure, head held high. A streak of violence, suppressed beneath ideas of nobility and chivalry. An obsession with protocol and military rank . . .

He let out a slow breath. "Heir?"

Water dripped down the wall, plunking its song on the stones.

Tortha spoke in a raw whisper. "All my life, I've been trainin' for it. When I was just a hatchlin', they chose me. The strongest. The bravest. The noblest . . . That's why I was out on patrol, even though I'm young. I had to start learnin' what war was like. I had to be ready to fight. To kill. To take a life without hesitation." She looked at him, her face bleak. "And I failed."

Eleri didn't speak.

"What we were doin' out there, the plan we were workin' on—it was so important. It was gonna change everything. The elders trusted me to help with it, and I . . ."

Tortha cut herself off. She looked uncomfortable, as if she had been about to say more than she should.

Eleri opened his mouth, about to press for details of this "plan." But before he could speak, Tortha shook her head.

"My herd tried fightin' to keep me," she said. "But the ankylosaurs who led that scoutin' party . . . they came from the Scrub Plains. Always been our rivals, jealous of our herd, you see. They reckon we're just a bunch of hicks—upstarts from the outer prairie. They figure we don't deserve a place so high in the Alliance ranks. So when they got themselves a chance to exile me, to shame my herd . . . Well, course they took it. Just how it goes, ain't it?"

"Tortha, I didn't—"

"I can do it!" Her voice cracked. "I don't care what it takes, I'm gonna rejoin my herd. Flamin' feathers, I'll prove myself to 'em! It's all I want, Eleri. It's all I care about."

Eleri hesitated. "Sometimes we can't have what we care about. Sometimes the things we want are impossible."

"You're a storyteller, ain't you? Don't you know what they call us in the Old Stories?"

"Moonchasers."

"Yeah, that's right—and know why? 'Cause we ain't scared to chase a challenge."

Eleri released a slow breath, staring at her horns. "No matter how hard you chase those moons on your face, you'll never catch them."

"I don't care what you say! I'm gonna take back my place in my herd—and if you've got any guts in that tiny body of yours, you'll try to do the same. Even if you're just a dirt muncher, it's better than livin' out here."

Eleri faltered.

Staring into the darkness, he fixed his gaze on the water. It drizzled down the stone of the wall. He watched it fall, focusing on the progress of each individual droplet. Was it possible? Could she be right?

He imagined rejoining his herd. The dark wall blurred into faces: joyous, warm, welcoming. The warmth of their warren, the safety of his lichen nest . . . the rush of forgiveness.

The image crumpled. Eleri remembered his herd on the Exile Cliffs, watching him trek into the Deadlands alone. His breath hitched. His life was nothing like Tortha's. His herd had never loved him.

Unless . . . What if he proved himself a hero?

In the silence, Eleri remembered his father at the Mountain Court, taking a step backward. His father, voting to spare him. His father had tried to give him a chance, even when he was just a "disappointment."

What might his father try if Eleri could prove he was so much more?

His skin tingled.

Perhaps it *was* possible. Perhaps he could win back his place in the Mountain Kingdom. But it would require an act of true bravery. To overturn the Mountain Court's decision, he must prove himself worthy beyond all other citizens of the kingdom. He must prove himself indispensable: a hero of the Broken Ridge herd.

Could he do it?

Eleri remembered his terror in the raptors' larder. He'd been afraid—and yet he'd survived, hadn't he? He'd tricked them. He'd won. If he could defeat his enemies on a grander scale . . .

Perhaps he *could* go home.

CHAPTER FOURTEEN

BLOODSTAINED TEETH

Morning light leaked through cracks in the Grotto's ceiling. It trickled slowly, keeping time with the *drip, drip, drip* of water on the wall.

"Right," Tortha said. "We've gotta make a plan."

The four young dinosaurs gathered by a boulder, which Tortha had designated the Speaking Stone. Back home, every herd had a formal place for speeches, meetings, and proclamations. It might be a plateau, a ridge, or a gully. In the Grotto, this boulder was the most obvious choice—even if Lerithon was distracted by its stellar formation of granite crystals.

"Ooh, goody! That sounds like fun." Sorielle beamed, then faltered. "Um . . . a plan for what?"

"To win back our honor, of course. To win back our

rightful roles as soldiers. To reclaim our dignity, our roles in our herds, and—"

"To go home," Eleri said.

They all fell quiet. There was only the drip of the water and the soft murmuring of the river.

"Home is a wandering path beneath the moon," Lerithon opined. "To walk is to find one's home within oneself."

"Yeah, well, I'm sure that's all hunky-dory for sauropods," Tortha said. "But the rest of us are keen to achieve more in life than wanderin' up and down a blasted canyon."

Sorielle shook her head. "But we've all been exiled, haven't we?"

Her voice was high-pitched, tempered by a hint of fragility. She stared at them with wide eyes, as if hardly daring to hope.

"Sentences can be overturned," Eleri said. "In extreme circumstances, after acts of true courage and bravery on behalf of your kingdom, the court can reconsider."

"It's never happened though, has it?"

"Not until now," Tortha said fiercely.

Eleri pressed a foreclaw to the Speaking Stone. How long had it stood here, alone in the darkness? He refused to live out his days alone, separated from his herd. "We'll need to do something to impress the courts."

"We're sittin' on opposite sides of this war, dirt muncher," Tortha pointed out. "If we do something brave to help the

Prairie Alliance, you'll be stuffed. And if we do something brave to help the Mountain Kingdom, *we'll* be stuffed."

"Ooh, let's find a way to help both of them!" Sorielle said.

Tortha scoffed. "Don't be a numbskull! What part of 'enemies' can't you wrap your head around?"

"So we've got to split up?" Eleri asked. "Work against one another?"

Even as he spoke, his voice cracked slightly. They were already so alone in the world; the idea of fighting his only allies made his claws clench.

Sorielle drew a sharp breath, her expression tightening. Again, there was a flash of something brittle in her gaze. It struck Eleri, suddenly, that the ankylosaur had survived here by herself for a long time.

Tortha hesitated. "I . . . Well, I suppose so. Don't see how else it can work."

A long pause.

"What if we didn't *help* the fighting?" Sorielle tilted her head. "What if we tried to stop it?"

Eleri blinked. "What?"

"Are you mad?" Tortha whirled on her, bristling. "You'd let them mountain-dwellin' scoundrels beat us?"

"No! It's just—"

Tortha scuffed her foreclaws on the stone. "The war is a fight for vengeance, to claim back what was stolen from us! The mountain dwellers took all the best food from us! They stole the streams, the flowers, and the valleys, where they hide like a bunch of snivelin' cowards . . ."

"Oh yeah?" Eleri fired back. "Well, our Wise Ones said that prairie dwellers started the war. They wouldn't share the fern prairie—whenever we tried to build our burrows down on the plains, they'd stampede across and cause cave-ins."

"Oh, and that's *our* fault? If you don't want your burrows cavin' in, maybe you oughta make 'em structurally sound." As soon as the words left her mouth, a strange expression overtook Tortha's face.

But Eleri was too angry to care. He glared. "It's not just the burrows! Flaming feathers . . . Everyone knows that the ankylosaurs stole the Scrub Plains after the Fallen Star fell. Those plains used to be shared territory until—"

"Ha!" Tortha cut in. "You reckon stealin' the *Scrub Plains* is comparable to stealin' a whole damn mountain? If you want a sight of greed, dirt muncher, go bend over that there river and take a peek at your reflection."

Eleri grimaced, preparing a retort. But before he could speak, a low booming voice cut through the cacophony of their argument.

"The Fallen Star still burns, slaying its victims through the folly of war," Lerithon said. "Those who win are those with bloodstained teeth."

Tortha glared. "What's that supposed to mean?"

"Bloodstained teeth," Eleri repeated, frowning. "Like the carrion eaters?"

As he spoke, his throat tightened. He pictured a battlefield, hours after the fighting had ended. A sea of fallen soldiers, ripe for the picking. And then the carrion eaters would swoop in, gathering the remains for their larders . . .

Bloodstained teeth. He felt nauseated.

"That ain't on purpose, though," Tortha said. "It's just good luck for 'em."

"Is it?" Sorielle asked.

They all looked at her.

"What do you mean?" Tortha demanded. "Of course it's just luck. You reckon we're fightin' this dang war to fill their bellies?"

Eleri stiffened. A memory flashed into his mind—an image he hadn't considered since his exile. He'd been so distracted, tormented by his fear of the Mountain Court, that he'd pushed the memory aside. But now it blasted back, sharp and vicious. "Maybe we are . . ."

"What?"

"Maybe we *are* fighting this war to fill the carnivores' bellies." Eleri's speech grew faster. "The day of my exile, I saw King Nylius holding a meeting with a raptor."

Tortha stiffened. "In secret?"

Eleri nodded. "They were lurking by the back entrance of the King's Domain—that's a private cave for the royal family. They were trying to hide in the shadows, I think. I only saw them by accident, on my way to the court."

Tortha bristled. "Filthy mountain dwellers! I should've guessed they'd be workin' with the corpse munchers."

In the darkness, there was a faint scraping sound. Eleri whipped his head around, searching for the source of the noise—but again, there was nothing.

Sorielle gave an odd little gasp.

"What's wrong?" Eleri asked.

The ankylosaur stared at him, her eyes wide enough to rival her backplates. "Now I understand," she whispered. "Oh golly, now I know why . . ."

"Why what?"

"Why I was exiled!"

Belatedly, Eleri realized that he'd never asked. He knew why Tortha had been exiled, of course, since her fate was tangled with his own. But he'd never asked why Sorielle—sweet, harmless Sorielle—had been sent to die in the Deadlands.

Sorielle hesitated. "My herd was staying near the heart of the Prairie Alliance territory—near the court itself, actually. I went for a walk at night. It was ever so dark, but I wanted to measure the perimeter of the king's central territory and use the external measurements to calculate the area, in order to estimate a soldier's speed of travel from—"

"Get on with it!" Tortha cut in.

"Oh." Sorielle blinked. "Yes, well, I was counting my steps along the boundaries of the Prairie Court. Then I heard voices. I didn't want to be rude and interrupt their conversation, so I hid behind the rocks."

"And then . . . ?"

"Well, their voices were very low, as if they were talking in secret. I peered out from behind my ridge—and it was a group of carrion eaters! It was the Night of Round Moon, so I had just enough light to see their faces. Two raptors and a carnotaurus, right in the heart of Prairie territory. They gave me a jolly good fright, I can tell you."

Tortha stiffened. "Did you fight 'em off? It was your duty to attack!"

"Oh gosh, perhaps you're right, but they weren't hurting anyone. They weren't even going near the nests. They were just . . . talking." Sorielle released a slow breath. "And even worse, there was someone else with them. An ankylosaur— one from our own kingdom, chatting with the carnivores!"

Silence.

"Well?" Tortha demanded. "What were they sayin'?"

"Oh, it didn't make much sense to me," Sorielle said. "It was all rather peculiar—the tyrannosaur kept saying that 'the Third' was losing patience, that offerings of late had been too meager."

"The Third?" Eleri frowned. "What does that mean?"

"I haven't the slightest idea," Sorielle said. "At dawn, I went to the Prairie Court and I told them what I had seen. I thought that King Torive should know there were predators loose in our territory."

"What did they do?" asked Eleri.

"The king exiled me. Right on the spot. His guards surrounded me and escorted me to the Deadlands—right then and there." Sorielle looked down, her voice cracking. "I didn't . . . I didn't even have a chance to say goodbye to my family."

"I don't like this," Eleri said. "Something shady is going on."

Tortha gave him a withering look. "Dug up some brains under all the dirt in your skull, did you?"

"The carrion eaters aren't supposed to be organized," Eleri continued. "All the stories say that they work alone, that they're just stupid brutes. But out here, we've seen them working in groups—like squadrons of soldiers."

In a cold flash, he remembered General Korvia: the tyrannosaur who held command at the oasis. He thought of the pterosaur who had brought a carcass from the battlefield—and of the raptors who had dragged Eleri to their larder, obeying their general's orders . . .

"Like they've got a kingdom of their own," Tortha said darkly. "A kingdom that's been hidden from us, all our lives."

"A third army of Cretacea," Sorielle whispered. "Oh gosh . . . What if that's what they meant? *The Third is losing patience . . .*"

"Exactly," Eleri said. "If our kings are working with the

Carrion Kingdom, they must have some kind of secret deal, right?"

"But why?" Sorielle asked. "How could anyone be so horrible?"

Eleri considered this. "The carnivores could be threatening them . . ."

"Yeah, I bet they are," Tortha said quickly. "Ain't too hard to guess the deal either. The royal families can keep their territory and their power, never riskin' their own lives, so long as they keep the war goin'."

"But if the war ends . . . ," Sorielle began.

"The predators are still gonna need prey," Tortha said, nodding. "The Carrion Kingdom will launch its own assault— and our kings'll be potential prey, just like the rest of us."

"But that's awful!" Sorielle exclaimed. "The kings are trading hundreds of soldiers' lives to keep themselves safe?"

"Sounds like it," Eleri said. "The royal families stay safe and keep their kingdoms under control. Flaming feathers . . . they teach us to *want* the war. To think it's the right thing."

Memories flashed into his mind—tales and legends of Mountain Kingdom heroes, battling the savage hordes of the Prairie Alliance. With a chill, he remembered King Nylius's words at his trial. *Year after year, those Prairie beasts are stealing what is ours . . .*

Eleri's stomach flipped.

"Keeps us loyal, doesn't it?" he said. "Meanwhile, the

carrion eaters have an endless feast, without ever risking their own lives. Everybody wins . . ."

"Except for our soldiers," Sorielle said.

"Our herds." Tortha spoke through gritted teeth. "Our families."

"We've got to end this," Eleri said. "If we can stop our kingdoms from fighting each other, we can unite. Together, we'll be strong enough to fight off the Carrion Kingdom."

"It'll never happen," Tortha said. "No way. My herd ain't about to work with a bunch of filthy mountain dwellers. We hate 'em too much."

"But don't you see? That hatred is the carnivores' plan! It's what keeps their bellies full, year after year "

A trickle of water ran down the wall, twisting around knobbly lumps of rock. They all watched it, momentarily silent. When it finally splattered on the cave floor, Eleri twitched.

"I've gotta tell you something," Tortha said. Something odd curled inside her tone . . . an unusual weight, as if she wasn't about to deliver her usual bluster and insults but something more serious.

Something like a confession.

Eleri's skin prickled. He remembered Tortha's hesitation earlier, when the triceratops had seemed on the verge of spilling a secret.

"All these years, the war's been draggin' on. The Alliance

131

claims a foothill here, a gully there. But it's been too slow. Every battle it's the same—weeks, maybe months of bloodshed for the sake of a few scraps of land."

Eleri stared at her. "What's your point?"

"Folks are gettin' impatient with all these little skirmishes. The Prairie herds want better territory—and we're done playin' games." Tortha exhaled. "There's a plan . . ."

Eleri blinked. "What? When?"

"In five nights' time. On the Night of Half Moon, we'll be strikin' the most terrible blow against the Mountain Kingdom in history. We're gonna take your territory for our herds—*all* of your territory. Hundreds of enemies are gonna die." Tortha hesitated, staring at her feet. "But not soldiers this time. Civilians."

Eleri's flesh chilled. "What do you mean?"

Tortha drew a sharp breath. "On the Night of Half Moon, the Mountain Kingdom will fall."

CHAPTER FIFTEEN

THE PLAN

*T*he *Mountain Kingdom will fall.*

Tortha's words echoed around the Grotto, cold and hard as a slap. Eleri stared at her through the murk, his own heart racing.

"It's what I was doin' that night, when we met." Tortha refused to meet his eyes. "We found a tunnel, see, leading from the foothills into the heart of your kingdom. I was helpin' to map it out, gettin' ready for a full invasion."

Eleri shook his head. "No, it can't be . . ."

"How do you reckon we got so close to your warren?" Tortha said. "Broken Ridge ain't down in the borderlands, is it? We had a secret route."

Eleri stared. At the time, he had wondered how the scouts had trespassed into the heart of the kingdom without being caught, but the question had been superseded by the shock of the pterosaur's swoop—and the horror of his exile.

Now he knew.

"A hundred Prairie soldiers are gonna rush through that tunnel," Tortha said. "All your soldiers will be on the battlefield, so there'll be no one left defendin' the civilians. Our squadrons are gonna smash their way into every cave, every nest, every warren."

Eleri's insides tingled. Tight with horror, he pictured the warren at the Broken Ridge. His father, dozing in a nest of lichen. His brother, safe and sound in the Heir's Cavern. The elders, the mothers, the eggs and hatchlings.

A bang. A crash. A roar. And then . . .

In the silence, Eleri remembered another conversation with Tortha. When he had remarked that tunnels were nothing to be scared of, the triceratops had looked oddly uncomfortable. *You'd be surprised, dirt muncher* . . .

Eleri's blood ran cold.

"But why would King Torive destroy the Mountain Kingdom?" Sorielle frowned. "His deal with the carnivores depends on the war continuing without end . . ."

"It can't go on forever," Eleri said. "Every year, there are fewer soldiers left, and there aren't enough hatchlings to replace them."

They all paused to consider this.

King Torive must have known that the end was nigh. Sooner or later, the carnivores would abandon their deal and launch their own invasion. If that happened, how could King Torive save his own skin?

"The Mountain Kingdom is superior territory, isn't it?" Sorielle asked. "It's a better defensive position than the plains."

Eleri nodded. "If King Torive thinks that the carnivorous army is gonna attack, I bet he'll want to snare the peaks for himself. He'd have the Mountain Stronghold to retreat to — and if all else fails, he could flee to higher ground."

"Coward," Tortha muttered.

She sounded broken. Bitter. As if her entire world had shattered: an empty skull in a predator's jaws. As Eleri stared at her, he realized that she'd been *excited* about this secret attack. It had been her great chance at victory. Her chance to help defeat the Mountain Kingdom—and to confirm her place as the future leader of her herd.

"And now?" Eleri asked. "Will you help us stop the invasion?"

For the first time, Tortha met his gaze. "Of course," she said. "Yeah, of course I will." Her voice grew bolder. "I fight for my kingdom, Eleri. For honor. Not to protect a coward—or to fill our enemies' bellies."

Our enemies. An odd little thrill ran down Eleri's spine. It was the first time that Tortha had acknowledged that they were a team. Allies, pitted against a ruthless foe.

"Dark is the night that we face alone," Lerithon said. "Light is the gift of the stars and the shine in eyes that meet our own."

135

"Yeah, yeah," Tortha said. "Don't go gettin' all soppy on me."

"But how can we stop the attack?" Sorielle asked, eyes wide with worry. "I hate to say it, but I don't think we can fight off the entire Prairie army."

"Destroy the tunnel before the attack can take place," Eleri said. "It's the only way."

Tortha tilted her head. "And how are we supposed to do that?"

Eleri ran his forelimb along the Speaking Stone, feeling the cold rock beneath his palm. Coarse stone. Ancient rock, lying undisturbed for decades . . .

Deep inside him, a story stirred.

Astrilar the Wise was the first Eye of the Forgotten. As the world had collapsed around her, Astrilar had used fire-blast stones to create an enormous warren in the Fire Peak itself. These combustible stones had been formed by the crash of the Fallen Star. They had lain dormant for decades— but a spark or flame would set them ablaze.

And when they burned, they exploded.

Once the earth had settled, Astrilar the Wise had led her herd across the Deadlands. They had found a wondrous mountain range, where streams still ran and flowers still bloomed. They had called their new home the Mountain Kingdom—and their descendants had lived there ever since.

It was a fairy tale, really. But Eleri had always loved the story. When he was younger, he had secretly played a game of Astrilar's Labyrinth, pretending that their warren was built into the side of the Fire Peak. Most of the adults claimed that it wasn't real, and Agostron had always mocked the very idea of it. *Don't be so stupid, Eleri!* he would say. *It's just a tale for hatchlings.*

Now the memory made him ache. The image of Agostron's mocking smile mingled with his memory of the Exile Cliffs—and that lone silhouette of his brother, watching Eleri stumble toward his death.

"Well?" Tortha said, her voice sharp with impatience. "Any ideas?"

Eleri drew a deep breath. "Fireblast stones. Like Astrilar the Wise."

The others stared.

"Ooh, that would be quite dangerous, wouldn't it?" Sorielle asked. "Their combustibility levels are extremely high. Even the tiniest spark is enough to trigger an explosion."

"Blow up the tunnel?" Tortha perked up. "I like it!"

Eleri nodded. "The stories say that a single fireblast can shred a tyrannosaur."

"How large is the tunnel?" Sorielle asked, turning to Tortha.

Tortha frowned as if struggling to remember. "About three feet taller than a full-grown ankylosaur. And wide enough for two of my commanders, but only if they were pressed side by side. A few bits were narrower, so we had to go through one at a time."

Sorielle began to gabble aloud, running her calculations by the group. Eleri caught the words "load-bearing," "combustibility," and "blast radius," but none of it made much sense to him. Even as an oryctodromeus, he'd never been interested in tunnel engineering.

Finally, Sorielle beamed. "Righty-o! If my calculations are correct, we'll need at least three fireblasts. Four would be better, to be safe. That's if we attack one of the narrower sections, of course."

"But where can we find 'em?" Tortha asked.

A strange chill ran through Eleri. "The Forest of Smoke."

They all knew the tales of the Forest of Smoke, an ancient, fossilized woodland of dead trees. The earth was cracked and broken, spewing ash and smoke into the air.

Worse, it was a lair for carnivores. Predators lurked in the smoke, preying on any fools who wandered into the maze of petrified trees. When the carnivores lacked fresh meat, they were even said to prey on each other.

"We'll have to risk it," Eleri said.

"And how are we supposed to get there?" asked Tortha.

"To find one's way, a traveler knows the night," Lerithon said. "For the stars are my map, and the clouds are my foes."

Sorielle perked up. "Ooh, can you find the Forest of Smoke?"

"The stars are my map. When I see them, I cannot be lost."

Tortha frowned. "But the Night of Half Moon is only

138

five nights from now. It's at least two days' travel there, and two days back . . ."

"We can make it," Eleri said.

Why was he so certain? Perhaps it was the great, reassuring weight of Lerithon beside him. Perhaps it was the spark of hope in Sorielle's eyes or the restless energy in Tortha's stance. Perhaps it was the Tale of Astrilar the Wise, who had used fireblasts to save her herd. If she could do it, Eleri could too.

But as he thought of that tunnel, his limbs stiffened. On the Night of Half Moon, an army would rush along that tunnel into his kingdom. They would smash their way into caves and burrows and warrens. They would slaughter hatchlings in their nests.

Unless Eleri and his friends could stop them.

CHAPTER SIXTEEN

A STICKY SITUATION

The Deadlands stretched before them, scorched and bare. The landscape groaned in the heat, as if its old joints were aching. It was barely noon, but the unlikely band of allies had already been traveling for hours.

Rudimentary sacks dangled from their backplates, horns, and limbs. Eleri had woven them from fronds in the Grotto before stuffing them with clawfuls of foliage. Sorielle had filled one pouch with dripping waterweeds, plucked from the underground river, and draped the sodden weight across her shoulders.

"It will help me to stay cool!" she said, beaming. "Won't that be splendid? And at the end of the day, we can eat the weeds."

Lerithon took the lead, ambling slowly across the great

plains. No constellations shone in daylight, but he was confident that he could find his way. Sauropods were born travelers, weren't they? Lerithon had studied navigation since the day he hatched.

Eleri's exhaustion had caught up with him. He hadn't slept properly for several nights, and his skin seemed to sprout more injuries than feathers. Every step twinged: a scrape or a graze, a cut or a blister. His dry throat stung, and the sun stabbed his eyes.

To motivate himself, Eleri tried to think of his herd. If this plan succeeded, the exiles would be heroes. He imagined himself old and wise, sitting around a circle of awestruck hatchlings as he told the tale of how he saved the Mountain Kingdom. One day, this would be a grand story.

But for now, it was torment.

"Isn't it a lovely day?" Sorielle glanced skyward. "A bright sky and a cheerful sun, smiling at us like an old friend . . ."

Tortha pointed her horned face in the ankylosaur's direction. "You'll be gettin' a permanent smile if you don't watch it."

Sorielle brightened. "Oh, you're so sweet."

Tortha ground her teeth.

Eleri trailed at the rear of the group, glancing back and forth as he watched for predators. After a while, he moved into Lerithon's shadow, using the sauropod as a shield against the sun. When he glanced skyward again, staring at a speck on the horizon, his heart dropped into his belly. "Find cover!"

The others didn't stop to ask questions. They sprinted for the nearest crater, scrambling into the shadows beneath its lip. Their supply sacks slapped against their sides, and Sorielle's waterweeds fell with a thump into the sand. Eleri's breath heaved, fast and rasping, as the shape approached. An enormous pair of wings wheeled overhead—and then it was gone, prowling across the Deadlands toward the Cold Canyon.

"Do you suppose it saw us?" Sorielle whispered.

Eleri shook his head. "I think we took cover just in time."

But when he thought of the direction the pterosaur was flying in, his insides constricted. Whether it had seen them or not, it would find easy pickings on the battlefield. Tonight, its belly would bulge with prey.

"Come on," he said. "We can't waste time."

They retrieved Sorielle's sack of waterweeds and toiled on, pressing their bodies into the heat. The wind picked up, whipping and scorching. Sometimes it carried acidic flecks, which burned Eleri's eyes and skin. Luckily, it wasn't a proper Burning Dust storm: just a few random specks, as if the desert had spitefully decided to sting them.

Once or twice, movement danced in the corner of his eye. He craned his neck skyward, searching, but there was nothing. No sign of the gigantic pterosaur. Still, the back of his neck prickled. He had the odd sensation that something was following them . . .

"What's wrong?" Sorielle asked, sensing his nerves.

"Nothing," Eleri said. "It's just . . ." He shook his head. "Nothing. Just a bit jumpy, that's all."

Tortha glanced skyward, following Eleri's gaze. "Did you see something up there? The pterosaur?"

"No, nothing like that!" Eleri hesitated. "Something smaller, maybe."

"Like an insect? Or a bird?"

"Yeah, maybe."

They stopped only to eat Sorielle's waterweeds, which had mostly dried up in the desert sun. Lerithon happily crunched up the sack itself, apparently enjoying the tangle of fronds.

By the time the sun began to sink, they had reached the edge of the crater field. They faced a vast plain of tar pits, stretching as far as Eleri could see. The tar gurgled and burbled, spitting bubbles of gluggy black oil into the air.

"That looks . . . sticky." Tortha eyed the pits dubiously. "Wouldn't fancy topplin' in."

"Well then, we'll just have to try not to," Sorielle said. "It's jolly lucky that there are paths, isn't it?"

Sure enough, stone ridges ran like rivulets between the tar pits. Narrow and gravelly, they wove a spiderweb through the morass of sticky black, forming junctions where they crisscrossed.

"How far does this stuff go?" Eleri asked, glancing up at Lerithon.

The sauropod raised his great neck, squinting as he

searched the horizon. "Beyond the black, a land of low clouds lies."

"Low clouds?" Eleri repeated.

"No idea," Tortha said, "but it's gotta be better than this stuff. Probably just fog. Come on—if we get through here quickly, I reckon we can camp out in the cloudy place."

Eleri hesitated. "It's getting dark. Maybe we should camp here and try to cross the tar tomorrow?"

But Sorielle shook her head. "If my calculations are correct, we are traveling at approximately six miles per hour. It's a jolly good effort, but I'm afraid it's not fast enough to stop the attack in time."

"Well, in that case . . ."

After a moment's hesitation, Eleri decided to take the lead. As the smallest and lightest, he could test each patch of footing. If Lerithon placed his weight on a crumbling piece of path, the entire ridge might collapse.

"Follow me." Eleri tried to sound braver than he felt.

And with a deep breath, he set out into the field of tar.

Zyre wheeled overhead, her breath tight. She rode an updraft, skimming between the rising pockets of warm air.

After spying on the exiles in their grotto, she had followed them out across the desert. Even now, her mind still churned with their discussion. Could the herbivorous kings really be conspiring with the carnivores to hold on to power?

If it was true . . .

That would mean everything else was a lie. Everything she had known, everything her parents had taught her. *Profit isn't personal.* But this *was* personal, wasn't it? Lies and betrayal, all wrapped in a royal bow. The windwhispers weren't masters of the sky. They were just another set of fools, crawling along to fill their true masters' bellies. Every secret they sold, every plan they betrayed . . .

All to feed the carnivores.

Zyre drew a short breath. There was no proof, was there? Without proof, it was just a wild theory. A conspiracy. It would be irrational to let it affect her own mission. Each day brought Shadow's deadline closer—and she had to take decisive action.

But more than ever, the idea made her queasy. She had watched Eleri in the Grotto, and in a strange way, she had come to respect him. The way he had unraveled the carnivores' plans. The way he had devised the fireblast scheme. And the way he had comforted Tortha . . .

Profit isn't personal, she reminded herself. She couldn't grow fond of the exile, not when her future depended on his death. At least that seemed fairly well assured now, if he was venturing into the Forest of Smoke.

Zyre flapped harder.

Below her, Eleri squinted, staring into the sun as if something had caught his eye. With a burst of nerves, Zyre fluttered higher.

Had he seen her? She didn't think so—at least, there had been no shout of alarm. But he had definitely seen *something,* and his suspicions were aroused.

The wind gusted and buffeted, sending Zyre reeling. She let it carry her a moment, whooshing sideways to find the best angle for viewing the exiles' trek. When she saw what lay ahead, her insides contorted. Tar. A labyrinth of black, gurgling tar . . .

The exiles were going to die. Zyre knew it just as she knew how to breathe or fly or feed. The tar pits would swallow them, leaving nothing behind. Not even a shred of proof for Zyre to carry back to Shadow. Her parents' faces swam before her, cold with disappointment. She had left it too late. Zyre's weakness—her hesitation—had cost her the most lucrative trade of her career.

Eleri would die. Nineteen starflecks would slip through Zyre's claws.

And there was nothing she could do to stop it.

One, two, one, two . . .

Eleri moved slowly, weighing the risk of each clawstep. He tested the path with bated breath. Some portions crumbled, collapsing into gravel flecks that sprayed the tar. As each tiny rock hit the goo, the tar gurgled and popped. Then the pebbles sank, sucked into the sticky black morass.

"Back!" he cried.

The exiles reversed slowly to the last juncture point. Eleri set out again, choosing a different path and praying to the stars that it would hold.

In the shallow pits, bones jutted above the surface. Eleri flinched as he passed the skeleton of a long-dead triceratops, its white horns stark and bare in the twilight. Beside it lay the twisted skeleton of a carnivore, contorted in desperation as it fought to escape the tar. Perhaps the beast had chased its prey into the pit—or else it had tried to feast on the dead triceratops and slipped to join its meal's fate.

Either way, it was an agonizing death. The pit was too shallow to drown in, but the victims' ankles and shins had been trapped by the sticky tar. They must have baked beneath the desert sun, slowly dehydrating as their skin cracked and their eyes stung.

No escape. No chance of hope. The tar was as ruthless as a raptor.

"The Fallen Star still burns within the heart of this land," Lerithon said. "One must not slip into its claws."

Eleri stepped with even greater caution, his pulse faster than a slicerfin's flippers. The sky grew darker by the minute as twilight sank into the final eddies of dusk. *Four nights to go,* he reminded himself. They had no time to waste.

They were halfway across the plain when a shriek split the sky. Eleri's heart stopped as he wrenched his gaze upward.

Pterosaur.

Sorielle gasped. "Run!"

Eleri was already churning gravel as he rushed along the next ridge. The others stampeded behind him, slower and more cumbersome, with supply sacks thumping against their bodies. Eleri paused at a junction to allow them to catch up. Tortha dropped her supplies and charged in front of him, snarling madly as the pterosaur dove.

The creature shrieked again, its claws outstretched as it reached for them—but Tortha was ready. She reared, throwing her horned head skyward, and one of her horns slashed the predator's talon.

The pterosaur screamed, tearing into the evening sky. A trail of blood splattered from its claw, mangled by the thrust of Tortha's horn. But prey was rare out here in the Deadlands, and it wouldn't give up its feast so lightly.

"Flamin' feathers!" Tortha swore.

It dove again, wild and vicious. Eleri was the easiest target, but he was shielded between Sorielle and Tortha—and so, with a wild flap, it veered behind the group and aimed for Lerithon's neck. Eleri's nerves jolted as he recognized its plan. If it managed to slash the sauropod's throat, Lerithon would go down. Even if it missed his jugular, Lerithon might stumble. If he slipped into the shallow tar, if his ankles were trapped . . .

One wrong step, and it would all be over.

But Lerithon refused to budge. With a great bellow, he whipped up his tail. It soared through the air with all the heft of a tree trunk, and the pterosaur banked, shrieking in a wild attempt to avoid it. One inch to the left, and the beast would have been smashed from the sky.

"Run!" Sorielle cried again.

Tortha took the lead, charging with her horns down: a protective shield for her companions. But her weight crashed in enormous crushing thuds on the stone—and as she ran, the path began to crumble.

Eleri couldn't let her go first. He *had* to take the lead, even if it put him in a more vulnerable position. He dashed around her at the next junction, darting low to emerge at the front of the group.

"Behind me!" Tortha roared.

Eleri ignored her. He sprinted forward, faster and faster, until his companions were several yards behind him. When the path began to collapse once again, he wrenched himself to a halt and spun to face the others. "Back! The other way!"

They reversed, stumbling and awkward, even as the pterosaur prepared to dive once more. But this time, it wouldn't risk a deadly injury. Its eyes had fixed on Eleri, isolated at the front of the group. He was beyond the reach of Tortha's horns or Lerithon's tail.

He was alone.

The pterosaur dove, its hunger fixated on Eleri. Blood streamed from its injured claw, ready to pluck him from the path. An oryctodromeus runt wasn't a true prize like the others, but he would have to do.

Eleri's breath caught. This was how his mother had died.

149

Was this the last thing she had seen? A shape in the sky, a flash of claws, and then . . .

His stomach churned.

Eleri cast his gaze around, desperate for an idea. The tar pits popped and blistered, shallow and steaming. But a few yards to his left, a deeper pit lay gurgling. It looked . . . *hungrier* than the others.

Eleri scrambled to the edge of the path, right on the brink of the tar. The others charged forward, shouting his name in desperation, but they would be too late to save him.

He had to save himself.

The pterosaur was six feet away. Five. Four. Three. Two . . .

As claws flashed for his face, Eleri dropped to his belly. He fell flat onto the path—and the predator missed him by half an inch. It had expected to smash into his body—but without that planned resistance, the momentum of its dive carried it forward—

Straight into the tar.

The pterosaur screamed. Eleri scrambled to his feet, panting and heaving as the creature's shriek was cut off. It hit the tar front-first, and it didn't take long for its beak to be consumed. The tar glugged and hissed, sucking it into the black.

The pterosaur writhed, madly flapping its wings, but they too were caught in the sticky black trap. A minute later, it stopped writhing. It lay limp and half-submerged, already dead as the tar consumed it. Minute by minute, it sank. Its torso. Its wings . . .

The tar gurgled. A bubble popped on the surface.

The pterosaur was gone.

Eleri stared, his body tight with shock. He was barely aware of his friends behind him, staring in wide-eyed horror.

"He's just . . . gone," Sorielle whispered. "Like he never existed."

Tortha glared at the tar, as if challenging it. "Good! He wanted to do the same to us, didn't he?"

It took Eleri a moment to realize that his limbs were shaking. He clamped down on the movement, trying to control himself, but his shock came in sharp little breaths, tight and sour.

As a hatchling, he had been taught that killing was necessary. The Prairie soldiers were invading beasts, threatening his life. To become a hero, he must end their lives. A true warrior—like Agostron—wouldn't hesitate to kill.

But Eleri was no warrior.

He was a storyteller. A collector of tales and memories. He hadn't even known the pterosaur's name—but by killing it, he hadn't just wiped out its life. He had erased its story.

The tar gurgled, hot and hungry.

Had there been another way? His mind churned with a dozen ideas—tricks and maneuvers that he might have tried, ways to injure the beast without killing it. He conjured story after story, memories of tales where the heroes had outsmarted their foes . . .

But it was too late now.

Eleri clenched his claws. He had only killed it in self-defense. And besides, a pterosaur just like this one had snatched his mother away forever.

"It was a monster," he said. "It deserved to die."

Eleri wasn't sure who he was trying to convince—Sorielle or himself. He drew a shaky breath. "Come on, it's getting late. We need to get past this tar before it's too dark."

"When comes the end," Lerithon said quietly, "darkness must consume us all."

No one replied.

CHAPTER SEVENTEEN

THE LAND OF LOW CLOUDS

On the far edge of the tar field, the moon was rising. Shadows sprawled across the land, dappled like lichen.

"Almost half a moon," Eleri murmured, glancing upward. "We're running out of time to stop this war."

"We can make it," Sorielle said. "I know we can."

But even the cheery ankylosaur sounded less hopeful than usual, her spirits worn by their journey. They all trudged slowly, limbs aching and faces downcast.

Beyond the tar pits, they emerged onto a small cracked plain. In the dark, a faint sulfuric stink hung in the air. The moon cast a shine across several knobbly hills, about two hundred yards ahead.

"Let's try aimin' for them hills," Tortha said. "Looks like a good defensive position, I reckon. We can camp behind a ridge—and with a rotatin' sentry roster, we'll be safe enough till daybreak."

"Can't we just stop here?" Sorielle asked.

Tortha gave her a scathing look. "Are you mad? Ain't no cover here. Soon as the sun comes up, we'll be invitin' every corpse muncher in this part of the Deadlands to snack on us." She shook her head and muttered, "It's like workin' with a bunch of hatchlings!"

"Hey, we haven't all had military training," Eleri said.

"No? Really? I never could've guessed."

Eleri decided not to argue. They were all on edge after escaping the tar field.

"Right," Tortha said, mollified. "Let's go."

The plain was low, flat, and cracked. As they traveled deeper into its grasp, the stink of sulfur grew stronger.

"Not too far," Sorielle said, her tone brighter. "At this rate, we'll reach the nearest hilltop in approximately seven and a half minutes. We'll be bedding down for a proper kip in no time."

But as they traipsed toward the hills, Eleri drooped. It started with his legs, which grew slower and heavier. His foreclaws hung lower as his torso buckled, and suddenly, he sucked in a whiff of dirt and clay.

"Eleri?" Sorielle asked, alarmed. "Are you quite all right?"

He couldn't decipher her words. They were meaningless

noise: strange cries that echoed inside the fog of his head. As if he'd eaten a poisonous plant or been struck by some invisible sickness . . .

"He's falling!" someone cried. "He's—"

Eleri hit the ground. A dull reverberation ran through his skull as the others thundered toward him, their enormous feet casting tremors in the earth. *Boom. Boom. Boom . . .*

The air stank. His head swam. Every breath tasted oddly bitter. Too late, he remembered what Lerithon had seen before they entered the tar field. *Beyond the black, a land of low clouds lies . . .*

"Gas!" Sorielle cried, her voice raw with horror. "It must be poisonous gas—that's what we can smell."

"Why ain't the rest of us sick, then?" Tortha demanded.

"It's coming from the ground," Sorielle said. "It's hovering low and then dispersing, so our heads are above the worst of it, but Eleri is much shorter than the rest of us! I suppose he's right in the thick of it . . ."

Eleri barely heard her. His head spun, thick and gluggy. He felt as if someone had filled his lungs with tar—and numbly, he realized that he was choking. He spluttered, fighting for a mouthful of air, but all he swallowed was another gulpful of gas.

"Higher!" someone cried. "You've gotta get him higher!"

Something sharp pushed Eleri's torso. He ignored it, too groggy to pay attention. "Get up!" Tortha barked. "Get up now, dirt muncher!"

With a hoarse groan, he staggered to his feet. Every breath was sharp and toxic, thick with the stink of sulfur.

". . . get to . . . higher ground . . . hills . . ."

Someone was speaking, but their words were beyond him. They sputtered in his mind, winking like sparks of flame in the mist. Sorielle was beside him, pushing him forward. Tortha shoved him and he staggered, barely able to catch himself.

Where were they leading him? They were too far from the hills; he could never walk that far. Not now. Eleri felt as if a raptor's claw had sliced into his skull, slowly squeezing the life from his brain . . .

"Climb!" someone shouted, right beside his ear. "Climb, Eleri!"

They were pushing him. Shoving him. Why couldn't they leave him alone? Didn't they know how tired he was? He only wanted to rest. To sleep . . .

"Climb!"

Eleri reached forward, pawing at the haze. His foreclaw struck something warm and enormous: a living hill, curving beneath his touch. *Lerithon*. The sauropod had dropped to his belly, lying on the ground in preparation for . . . what? Sleep? Oh, good. Perhaps it was time for a nap. Weariness engulfed Eleri, soft as moss . . .

"Climb!" Tortha's voice was a panicky choke. "Just do it, Eleri!"

Sorielle shoved him forward. "Get above the mist!"

Eleri blinked. They were right, weren't they? He had to climb. He had to get high onto Lerithon's back. But it was so hard to focus. So hard to concentrate. All he could do was . . .

"Climb, Eleri!" Sorielle cried.

And so he did.

Eleri dug his claws into the living mountain, wincing as Lerithon flinched beneath him—but he didn't let go. He struggled for breath—and was he imagining it, or did the air taste cleaner?

He had to get higher.

Choking and rasping, Eleri dragged himself up another few feet. He'd reached the peak of Lerithon's back, and with a short sob, he clung to the enormous body beneath him.

"Hold on!" Tortha called as Lerithon rose.

Eleri cried out, almost falling as the jolt dislodged him, but he managed to cling on.

Down below, Tortha and Sorielle were woozy now too, both staggering slightly. They were tall enough to escape a lethal dose of the gas, but short enough to inhale faint clouds of its poison. Only Lerithon seemed immune, his great neck protruding high above the deadly clouds.

"To cross the clouds, one must lose one's fear of falling," he said.

"Go!" someone cried below. "We have to reach the hills!"

Who had spoken? Was it Tortha? Sorielle? Perhaps it was Eleri himself. He could barely focus long enough to decipher his own thoughts, let alone any mangled voices. But Lerithon jolted forward, barreling toward the hills. Eleri clung on like a snail, pressed against the sauropod's coarse skin.

Step by step, they charged through the mist. Step by step, they picked up speed, careening forward like raptors on the hunt.

And step by step, Eleri clung to Lerithon's back with every ounce of strength in his claws, struggling to stay awake.

"Do not fall!" Lerithon gasped.

The cry slapped him back into wakefulness. He clung on tighter, trying to hold his head high.

Lerithon gave a little cry of pain.

"Sorry!" Eleri gasped. "I . . . I didn't mean . . ."

"Dig deep, little earthsinger," Lerithon said, his great voice cutting through the fog in Eleri's head. "Hold tight, and do not let go. Tonight, I am your warren. Tonight, I will keep you safe."

And so Eleri clung tighter, hating himself as his claws sliced into the sauropod's skin. But Lerithon didn't cry out again—and Eleri didn't let go.

At the peak of the hill, they stood high above the sea of fog. Eleri was vaguely aware of voices, of someone coaxing him from his perch. He finally released his grip and slid, stumbling and gasping, from Lerithon's back onto the rocks.

Sorielle appeared beside him, nudging him gently forward. He stumbled on as she directed and found himself behind a cluster of jagged boulders. It wasn't much cover, but he gratefully slumped into the stones.

"Sleep," someone said. "Sleep, Eleri . . ."

He was back in his warren, wasn't he? That was his father's voice. No, it was a female voice. His mother? No, that couldn't be right—he'd never known his mother. He only had his father, his herd, his brother . . .

Agostron. The image flashed before him, sharp and vicious. A pair of eyes, ripe with hatred as he spoke of Eleri's treachery. The herd, clustering around him. His father's disappointment—and then his choice at the Mountain Court, his vote for clemency . . .

The images blurred. Eleri's mind tangled. His body tingled, fizzing like a tar pit as the last of the gas painted confusion through his skull.

Eleri slipped into the dark.

CHAPTER EIGHTEEN

TRUTH AND LIES

Eleri woke to silence.

Dawn poured over the hills, cutting dusty streaks across the Deadlands. His head ached, but it was a dull pain now. The confusion from the poison clouds had ebbed, fading like gas in the night. The sunrise was a stark reminder of their deadline.

Three nights to go.

With a dry swallow, Eleri staggered to his feet.

He stood in a cluster of jagged rocks, shielded by shadow. Sorielle and Tortha slept beside him, their enormous torsos inflating with each breath. Only one supply sack remained, a pouch that had hung from Sorielle's backplate. Everything else had been lost to either the tar or the gas.

A trickle of water seeped down the slope. It tasted bitter

and brackish, but Eleri forced himself to gulp down several mouthfuls. If nothing else, it dampened the sting that the gas had scorched inside his throat.

Eleri tiptoed past Sorielle and Tortha, trying not to make a sound. He picked his way across a stony ridge, to where Lerithon lay alone beneath the rising sun. The sauropod was clearly on sentry duty, but his attention seemed more fixed on the shape of the clouds than the threat of carnivores.

A series of deep scratches scored Lerithon's skin. The gashes rose from his tail to his spine, as if something had sliced his skin during the night, like a predator . . .

. . . or a friend.

Eleri felt sick. He glanced at his claws, caked in dried blood. His stomach roiled as he brushed them in the dirt, hurriedly trying to scrub away the evidence. "Lerithon, I'm sorry," he said. "I'm so sorry. I didn't mean to hurt you."

The sauropod's gaze remained on the horizon, deep and distant. He seemed to be lost in thought, and for a moment Eleri doubted that Lerithon had heard him.

"Does it hurt?" Eleri asked. "I could find some healing leaves, when we get back to the Grotto. I could try to . . . I . . ."

He trailed off, feeling utterly useless.

Finally Lerithon spoke. "A wound is not pain, Eleri of the Broken Ridge. To lose one's friend is pain. To lose one's family is pain." He paused. "A wound incurred to save one's friend is a privilege."

Eleri stared across the plains, unsure how to respond. Something personal creaked in Lerithon's tone, as if he were speaking from his own experience. "Have you . . . Have you lost someone, then?"

Lerithon's great neck sagged slightly. "To lose one's herd is not to lose someone. It is to lose oneself."

Eleri's insides knotted. He thought of his oldest dream, still flickering inside him like a fragile flame: to finally earn his herdmates' acceptance. To find a purpose in their ranks. Not to be a burden or a traitor, but an asset to the herd.

Just like Agostron.

Eleri's throat was dry. He swallowed. "How *did* you lose your herd? Did they exile you?"

Lerithon took a long while to respond—but when he did, he sounded as ancient as the plains. "When one is different, one dreams of many things. Of the stars. Of the shadows. Of the past . . . and of secrets one should not know."

Eleri stiffened, blinking. "You're an Eye of the Forgotten?" he whispered. "Like Astrilar the Wise?"

Lerithon gave a slow nod. "In the darkness, stories may unfold. They flit before one's eyes like insect wings. They are difficult to catch—but sometimes, they unfurl and show their truth."

"You have visions of the past," Eleri whispered, slightly awed. "You see the shadows . . . echoes of the time before the Fallen Star?"

There was a long pause.

162

"One's herd did not believe in such things." Lerithon raised his head, staring skyward. "In the herd, one must obey the will of the stars. One must not pry into things that should remain unknown. To do otherwise is to . . . blaspheme."

"But you couldn't help it, could you? If you're an Eye of the Forgotten, you can't just stop the visions from coming." Eleri paused. "Why didn't you lie? If your herd thought your powers were blasphemous, couldn't you keep them secret?"

"One cannot hide one's true self," Lerithon said.

Eleri stared out at the plains. The sun hadn't yet fully risen, and shadows marred the rocks like wounds. He drew a shaky breath, trying to wrap his mind around Lerithon's words.

He knew, of course, that the sauropods were deeply religious. They migrated along the Cold Canyon each year, following the will of the stars. They were wise. Ancient. Mysterious and mystical . . .

And yet, they had turned Lerithon away.

"What happened?" Eleri whispered.

Lerithon drew a long, slow breath. "Together, we walked beneath the stars. In the Cold Canyon, one's vision sang of blood, of death, of pain. Of a land nearby where the earth was angry and great stones fell to crush many souls."

Where the earth was angry . . . "The Land of Falling Sky," Eleri whispered. It marked the outskirts of the Mountain Kingdom—a place prone to violent rockslides, where clifftops crumbled onto the plain below. "You sensed it was nearby, and you told your herd about it. And so they exiled you?"

"In the Cold Canyon, a tunnel lies. It passes into the Land of the Fallen Star, which other herds may call the Deadlands. One was forced to walk this tunnel alone."

Eleri's breath hitched. He could picture it now: a cold night, a dark sky. A herd of gigantic sauropods, pausing in their great migration. Lerithon must have been the smallest among them—the only youngling left to the herd. And yet they had forced him into the darkness.

They had forced him out alone.

Agostron had been right. The last sauropod herd *was* dying—but it wasn't due to fate. It was due to their own cruelty. Their own arrogance. Eleri had spent his life admiring the sauropods, and for what? Because they seemed majestic? Because they crossed the world like kings and queens, unknowable and untouchable? Because their tails had swept the stars across the sky?

They might look wise, but they were fools.

"I'm sorry," he said, his voice raw. "I'm sorry they exiled you."

"Be not sorry, Eleri of the Broken Ridge. Dreams may guide one through the darkness. One dreamed of ancient creatures, sheltering in a place of sanctuary. Water is the path of life, leading one from past to future."

Eleri tried to decipher this. "You dreamed about the Grotto? That's how you found us? You knew to follow the river!"

164

Lerithon gave a slow nod. "Water is wise, for it knows where to run."

The sun continued to seep upward, casting fresh rays of light across the Deadlands. As Eleri focused, his eyes fixed on the remains of an ancient riverbed. It took him a while to realize that this was what Lerithon had been staring at for their entire conversation. *Water is wise, for it knows where to run . . .*

The river had dried up years ago. Generations ago, most likely, when the Fallen Star had scorched this land. But its path still meandered to the east, trailing toward a shape on the horizon: a bristle of dark claws, gnarled and broken. They reached weakly to scrape the morning light, as tendrils of ash spiraled skyward.

"Is that the Forest of Smoke?" Eleri said, eyes widening.

"One must trust in one's own vision."

Eleri took this as a "yes." But as his gaze flitted along the horizon, another shape loomed, a mile or two beyond the Forest of Smoke: a vast peak, craggy and jagged.

Instantly, Eleri recognized its shape, though he'd never seen it so close. "Hey, isn't that the Fire Peak?"

Even as he spoke, a fresh ray of light spilled across the landscape—and with a surge of horror, Eleri understood what he was staring at. Yes, it was the Fire Peak. But it wasn't just a mountain.

It was a kingdom.

The Fire Peak was a hive of activity. Squadrons of soldiers

prowled along its crests and ridges, their bodies silhouetted against the rising sun. Pterosaurs soared overhead, circling in slow loops as if on sentry patrol. On the plain, rows and rows of soldiers lay sleeping: a carnivorous army waiting to strike.

Eleri thought again of General Korvia. He thought of the raptors at the oasis, obeying her orders—like soldiers in a secret army. Now there could be no denying it.

"Well," Eleri said hoarsely. "I guess we know where the Carrion Kingdom has been hiding."

CHAPTER NINETEEN

THE CARRION KINGDOM

Hidden by a rocky ledge, Zyre stared at the distant Fire Peak. Her mind churned. Flocks of massive pterosaurs swarmed above its crater, infesting the mountain like termites in an ancient mound.

This was proof.

A kingdom of enemies lurked in the Fire Peak. The Carrion Kingdom ruled the wastes—and the herbivorous kings had betrayed their citizens. Zyre couldn't claim ignorance or tell herself it was just a wild theory now. She couldn't look the other way to salve her conscience. Her insides twisted. *Profit isn't personal* . . . But how many must die to satisfy the hunger of this secret army?

And how long could Zyre's kin profit from those deaths?

Close to Zyre's perch, the exiles gathered for an emergency

meeting. Zyre watched as they banded together, gawking in horror at the sight of the Fire Peak.

"We've gotta destroy it!" Tortha said.

The others stared, clearly flabbergasted by what lay before them. Zyre watched in secret, her talons curling. As her own initial shock subsided, her spy training began to kick in. No matter how shocking it was, new information should be analyzed with calm logic.

"We can't destroy it." Sorielle looked anxious. "I'm so sorry to be rude, Tortha, and I do admire your zeal, but I suspect that it's impossible."

"Our best revenge is to stop the war," Eleri said.

Tortha growled, scuffing her foreclaws in the dirt. "I can't stand the sight of 'em! Hidin' out here in the Deadlands, playin' filthy tricks so they can blackmail our kings . . ."

"Yeah, we all agree." Eleri straightened, as if trying to hide his own anxiety, but Zyre wasn't fooled. She knew when her quarry was bluffing: "But isn't there some military protocol for this kind of situation?"

Tortha bristled. "Of course there is! Not that I'd expect a *storyteller* to know about it."

To his credit, Eleri didn't rise to her bait. "Go on, then."

"Well," Tortha said, speaking slowly as if he were stupid, "you've got to start by gatherin' intelligence, sniff out the details of the enemy encampment. Flamin' feathers, a hatchlin' could figure this out . . ."

"Right," Sorielle said brightly. "In that case, we should

figure out what we know about their kingdom, right? Think about this logically?"

Finally, Zyre thought.

"They need a food source," Eleri said, as if thinking aloud. "They send out pterosaurs to gather carrion from our battlefields. That's why they keep larders across the Deadlands, so they've got a constant food supply filtering back to the Fire Peak."

"What else do they eat?" Sorielle asked. "We know that their prey supply is dwindling each year . . ."

"Each other?" Tortha suggested.

The others looked at her, horrified. Zyre's flesh prickled.

"What?" Tortha said. "I bet it's true. In the Prairie army, if you ain't good enough or you disobey an officer, you get punished by missin' dinner. What if the carrion eaters have got a different punishment?"

"You get to *be* the dinner?" Sorielle asked.

"Exactly."

"Fear is the foe of true leadership," Lerithon said.

Tortha snorted. "Might not be 'true leadership,' but I reckon it's plenty effective."

"But why are they gathering on the plain?" Sorielle asked. "It's like an army preparing to march somewhere, isn't it? As if they're ready to go to war."

"Or to a feast," Eleri said. His eyes widened, as if struck by a horrible thought. "What if they know about the tunnel invasion plan?"

"How could—?"

"They've got raptors sneaking around having secret meetings—they could've heard something, or someone might've sold the secret. Or they could've hired wind-whispers to keep an eye on our kings . . ."

In her hiding place, Zyre stiffened.

"The tunnel attack is only three nights away!" Eleri went on. "It can't be a coincidence that they're gathering now, ready to march."

Tortha looked nauseous. "So they'll get my comrades to do the dirty work, and then they'll swoop in and . . . ?"

No one needed to complete the sentence.

"This doesn't change anything," Eleri said. "If we destroy the tunnel, the Prairie soldiers can't get into the Mountain Kingdom in the first place. The attack will never happen."

"And the carnivores will be stranded far from home, without that easy feast they were promised." A spark of nasty pleasure filled Tortha's eyes. "I bet they'll be furious . . . Hey, maybe they'll start turnin' on each other!"

Eleri looked hopeful. "In their moment of weakness, maybe our own troops can strike against them!"

"'Our' troops?" Tortha frowned. "Do you mean the Mountain or the Prairie?"

"Both," Eleri said. "United."

In the shadows, Zyre's heart skipped a beat.

"After we stop the tunnel invasion," Eleri said, speaking

faster, "we'll tell our herds the truth . . . and maybe we can convince them to work together."

Tortha barked a laugh. "You've gotta be kiddin'."

"I'm dead serious," Eleri said. "Alone, the Prairie Alliance can't fight off the carnivores. Neither can the Mountain Kingdom. But if our troops work together against a common enemy . . ."

"We're exiles, dirt muncher," Tortha said. "Traitors, remember? Accordin' to the Laws of Noble Combat, our herds should kill us on sight."

"My father leads the Broken Ridge herd," Eleri said. "If I can talk to him, he might listen. He has some influence—he could get us an audience with the Mountain Court! And if we can stop the tunnel invasion, we'll be heroes, won't we? They'll have to at least *listen* to us."

A long pause.

"We can try," Sorielle said gently. "It's a lovely idea, Eleri—it truly is. But before we get ahead of ourselves, we still need to destroy the tunnel." She paused. "And for that, we need fireblasts."

They all stared at the horizon, their gazes settling on the Forest of Smoke. Zyre's attention darted between the exiles and the forest, imagining the dangers that lurked within. The forest wasn't just a tangle of petrified trees. It was a labyrinth of smoke and ash, right on the border of the Carrion Kingdom. Were the exiles mad?

"We'll have to be careful," Eleri said. "But if we sneak in and out quickly, I reckon we can grab a few fireblasts."

"There'll be carnivores in there," Sorielle said doubtfully. "Scouts from the Fire Peak, I suppose."

"Well then," Eleri said, "we'll have to make sure they don't catch us."

No one replied.

Lurking in the shadows, Zyre gripped her starfleck pouch. One starfleck. One precious speck of value—and her only possession in this world. If she obeyed Shadow's orders, she could earn nineteen more. She could earn a nest on Lightning Peak, where the world had softer edges . . .

Where her grandmother was waiting.

It would be so easy. All she had to do was sell Eleri to the carnivores. If she flew hard, she still had time to carry his claw back to Shadow by the deadline. There would be countless predatory patrols in the Forest of Smoke. All she had to do was whisper . . .

But how many innocents would die?

Eleri and his companions were the only ones who knew the truth. The only ones who could stop the war and stand against the Carrion Kingdom. If Zyre sold Eleri to the carnivores, she would be sacrificing more than one oryctodromeus runt.

But if she reneged on Shadow's deal, she would be sacrificing her own future. Her parents' creed rang in her mind, cold and ruthless. *A master of the sky—and all those fools who crawl beneath it* . . .

Was she doomed to remain Zyre of the Prairie—pitiful, poor, and alone? Or would she finally become Zyre of Lightning Peak?

As she stared at the horizon, Zyre made her choice.

The Forest of Smoke smoldered.

Dead trees reached skyward, petrified and black. Their branches twisted, gnarled like claws. Ash and soot hissed from long cracks in the earth. Just harmless smoke, nothing like the lethal gas they had encountered last night—but still, it was enough to clench Eleri's claws.

He tried to focus on his strengths rather than his fears. His belly was full, thanks to Sorielle's final sack of foliage. He had drunk his fill from the brackish "stream" by their hill camp, and thanks to the gas, he'd managed a full night of sleep.

If there was ever a time to face the Forest of Smoke, it was now.

"All right," Tortha said. "This whole thing was your plan, dirt muncher. Where do we start lookin', then?"

Eleri tried to sound more confident than he felt. "Well, fireblasts are super flammable. Any that formed near the smoking cracks must've exploded years ago, right?"

"So . . . look where it's not so smoky?" Sorielle asked.

"Exactly."

Lerithon ambled along behind them, his great neck rising above the haze. "Where smoke does not blow, the stars may show."

"This whole dang place is smoky!" Tortha said, exasperated. "That's like sayin' to look for a spot in the desert where it ain't sandy."

"Oh, it's not so bad," Sorielle said brightly as they edged past another smoking crack in the earth. "It's rather relaxing in a way, isn't it? Like a nice warm bath on a cold morning."

Tortha scuffed at the dirt. "Sure, a bath that'll scorch you alive."

"We had hot springs back home," Sorielle said. "Oh, how I used to beg my parents to let me bathe in them! Especially during the cold months, when the ferns would wake with crowns of frost. It was such a delight to snuggle in a warm pool of bubbles—just lovely, it truly was."

"I'll give you 'lovely,'" Tortha muttered.

"Oh, thank you! You're such a good friend, Tori."

The triceratops bristled. "What did you just call me?"

Sorielle blinked. "Oh, don't you like it? I think it sounds rather sweet. My mother always gave us such lovely nicknames—you know, she used to call me 'Sori' because I was always apologizing for things. 'Sorry Sori,' she called me. Isn't that funny?"

Tortha opened her mouth to snap back—no doubt with

a promise to make her companion truly "Sori" if she didn't shut up—but the argument was cut off by a booming voice.

"Left!" Lerithon called.

They all turned, squinting through the soup of smoke. Eleri leaned forward, every instinct prickling. Could it be a predator? A carnivore, lurking in the shadows . . . ?

Then he realized what had caught Lerithon's eye. There was a gap in the smoke, where the dead trees bristled in thickets. The forest grew denser: a tangle of fossilized twigs and branches.

"Ooh, do you think there'll be fireblasts in there?" Sori-elle asked eagerly.

"Well, if the trees have survived in such a thick cluster, there can't be too many sparks in that area, right?" Eleri said. "If any fireblasts formed in there, they might still be intact."

"Hmm," Tortha said. "Glad there's room to cram a *few* brain cells in your skull with all the dirt."

Lerithon's long neck craned forward as he squinted to make out the details of the thicket. He slowly shook his enormous head. "I cannot walk in the place of shadow."

"You mean your ginormous sauropod rump is too huge to squeeze in there?" Tortha translated. "Yeah, already figured that one out. Try stayin' here to guard us or something."

"I watch my herd, as the stars watch me."

Tortha threw him an irritable scowl. "For the last time, this ain't a *herd*, all right?"

"But we'll still be friends when this is all over, won't we?" Sorielle asked.

"You're kiddin'!" Tortha gave a dismissive laugh. "I was on my way to a high-rankin' military career. When my exile is over, I ain't keen to hang out with a bunch of misfits."

Sorielle stiffened, something brittle in her gaze. A flash of . . . dread? Loneliness? Again, Eleri thought of her time in the Grotto before the others had been exiled. Sorielle knew what it meant to be alone.

"Come on," Eleri said, ignoring Tortha's jab. "Let's find some fireblasts and get out of here."

They ventured into the thicket, edging between the petrified remains of trees. Eleri had it easier than the others. For once, his small stature worked to his advantage. He slipped between twisted tree trunks, ignoring the prickle of long-dead foliage.

Tortha and Sorielle trudged more slowly, detouring around the bristliest outcrops.

"Ooh, look!" Sorielle blurted.

Eleri scurried back toward her, ducking under low-hanging branches. The ankylosaur had halted in her tracks, eyes fixed on an oddly colored stone. It glinted, rippling with veins of crimson crystal—and as the shadows shifted, it seemed to glow.

"Be careful, all right?" Eleri said, staring at the fireblast. "Don't want these things going off while we're holding them."

"Good point!" said Sorielle. "I suppose that scraping them with claws or teeth might cause a spark, mightn't it?"

"Then how in the blazes are we supposed to carry 'em?" Tortha demanded.

"Delicately," Eleri said.

"I'm a soldier, not a blasted dancer!"

"Well, let's hope that you're not 'blasted' in any way," said Eleri, studying the explosive crimson stone.

Ever so carefully, he bent to lift the fireblast. Touching the stone was the last thing he wanted to do, but he had no choice.

This was his chance to earn his place back home.

Eleri avoided the seams of crystal, instead focusing his grip around the rockier parts of the stone. As soon as he touched it, an odd little quiver ran through his forelimbs. He forced himself to be still, counting his breaths until he was calm enough to continue.

With a tight breath, Eleri plucked the stone from its resting place.

Nothing happened.

Eleri balanced the fireblast gently, encasing it in the fleshy palm of his forelimb. He kept his claws well away from the stone, avoiding any scrapes that might spark an explosion.

He let out a slow breath. "I think it's all right."

"Jolly good work, Eleri!" Sorielle beamed. "Oh, this is going splendidly, isn't it? I wonder if—"

"What was that?" Tortha snapped.

Too late, Eleri heard it as well. A crunch. A clawstep in the undergrowth, somewhere deeper in the thicket. "Flaming feathers . . ."

A pack of raptors leaped through the thicket, their eyes alight with fury and hunger. They swarmed toward Eleri and his companions, claws outstretched and long tongues flickering. Their leader wore a starfleck on his brow, slicing light between the branches.

"Lerithon!" Sorielle cried, but it was hopeless. Their enormous ally was on the far side of the thicket—and he could never save them now. His body couldn't fit between the trees.

It was up to them.

The raptors streamed forward. How many were there? Nine, ten, eleven? Their greedy eyes roamed across the feast before them: an ankylosaur, a triceratops, and an oryctodromeus. If they brought down even *one* of the exiles, the gang of carnivores would feast for days.

"Go," their leader hissed. "Bring me a banquet."

CHAPTER TWENTY

THE FOREST OF SMOKE

The raptors charged.

They hurtled at the herbivores, claws raised and teeth bared. Tortha lunged in front of Eleri, ready to shield him. Her neck frill flushed a murky red, the membrane shifting hues to daunt the carnivores.

"Go!" Sorielle cried. "Eleri, run!"

Eleri jerked backward—but where could he go? The Forest of Smoke was an endless trap of dead trees and pale smoke. His body shimmered, a beacon of scales and sapphire feathers. Among the stones and streams of the Mountain Kingdom, he could camouflage easily. But here . . .

"Go, Eleri!" Sorielle yelled again. "If you stay here, I estimate an eighty-four-point-nine percent risk of mortality in the next three minutes."

Eleri hesitated. He couldn't run—not now, when his friends were in danger. If the entire pack of raptors leaped on Tortha, or even on Sorielle, one might manage a killing bite to the throat . . .

"No!" Tortha roared, rearing on her hind legs. She crashed into the nearest raptor, smashing him down with a horrific crack. The creature fell and did not rise—but more poured forward, eager to tear apart their prey.

Sorielle turned and gave a huge sweep of her tail. She almost took out Eleri, who ducked frantically beneath it as she smashed through the line of attackers. Her tail-tip bristled with hefty spikes, which sent the raptors scattering like wind-tossed twigs. But two slipped past her, ducking beneath her tail with vicious snarls.

With two bloodthirsty predators charging at him, Eleri had just one fiery choice.

He hurled the contents of his claw toward the raptors.

The fireblast sailed through the air, fast and lethal, and smashed into the ground between the two carnivores.

Eleri drew a single breath.

An explosion engulfed the forest.

Flames rippled from the crimson stone, scorching the air and sending tendrils of bitter smoke everywhere. The sound smashed into Eleri's ears, as sharp as a physical blow. The air rang oddly, echoing as if the explosion still lingered. Or was that just his ears? He staggered behind a tree, closing his eyes and struggling not to cough. With mangled screams, the raptors hit the ground. *Thud. Thud.*

They didn't rise.

Again, Eleri's insides roiled. For a moment, he felt as shaken as he had when the pterosaur had hit the tar pit—again, he had taken a life. Worse, he had taken two. But this time, for some reason, the act hadn't shaken him so deeply.

He felt . . . callous.

In some ways, that was more frightening than anything. Was he becoming numb to death? Agostron would say that was a good thing—that it was the mark of a hardened warrior, ready to fight his enemies.

But he'd had no choice, had he? This was a fight for survival—and if the raptors had their way, Eleri and his friends would all lie dead at the end of it.

With a shaky gulp, Eleri burst from behind the tree, searching for more attackers. His ears rang and his heart pounded. If he could find another fireblast, perhaps he could defend his friends . . .

Tortha and Sorielle had whittled the pack down to six raptors, including their leader. The gang retreated, spitting curses at the prey who had brought down their comrades.

"Don't be cowards!" their leader roared. The starfleck jolted on his brow, casting slashes of light as he shook his head in fury. "That's fresh meat there, waiting for us!"

"Oh yeah?" a younger raptor hissed. "Don't see you rushing in to grab it, sir."

The gang moved in jerky jolts, their beady eyes weighing their chances of a meal. Their tongues flickered as they ran the calculations: risk versus reward. If they worked together, they could still win a meal—but which prey should they choose?

One by one, their gazes fixed on Eleri.

Their leader licked his lips. His cold eyes flashed. He crept forward, claws outstretched—and when he spoke, his voice was a rattling hiss. "Uriela, take the lead. Bring me the little one!"

A female raptor prowled forward. A sadistic smirk lit her eyes as the rest of the pack fell in obediently behind her, flexing their claws.

Eleri ran.

This time, he didn't wait to protect his friends. They didn't need protection. The carnivores had chosen their prey, and without a fireblast, Eleri could never fight them off. A roar exploded behind him, spliced by the smashing of Tortha's great legs as she charged. A mangled cry, a horrible thud . . . Eleri offered a silent prayer to the stars that she'd taken out another raptor.

Sorielle shrieked, and Eleri heard the thud of her tail. Another foe thwarted, perhaps?

Clawsteps scrabbled behind him, and Eleri's heart almost exploded in panic. At least one raptor had slipped past his friends, perhaps more. Tortha and Sorielle could never keep up with a sprinting raptor; their hefty frames left them slow and cumbersome.

Eleri was on his own.

He put his head down and fled, darting between the dead trees. Charcoal skittered around him as he plowed through ancient twigs, crushing them into clouds of dust. Something flittered in the trees above him, but all that mattered was his own ragged breath and the pounding of the raptors' claws.

Was he fast enough? He was built for short sprints—but so were the raptors. It would only take one beast to bring him down. If he tripped, or faltered, or . . .

He couldn't run forever. He needed a plan.

Eleri ducked behind a cluster of trees, shaking in wild spasms. *Be still. Be still . . .* He plucked a pebble from the soil: not a fireblast, but a simple dark stone. He fought to hold his breath, still and silent. Would the raptors run straight past him? It was a desperate hope, and yet—

His hope faltered.

Two raptors scurried closer, their beady eyes flickering. The first sprinted straight past, half-crazed and salivating at the prospect of a meal.

But the second was not so easily fooled. It was Uriela, the raptor given command of the hunting party. She jerked to a halt, sniffing the air. In one sharp movement, she whipped around to face Eleri's hiding place.

"Come out, come out, little friend," she crooned, raising her claws. "We're so very pleased to *meat* you . . ."

Eleri launched himself from the trees.

But he didn't run from Uriela. He ran straight toward her—and with a flying leap, he hurtled into her flank. The raptor was at least double his size, but with a mad scramble, he whipped himself up onto her spine. Uriela yowled as Eleri gouged her skin. His claws were built for digging dirt—and right now, for digging flesh.

Uriela writhed. "You pathetic little . . ."

Eleri decided to take a gamble and pressed the stone into the back of her neck. "Feel that?" he panted. "That's another fireblast."

Would she call his bluff? Eleri felt a prickle run down his spine.

The raptor hissed a spattering of curses. She tried to twist her neck around to confirm that the rock was laced with lines of crimson crystal, but Eleri pressed it harder into her neck, and she froze.

"I can set this off with a swipe of my claw," Eleri rasped. "You're gonna stay here and not move a muscle while I leave. If you come after me, I'll throw it at you. If you attack me now, I'll take us both out."

She barked a cold laugh. "You would take your own life? I don't believe it. Herbivores are cowardly little—"

"I'd rather go down fighting than make a meal for your pack! And if you don't believe me, believe *this*." Eleri dug a claw into her back again, reminding her of his ability to set off a spark.

184

Uriela stiffened. "When I catch you . . ."

Eleri didn't wait to hear the rest of the threat. He sprang down and hurtled into the trees, taking the route away from Uriela's companion. He had to find Lerithon! The sauropod could smash these predators with a single sweep of his tail.

But which way to run?

Dead forest sprawled in every direction, an endless maze of blackened trees cast in a swamp of smoke and soot. Eleri hesitated, and a crunch of clawsteps warned him that Uriela was on the prowl again.

Eleri swallowed.

He tossed the pebble aside and sprinted. He didn't know which way he was running, only that he *had* to get away from Uriela. If she guessed that his "fireblast" had been a ruse, she would make him pay.

Eleri ran faster. He hurtled across a clearing, ducked around a blast of steam from the ground, and bounded through a fresh cluster of trees. Branches thwacked his skin and scales, still healing from his journey down the Exile Cliffs. A twig snagged his feathers, and he paused, yanking it free, before racing down a slope.

Suddenly, Uriela was behind him.

He heard her claws in the undergrowth and the ragged snarls of her breath in the air. In less than a minute, she would be on him. With a sickening flash, his memory conjured the moment at the oasis when Yirian had leaned in, preparing to feast . . .

"Take this!" someone cried.

The voice was high—not just in pitch, but in location. It shrieked from somewhere in the canopy, lost in a tangle of leaves and smoke.

Eleri wrenched his head up, panting. It took him a moment to spot her: a tiny anurognathid, perched above him. She was a knot of scales and sinew, as scrawny as a warmblood bird.

The petite pterosaur skittered along a branch, flapping her wings in a frantic beat. She gestured for him to open his claw before dropping a cold object into his grasp.

Eleri looked down. His eyes widened as he recognized the object. Too small to be a fireblast, but it was the next best thing: a starfleck.

"Thank you," he rasped, eyes wide. "But I can't . . ."

"Use it!" she hissed.

Eleri crushed the fragile crystal in his grip—and instantly, it exploded into light. Its magic flooded his veins with strength. Energy rushed through his limbs, wild and raw and rippling with the promise of survival.

The starfleck had crumbled, but its energy pulsed through his veins. Eleri ran faster, hurling every ounce of strength into his stride. Uriela snarled behind him, picking up her own pace as he skittered through the trees.

Something shot through the canopy above him, and Eleri knew that the anurognathid was on his trail too. Who was she? Why had she helped him? She had gifted him a precious starfleck . . .

186

It didn't matter. Right now, Eleri would take any help he could get. The knowledge that he had an ally nearby, that he wasn't alone, filled him with a rush of strength as miraculous as the starfleck itself.

The earth tilted violently, sloping toward a narrow ravine. It looked like the remains of an ancient riverbed. The Fallen Star had destroyed the river, just as it had destroyed the rest of the forest. In its place, a cavernous crack ran along the bottom of the ravine.

And from the crack, smoke poured skyward.

Eleri skidded to a halt, grasping at gravel and ash. He barely stopped in time, just inches from plunging over the edge.

"Got you!" Uriela cried.

She appeared at the top of the ravine, staring down with a glint of cruel delight. He could never cross the smoking fissure, and Uriela had the advantage of higher ground.

He was trapped.

With a wild shriek, a tiny figure dive-bombed Uriela. *The anurognathid!* She plunged through the air with claws outstretched.

But with a snarl, the raptor swatted her aside. The movement was so casual that it made Eleri's guts twist.

"No!" he choked.

The tiny pterosaur hit the ground, crumpled and unconscious. Her body lay too far away, and Eleri couldn't see whether she was still breathing . . .

Either way, his only ally was gone.

As Uriela picked her way down the slope, sending burnt-flecks skittering, Eleri cast his eyes around for a weapon. The strength of the starfleck still pulsed in his bloodstream, but he could sense it was beginning to fade. Smoke and sparks spat from the fissure, filling the ravine with a gray haze. With a burst of hope, he spotted a glint of crimson. Another fire-blast? But it lay on the far side of the fissure, out of reach . . .

Out of time.

Uriela was on him, her teeth and claws flashing. Hot breath panted across his face, ruffling his skin and feathers with the stink of rotten flesh. Eleri gagged, trying not to imagine her last meal. As Uriela pinned him to the hot earth, a blast of steam exploded beside his face. He twisted his head away, exposing his throat.

"Oh, don't worry," she hissed. "Normally I grant my prey a quick death. I rip their throats out first, you see, so they never feel the rest of it. I like to consider myself . . . merciful."

Uriela paused. "But your little herd has torn apart my pack. With you, I think I'll start my meal somewhere less lethal. I want you to *feel* what's happening to you . . ." Her teeth glinted. "Bite. By. Bite."

Eleri froze, his body churning with terror. His prey instincts told him to freeze, to play dead—but right now, that would only seal his fate. He had to escape.

He had to fight.

"Eleri!" someone screamed.

188

In the corner of his eye, Eleri saw the figures at the top of the ravine. Even through his panic, he recognized the shapes of a triceratops, an ankylosaur, and a sauropod. They charged down the slope, spilling gravel and stones toward the rift below. They were here—his friends were here!

But Uriela's claws were at his throat, and her teeth were bearing down on his torso. The starfleck's strength pulsed in Eleri's limbs, its power dwindling with each breath. His friends could never reach him in time . . .

Somehow, he had to save himself.

With a violent cry, he kicked upward with his hind legs. The fading starfleck lent power to his kick, providing a wild surge of strength. His claws gouged the raptor's belly, and Uriela lurched backward with a cry of agony. Eleri scrambled to his feet, readying his forelimbs for another swipe. As soon as Uriela lunged at him, unsteady with rage, he raked his foreclaws across her face.

Uriela screeched. She hurled herself at him, a twisted knot of teeth and ire, but he danced aside—and the raptor's momentum carried her toward the edge. For a moment, Uriela teetered. Her tail swiped madly, fighting to balance herself, to drag her center of gravity backward . . . and with a ferocious cry, she regained her balance.

Eleri flinched.

"You'll pay for that!" she snarled.

The raptor threw all her strength into her tail, whipping it around in a furious attempt to smash Eleri down. But instead of ducking, Eleri was driven by some wild instinct to seize her tail. Uriela shrieked as his claws dug in, breaking the skin. Frantic, she fought to shake Eleri loose—and in her fury, she misstepped.

The world stopped.

For the second time, Uriela wavered on the edge—but this time, she had no tail to rebalance herself. Eleri clung to her tail with all his might, until Uriela's entire weight jolted into his claws. For a mad moment, he thought that he might save her.

Then the full impact of her weight hit him.

If he held on a moment longer, she would drag him down too. She began to slip from his claws. With a gasp, Eleri lost his grip—and Uriela cried out, scrambling to regain her footing . . .

Screaming madly, she plunged into the fissure.

CHAPTER TWENTY-ONE

PREPARATION

In the end, they quickly but carefully collected only two fireblasts—they couldn't risk searching further. The carnivores might send reinforcements, and they were running out of time.

"Three or four would be better," Sorielle said, after running the calculations in her head once again. "But we'll find a way to make it work."

Sorielle carried the anurognathid, who had been knocked unconscious by Uriela. Eleri had placed their tiny ally on the ankylosaur's back, propped between two of Sorielle's backplates. Tortha had greeted this decision with a growl.

"You can't trust her!" she snapped. "Filthy little windwhisper—a bunch of spies and liars, the lot of 'em. What was she doin' there, anyway? Was she followin' us?"

"She saved my life," Eleri said.

"She might've been spyin' for the Carrion Kingdom!" Tortha went on. "My pa always said that only a fool trusts his life to a windwhisper."

"She could be a crafter," Sorielle said. "Not all of her kind are spies."

"Out here, in the Deadlands?" Tortha scoffed. "What's she craftin', decorative sand art? Of course she's a spy!"

Eleri glanced at the tiny pterosaur, helpless and unconscious. "I don't care what she is. She'll die if we leave her here."

And in the end, that was that.

When dusk settled in, they camped again in the hills. Eleri was so exhausted that he slept through the night, apart from his rostered turn on sentry duty. During his shift, he stood at the peak of the hill, staring at the dark horizon.

His fireblast had killed two raptors today. Eleri knew it had been necessary, that it was the only way to defend his friends. But his reaction still made him queasy. In the heat of the moment, he had felt almost numb to their deaths.

The raptors had to die for the exiles to live. Eleri could accept that, perhaps. But that didn't mean that their lives were worthless, that their stories didn't matter.

If killing meant nothing, was he any better than the carnivores?

But what about Uriela? In the heat of the moment, wild

instinct had driven him to hold on to her tail. To try to save her. It was madness, wasn't it? If anything, it made Eleri feel even more unsettled.

What had been the difference between the first two raptors and Uriela? Why did instinct drive him to kill in one case but hesitate in the other?

As he stared at the dark horizon, Eleri understood. In the first case, his friends had been in danger, and Eleri had acted to save them. In the second case, the only one in danger was Eleri himself.

Perhaps he was less callous than he feared.

Eleri gazed into the dark, his insides tangling. Somewhere out there, the Carrion Kingdom lay waiting. An army of ravenous predators was massing on the plains, waiting to march to the Mountain Kingdom.

Waiting to devour Eleri's herd.

He would do anything he could to stop them.

If he had to kill again, could he do it? In the heat of the moment, to save innocent lives . . . yes, he could. Not to save himself, perhaps, but to save countless hatchlings and elders from the carnivores' jaws.

In the morning, they traveled back toward their homelands. The tunnel attack was due the following night, and each hour pressed on Eleri's shoulders like a physical weight.

They took a longer yet safer route this time, bypassing the field of toxic gas—and the bubbling tar pits—and Lerithon seemed confident that they could arrive before the attack.

The anurognathid perched on Lerithon's back. The tiny spy was awake, but visibly strained by her injuries.

"What's your name?" Eleri asked as they trekked across the sand.

She glanced at him, her expression cagey. She seemed unwilling to share personal information—as if he were asking her to give up a deep secret. Then again, she *was* a windwhisper, wasn't she? Secrets were their currency.

"Zyre," she said. "Of Lightning Peak."

Eleri gave a slow nod. "You've been following us, haven't you? For the last few days, I kept catching little bits of movement. I thought I was imagining it, but . . ."

Zyre hesitated. "Yes."

"Why?"

"I thought your story might prove valuable. I . . . I needed some new information to sell to the kings."

"Like what?" Tortha demanded.

"Information from the Deadlands is always valuable," Zyre said. "Not many of my kind venture out here. It's too . . . risky."

A long pause.

Memories of the Forest of Smoke flashed into Eleri's mind. When all seemed lost, Zyre had dropped a starfleck into his claws, lending him strength as he ran for his life.

Then she had lunged at Uriela's face, claws outstretched, and been smashed from the sky for her trouble.

"Twice," he said. "You saved me twice yesterday. Why?"

Zyre hesitated. She gave her head a slow shake. "I know about the Carrion Kingdom, and the war, and the kings' betrayal. I know about the tunnel into the Mountain Kingdom. I know you're planning to destroy it."

"And?" Tortha's eyes were sharp.

"I want to help."

Tortha snorted. "You're a creepy little bug muncher. You reckon we're fool enough to trust you?"

"She saved my life!" Eleri protested.

"Don't mean she's here to help us!" Tortha snapped. "I bet she wants to sell us out to King Torive, or one of the generals in the Prairie Alliance. We could be valuable prisoners if she plays this right."

"She gave me a starfleck," Eleri said. "If she only cared about profit, why would she give me something so valuable?"

After carrying the anurognathid's unconscious form, he knew that her starfleck pouch was empty. Zyre hadn't just given him a starfleck, but given him her *only* starfleck. It was a startling gift.

"I trust her," he added. "I want her to come with us."

"Well, I don't," Tortha said.

No one met her gaze.

Sorielle finally broke the silence. "I vote in favor of trust. That was a jolly good turn she did for us yesterday."

They all glanced at Lerithon.

"Sad is the star who shines alone." He stared dolefully at the horizon. "Only together may they form a constellation."

Eleri turned to Tortha. "Looks like you've been out-voted."

The triceratops ground her teeth. "Mark my words," she muttered, "we're all gonna regret this."

Eleri could only hope that she was wrong.

They traveled slowly, choosing each clawstep to avoid any unnecessary jolts. Eleri was the only exile to walk on two legs, and so he carried a fireblast in each of his foreclaws. He'd wrapped the deadly stones in leaves, which grew in a few sporadic patches in the otherwise dead forest. He had first soaked the leaves in a briny pool to minimize the risk of a spark.

Still, his entire body tensed. If he stumbled, they might all die in flames.

When darkness fell, they camped in a shallow crater. No time to head back to the Grotto. The Half Moon would shine tomorrow night, and so Lerithon was leading them straight to the battlefield. No food grew here, but rivulets of dirty water seeped up when they scrabbled at the earth.

Zyre perched on a boulder, staying very quiet. The anurognathid seemed shy, unwilling to draw attention to herself—or perhaps it was her spy tendencies coming through. Shy or spy, she seemed keener to listen than to join their discussion.

"I know where the tunnel entrance is," Tortha insisted. "Just get me to the battlefield, and I can get us inside."

"A battle can always be found." Lerithon gazed at the stars. "The land weeps where life is spilled."

"Thanks," Tortha said. "Very helpful."

Sorielle stood near the outskirts of the camp, taking her shift as sentry. She turned to Eleri with an excited smile. "Ooh, that sounds like the Tale of Yari the Strong! Do you know that one, Eleri? Can we hear it?"

"Sure, if you want." Eleri brightened a little. "I've practiced telling it to hatchlings before, so I think I remember all the—"

Tortha bristled. "We ain't hatchlings, dirt muncher! We don't need a bedtime story."

"As bright as stars, tales tell us who we are," Lerithon said.

Tortha ground her teeth. "Fine! You all have fun tellin' fairy tales. I'm gonna look for some food, since you numbskulls lost it all."

She stomped away from their campsite before scrambling up the side of the crater. Tiny stones skittered behind her, clattering into the bowl of stone. Eleri thought it best not to mention the fact that Tortha had lost her own food supplies in the tar pits.

Sorielle turned back to Eleri. "Go on, then! Oh, it will be lovely to hear a storyteller tell a tale again."

Eleri felt an odd flush of warmth. *A storyteller.* No one

had ever called him that before—at least, not as a compliment. He cleared his throat, feeling self-conscious as Lerithon craned his great neck to listen. Even Zyre lifted her head to watch, her tiny eyes intense.

"This is the Tale of Yari the Strong, who lived in the Time of the Fallen Star. When all the earth was drenched in blood, he strode forth from the wastes and saved a clutch of hatchlings from those who fed on death and despair . . ."

As he went on, Eleri's confidence grew. He remembered the rhythm of the story now, the way each syllable slipped between his teeth and tongue.

"It began in blackness, on the Night of No Moon, just weeks after the Fallen Star struck. Mist still encircled the world, and the land lay smoldering in ruin. But in a steep ravine, where trees still grew and water still ran, a spike-grip herd took shelter," Eleri said, using the Old Name for iguanodons. "The eldest of them was called Yari. He looked old and weak, and many thought that he would not survive the month. Some had even called to leave him behind."

Eleri paused.

"But as frail as he seemed, Yari had the courage of a much younger dinosaur. In the night, he heard a cry—and while his herdmates slumbered, Yari ran toward the sound. It came from a nest of hatchlings. While the spikegrips slept, a pack of nightslicers was circling." Eleri drew a breath. "Or as we would call them now, raptors."

Sorielle was a good listener, gasping at all the exciting points. Lerithon nodded sagely, his eyes distant. Eleri couldn't tell whether the sauropod was swept up in the tale or focusing on the night sky behind him.

"But Yari would not let the hatchlings be taken. He may have looked old and frail, but he carried a deeper strength. The strength of courage—and of wits. And so he gathered up a clawful of murkthorn vines from a nearby cave. These rare vines grow in darkness, with luminescent blooms, and a single prick from a thorn may force its victim into hours of feverish sleep."

Lerithon turned slowly to listen, his great neck curving beneath the stars. "Once, one found a grove of dreams within the dark."

Eleri considered this for a moment, before deciding to take it as a contribution to the story. "Yes," he said. "Thank you, Lerithon."

The starsweeper did not reply.

Eleri raised his own claws, as if to demonstrate the sharp spikes of a murkthorn vine. "After he had gathered a dozen thorns, Yari swept himself up in a haze of shadow and lurched from the dark: a monstrous spirit of the mists."

Sorielle's eyes widened. "Ooh!"

"Yari fought the nightslicers—and in the dark, he beat them down. He dodged and darted, aiming murkthorn stabs at their limbs. For Yari may have looked frail, but he possessed the wiry strength that sometimes comes to the aged.

It is a sharper strength, all claws and sinew, that is as rare and prized as a starfleck.

"The nightslicers fell, one thorn-prick at a time, and the air grew cold with startled cries. In the dark, the raptors heard their comrades fall and thought them slain, not merely sleeping. Lost in mist and shadows, they thought they faced a dozen monstrous enemies—not just one old herbivore."

Eleri lifted his head. "And so the raptors fled, and the hatchlings were saved. The herd rejoiced, and lauded Yari as the strongest and bravest of them all. And he lived out his days as the herd's greatest warrior, destined to protect them all from the dangers of the world."

Eleri finished the tale with a faint smile.

"Oh, that was just delightful!" Sorielle said, beaming. "Simply marvelous. You really are a wonderful performer, Eleri—you should be our herd's official storyteller."

Eleri snorted. "I don't think Tortha would agree with a single word in that sentence."

"Oh, piffle," Sorielle said. She leaned forward conspiratorially, as if about to say something controversial. "I don't know about you two, but I'm starting to suspect that Tortha is rather unhappy."

"Yeah, I got an inkling of that," Eleri said. "Think I'll go and find her."

"Oh, that's very kind of you!" Sorielle said. "I should probably stay here, since I'm on sentry duty, or she might decide to execute me. But I hope that you're able to have a lovely chat!"

Eleri didn't bother to invite Lerithon, whose attention had drifted to the clouds on the horizon. The great sauropod was humming a tune under his breath, but his neck was raised so high that most of the melody was lost on the breeze.

Zyre perched at the edge of the group.

She watched quietly as Eleri left, clambering up the edge of the crater. After he disappeared over its lip, she looked down again. Her starfleck pouch hung empty, dangling limply from her claw.

Everything ached. Nothing was broken, thank the stars, but her body throbbed like one enormous bruise. Zyre imagined her parents' faces, sharp with disdain as they watched her crawl.

She exhaled slowly.

"Would you like to tell me the truth?" Sorielle asked.

Zyre blinked, taken aback by the unexpected question. The ankylosaur's tone was light and friendly, but there was an underlying current of distrust that Zyre hadn't expected.

"I often find that it helps," Sorielle added.

"What?"

"Telling the truth. It helps to clear your conscience, don't you think?"

Zyre stared at her, bewildered. "I don't—"

"You understand perfectly well." An unexpected hard note undercut Sorielle's tone. "I expect that you find me rather foolish. Most people do. But I know the ways of the anurognathids, and I know that you've lied to us."

Zyre stiffened.

"You called yourself 'Zyre of Lightning Peak,' but you're too young to have earned a nest there. Ten starflecks, isn't that the price? You couldn't have earned that much so quickly without doing some rather questionable jobs."

"That's not—"

"And besides, if you're so wealthy, why would you travel with only one starfleck?" Sorielle's tone was pleasant but sharp. "Surely a rich and successful spy like you could afford to carry more in your pouch. And if you're so well off, why risk your life traveling into the Deadlands at all?"

Zyre faltered. "I . . ."

"Spies don't do jobs unless they're paid," Sorielle continued. "Someone paid you to follow us into the Deadlands."

Zyre finally found her voice. "I collect information first and find a buyer afterward. If the information is valuable, I can get customers to bid for it."

"I'm sure you can," Sorielle said. "Information about the war, at least. But who would bid to hear the tale of a bunch of exiles?" She shook her head. "You wouldn't risk your life on this mission unless you already had a buyer lined up."

Silence.

Zyre stared into darkness, her mind racing. Despite her smiles and sickly sweet words, the ankylosaur was no fool. If she tried to lie, Zyre was fairly certain that Sorielle would untangle her story as easily as arithmetic. But if she told the truth, Sorielle would inevitably tell Tortha, who might execute her on the spot . . .

"I was offered payment," she said finally.

"What job?"

"I was paid to follow one of you. To make sure . . ." Zyre trailed off. The silence stretched. "To make sure you were safe."

Sorielle stared at her. "What?"

"I don't want to elaborate," Zyre said tightly. "I keep my clients' identities secret. But I was paid by one of your family members to keep you safe in the Deadlands until your exile sentence could be overturned."

Sorielle's eyes widened. A faint flicker of hope shone behind her pupils. "Eleri's family?" she whispered. "That's why you gave him the starfleck, isn't it? That's why you saved him in the Forest of Smoke!"

Zyre didn't respond.

Sorielle broke into a relieved smile. "Oh, thank goodness for that! I was starting to worry that you'd come here to hurt us."

"No, of course not!" Zyre spoke a little too quickly. "I'm here to help you."

"And that's how you'll earn your client's payment?"

Sorielle brightened. "Oh, that's wonderful! We'll have a clever ally on our side, and you'll get to earn your nest at Lightning Peak—isn't that just the loveliest idea?"

Zyre squirmed. "The loveliest."

"It has to be Eleri's family, of course," Sorielle went on. "Lerithon's family exiled him, and Tortha's family are hardened warriors—I hate to be ungenerous, but I can't imagine that they'd pay to keep her safe . . ."

Sorielle trailed off.

For the first time in the conversation, Zyre was distracted from the strain of her lie. She studied Sorielle's face in the shadows, noting the ankylosaur's low gaze and downturned chin. "And *your* family?"

"Pardon?"

"Your family, Sorielle. How do you know they didn't hire me?"

A cool breeze trickled across the crater, stirring dust and secrets in the moonlight.

"They just . . . wouldn't."

Zyre hesitated. "You call yourself Sorielle of the Grotto. All the others have kept their original herd names, except for you." It was a statement, but it slipped out like a question. "Like you *want* to leave your family behind."

Sorielle didn't meet her eyes. "That's not true. King Torive exiled me. I didn't leave by choice."

"But you didn't fight to stay?"

A long pause.

"What was your original name?" Zyre asked gently.

Sorielle took a long moment to respond. "Sorielle of the Fern Lea," she said. And then the words came, tumbling out with all the rush of a waterfall. "You have to understand, it wasn't that I didn't love them. I had a jolly good childhood, I truly did, it's just . . ."

She faltered.

"They didn't understand you?"

"They were all soldiers," Sorielle said. "They were so strong and brave, like Tortha, but I . . . Well, I just . . . I never understood it, really. The whole war, you know. It seemed so pointless to me. I liked numbers. I thought it would be lovely to live in the Fern Lea, without ever fighting in the war, and find out things about the world."

"Like what?"

"Like the weight of a raindrop," Sorielle said. "Or the speed of a falling leaf. Or the way that snowflakes splinter into millions of tiny shapes during the Times of Cold Moon . . ." She sounded distant, staring at the stars. "It's all numbers, you know. I feel that if I had a chance, I could unravel it all. It would all make sense."

"The world?"

"Everything."

Zyre gave a slow nod. She knew how it felt to disappoint her family. "My parents expect me to earn a nest at Lightning Peak. My grandmother lives there, and I . . . I want to see her again."

Sorielle stepped closer, her eyes bright. "If you help us, you might," she said, and a hint of her smile returned.

Zyre's insides tightened. She glanced back up at the lip of the crater, where Eleri had disappeared into darkness.

"You can still earn your place at Lightning Peak," Sorielle said. "And I'm sure your parents will be so proud of you."

A cloud passed across the moon, painting darkness on the crater. Shadow's voice echoed in the back of Zyre's head, cold and clinical. *His name is Eleri of the Broken Ridge . . . I want you to track him down—and make sure he never returns . . .*

"Yes," Zyre said. "Maybe they will."

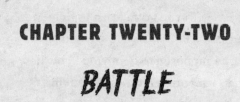

CHAPTER TWENTY-TWO

BATTLE

Eleri climbed the crater, ignoring the scatter of stones behind him. He crested its lip with a grunt of effort. It didn't take him long to spot Tortha, whose horns gleamed beneath the moon.

"Tortha?"

She ignored him. Eleri scurried forward, tilting his head as he studied her. "You look like Lerithon, staring at the stars."

"I'm thinkin'."

He gave a slight grin. "Got room in your skull with all those horns?"

Tortha turned to him. For a moment she looked ready to snap, but then she gave a weary laugh. "Suppose I've earned that one."

For a while, they sat in companionable silence.

"You shouldn't be wastin' your time on stories," Tortha said quietly. "They won't help you win a battle. You almost died today, Eleri. You've gotta learn to fight, not to tell tales for hatchlings."

"How am I supposed to fight? You know how small I am. I can't beat a carnivore ten times my weight."

"Don't matter a lick. It ain't about your weight, it's how you use it."

"Tell that to a tyrannosaur."

She met his gaze. "Back in my herd, we used to get pestered by bugs. They lived down in the Lowland Marsh, you see. They'd land all over us, bitin' and stingin', and we could never get rid of 'em. Know why?"

Eleri opened his mouth, but Tortha didn't wait for his answer. "'Cause they were small and fast. Our strength didn't matter. Our weight didn't matter. Those dang bugs beat us every time."

Eleri frowned. "Are you saying I'm a bug?"

"No! Well, you're as annoying as one, but no. I'm sayin' you've got traits you can use to your advantage, if you just try using 'em properly."

"Show me, then."

"You askin' for a lesson, dirt muncher?"

"Depends. Are you offering one?"

In response, Tortha hauled herself to her feet—and suddenly, she charged. Her horns flashed as she lowered her head, stampeding toward him with all the force of a boulder in a rockslide.

Eleri flung himself aside, barely avoiding her horns as she smashed past.

"Good!" she huffed. "Fast, decent reaction. But it ain't enough to just get away—you should've turned the situation to your advantage."

"But how—?"

She charged again, and Eleri cut off his own question with a startled cry. He had some serious qualms about Tortha's teaching style, but this was hardly the moment to discuss her technique.

He braced himself, ready to leap aside—but then he remembered his fight with Uriela, and the mad instinct that had driven him to grab her tail. The raptor had expected defense, so his offensive move had caught her off guard—and indeed, off-balance.

He might not have strength, but he had surprise.

Instead of darting aside, Eleri dropped to the ground and slid beneath Tortha. He reached up to rake her underbelly with his claws, careful not to break the skin.

"Ha!" Tortha cried. "That's better! If you're small enough to fit under an enemy, I reckon you can attack from below. That's where all the vital organs are, right?" She scraped a claw in the dirt. "And it's the worst place for bug bites!"

Eleri grinned, pleased with himself, but Tortha wasn't

about to let him enjoy his victory. She spun, throwing up a cloud of dust and gravel, and hurtled back toward him.

This time, Eleri took the initiative. He dashed to the right, looped around, and vaulted toward her from the side. With an almighty leap, he landed on her back. Tortha grunted, startled, as he reached for her jugular . . .

Sorielle clambered over the lip of the crater.

"Oh goodness!" Sorielle took in the scene before her. "What happened to having a nice chat?"

Eleri laughed, releasing Tortha and sliding to the ground. "My turn for sentry duty?"

"I'm afraid so," Sorielle said.

"All right, I'm coming."

As he trekked back toward the crater, Eleri's muscles ached. It wasn't the ache of a wound or even exhaustion. It was a satisfying ache. An ache that meant he was building his strength and living to fight another day.

In the morning, he and his friends would trek toward the Cold Canyon. They would sneak through a battlefield, dodging soldiers of the Prairie Alliance and the Mountain Kingdom alike. Tomorrow night, they would enter the secret tunnel . . . and blow it to smithereens.

And if Eleri was lucky, he *might* survive to tell their story.

It was late afternoon when they reached the battlefield. In just a few hours, the Half Moon would rise.

The sky was bruised, fading into dusk. It had rained an hour earlier. The droplets were dusty and bitter, but they had provided a much-needed drink. Eleri had remoistened the leaves encasing the fireblasts, reducing the risk of sparks.

They heard the battle before they saw it. Crashes and wails carried across the Cold Canyon, spilling into the Deadlands. Eleri stood at the canyon's lip, trying to drown out the cries. Could it be his father out there, dying on the battlefield?

Could it be Agostron?

"Which way?" Sorielle looked anxious.

"The tunnel entrance is on the other side of the canyon." Tortha stared forward, her expression bleak. "Down in the foothills, at the border of the Mountain Kingdom."

"Where they're *fighting*?" Eleri demanded.

"Yep. You scared, dirt muncher?"

"Of course I'm scared! You think we're all as mad as you?"

Tortha smirked as if he'd paid her a compliment. "Come on, then."

They descended into the Cold Canyon, picking a winding path down the sloped wall of the ravine. Eleri carried the fireblasts, wrapped in their nests of damp leaves. As he fought to keep his claws steady, it struck Eleri that they were breaking the Laws of Exile. Right now, by stepping out of the Deadlands, they were defying the sacred ruling of the Mountain Court—or the Prairie Court, in the others' cases.

If they were caught, they'd be executed on sight.

"We can't be seen," he said, huffing for breath as they reached the base of the canyon. "Not until we've destroyed the tunnel and earned a right to speak at court. If anyone recognizes us now, anyone from our herds . . ."

"Gee, you figure?" Tortha said sarcastically. "And here I was, plannin' to run straight up to a random Prairie squadron and holler madly. *Oh hey, I missed y'all so much! Hey, why are you sharpenin' your horns?*"

The Cold Canyon was vast. They crossed in silence, aware of their deadly proximity to the battlefield. With every step, the clashing and screeching grew louder, splintering the eerie quiet of the ravine.

Eleri had never explored this part of the canyon on foot. Adult soldiers occasionally patrolled here, but it was off-limits to civilians. A week ago, he'd watched the sauropods travel along this path, while Agostron stood by his side and a pterosaur swooped from above . . .

It seemed a lifetime ago.

"Have any of you been down here before?" he asked.

Lerithon gave a slow nod, but none of the others spoke for a moment. Zyre finally replied, stretching her wings cautiously as she perched on Lerithon's back. "I have. I was hunting for secrets to sell."

"Find any?" Tortha asked tightly.

"No," she said. "Just rocks and rubble."

Cracks and caves stippled the canyon walls, while scraggly

trees sprouted from the soil. Lerithon fixed his gaze on the mouth of a tunnel, on the Deadlands side of the canyon. "One must walk in darkness when one does not deserve the light."

Eleri glanced back over his shoulder. "That tunnel entrance . . . it's where your herd exiled you?"

Lerithon gave a slow nod.

"So it joins up with the tunnel network under the Deadlands?"

Another nod.

Eleri made a mental note. If their plan went awry, Lerithon's tunnel might be their best evacuation route. They could escape underground into the Deadlands—and perhaps even find Lerithon's original path to the underground river. No herbivorous soldier would dare to follow a pack of exiles into the Deadlands.

Of course, it would be a different tale if their pursuers were carnivores. Eleri's stomach churned as he imagined it. They'd be trapped in darkness, with killers prowling through the shadows toward them . . .

As escape routes went, this was definitely a last resort.

On the far side of the canyon, they climbed the slope slowly. The path was well worn by army patrols, but clumps still crumbled beneath their feet. Eleri's heart pounded as he took the lead, checking for the safest spots to place a claw.

Finally, they crested the lip of the canyon.

The battlefield was . . . stark. A natural plain of ferns and moss, dotted with conifer saplings—but right now, it seemed more lifeless than the Deadlands. Dead earth, trampled and bloodstained. Dead plants, crushed beneath a hundred charging claws.

And dead soldiers, lying in wait for the carrion eaters.

Nausea rose inside Eleri. "Flaming feathers . . ."

Tortha stared across the battlefield, her expression bleak. The armies crashed against each other, mad and wild, like waves of Burning Dust smashing into a crater. No hesitation. No mercy. Just stomps and horns and spikes and screams. Ankylosaurs battled iguanodons, groaning as their massive bodies collided. A squadron of stegoceras darted like water, separating a triceratops soldier from its squad. The triceratops buckled as its smaller foes piled on: a living torrent, gouging at its throat and eyes . . .

"We have to stop this," Sorielle whispered. "No matter what, we have to stop this."

No one disagreed. Tortha looked physically ill, as if the bleak reality of battle had crushed her daydreams of valor and victory. Zyre stared down, avoiding the sight. Perhaps it was guilt that weighed on her as she remembered how her kind had profited from this war.

"Come on!" Eleri tore his gaze away. "Let's go."

Tortha took the lead, a soldier on a mission. Eleri kept his distance, following several yards behind. By all rights, they should be fighting each other right now, not traveling together as allies.

Lerithon provided a decent distraction, drawing the attention of nearby soldiers. While startled eyes swiveled to gaze at the passing giant, the other exiles slipped between the hordes of fighters, avoiding being drawn into the fray.

"There!" Tortha rasped. "Behind that hill with the conifer trees."

Despite its girth, the tunnel's mouth was well camouflaged. It lurked in a crook-like valley, wedged between a foothill and a corrugated ridge. Conifers sprouted from the slopes above, their canopy concealing the rocky jaw of the passage.

"Remember the plan?" Eleri asked.

They all nodded. Eleri would place the fireblasts, with Tortha guiding him through the tunnel. Sorielle, Zyre, and Lerithon would wait outside, keeping watch for soldiers.

"Don't let anyone in," Tortha said, her voice tight. "That tunnel's comin' down, and any Prairie soldiers inside are gonna die. I won't be responsible for killing my comrades. Got it?"

Sorielle nodded, her eyes wide. "Oh yes, I understand," she said. "Gosh, what a responsibility! I promise I won't let you down, Tori."

It was a sign of Tortha's stress that she didn't even protest the nickname.

"I do hate to ask," Sorielle added, "but what if they're already inside?"

Tortha twitched. Eleri looked down. There was no answer

for that. If the Prairie Alliance soldiers were already in the tunnel, he and Tortha would just have to deal with them.

"In the darkness we must fall," Lerithon opined. "In the pain we must endure."

They all paused.

"Well," Eleri said, "on that cheerful note, we'd better get on with it."

CHAPTER TWENTY-THREE

THE CAVERN OF TEETH

The tunnel was pitch-black.

Tortha took the lead, using her horns to feel the way. Eleri crept cautiously behind her, a fireblast in each claw.

"Watch your step," Tortha warned. "There are some loose pebbles here. We're about to turn left, so try not to bump the wall . . ."

Every step seemed a potential death sentence. The fireblasts' wrapping had long since dried out, and the dead leaves crinkled in Eleri's claws. A single spark could set them ablaze. He imagined it now: the rush of flame, the sucking of air, the tunnel collapsing . . .

And all in darkness.

He'd give anything to return to the Grotto, with its streaks of daylight and luminescent fungi. A single shining mush-room might make this journey bearable.

But there was nothing. Every step was blind, and all Eleri knew was the *thud, thud, thud* of Tortha's steps and the *scritch-scratch* of his own claws on stone. The air tasted bitter. Each breath echoed in the dark.

The tunnel climbed slowly, weaving up into the Mountain Kingdom. Tortha walked steadily, but occasionally her nerves betrayed her. A footstep would falter, or the rhythm of her steps would run askew. Once she stopped in her tracks, trying to feel her way forward at a fork in the tunnel, and Eleri almost crashed into her.

"Hey!" he rasped, struggling to keep his grip on the fire-blasts.

"Sorry," she whispered. Her voice was raw.

His anger faded. "It's okay."

Step by step, the tunnel rose upward, ascending into the inner sanctum of the Mountain Kingdom. It resembled an enormous warren, clambering up toward the Broken Ridge from the heart of the earth.

To Eleri's immense relief, there was no sign of the Prairie troops. If hordes of soldiers were already in this tunnel, there would be evidence of their passage: broken rocks, or at least the echo of voices and footfalls ahead. Triceratops and ankylosaurs weren't exactly light on their claws.

"I think we got here first," he whispered.

With each twist of the tunnel, the air grew colder. Soon it

stung, sharp with the bitter chill of a midwinter frost. When Eleri's tail brushed the stone wall, it instantly retracted, yanking away from the ice-cold stone.

"It's like winter in here," he whispered.

Tortha hesitated before she responded. "Yeah. And it's gonna get worse before it starts gettin' better."

The exiles slipped into another narrow tunnel, barely wide enough for Tortha to squeeze through.

One step, two, three, four . . .

Eleri kept count in his head, trying to distract himself. But he often lost count, startled by an unexpected halt—or by Tortha's clawsteps faltering. Most often, the distraction was his own raw terror. It gripped the inside of his throat, drawing the flesh tighter, making it harder to breathe.

Suddenly, a rush of movement swept past. Eleri cried out and ducked, startled, as something scuttled along a ridge of stone above him. It shrieked, hissing and darting away into the blackness. "What was that?"

"A warmblood," Tortha whispered. "I think so, at least."

Eleri blinked. Unlike the dinosaurs, warmbloods couldn't speak or reason. The vicious scavengers gave birth to live young rather than eggs. They were small but wild, known for preying on eggs and hatchlings. They also ate carrion, if they could find it. A warmblood could decimate an unprotected nest but posed little threat to an adult dinosaur.

"Ignore it," Tortha said. "We're too big to eat."

The air grew colder and colder. As he gripped the fireblasts,

Eleri tried to keep his claws from shaking. If any trickles of water leaked into this tunnel, they would freeze: trapped forever in a sea of black.

"Almost there?" he whispered.

Tortha was aiming for the narrowest point in the tunnel, near the exit into the Mountain Kingdom. Their original plan had required at least three fireblasts, but Tortha and Sorielle had devised an alternative solution. Eleri wasn't clear on the details, but Sorielle had seemed fairly confident that it would work.

"Still a bit farther." Tortha sounded as if she was speaking through gritted teeth. "Just a few more bends, and then we've got the Cavern of Teeth to cross . . ."

"The Cavern of Teeth?" Eleri said, startled.

"Well, it ain't literally teeth. My commanders called it that because it's a bit . . . jagged. Kind of like a carnivore's teeth."

"You never mentioned that before."

Tortha hesitated. "I didn't want . . . Well, I didn't want you stressin' about it for no good reason."

Eleri's body tensed. "And you think it helps to tell me *now*?"

"It ain't too bad, really." Tortha sounded as if she was trying to convince herself. "It's just a bit . . . spiky."

"Spiky? Are you serious?"

"Stop stressin', dirt muncher! So long as we're careful, we'll be fine. And there's a bit of light in there, actually, so it's better than this place . . ."

Now that she mentioned it, Eleri *did* see a faint glimmer in the black ahead. His heart sped a little—not from fear now, but excitement. He could handle a few spiky rocks if it meant an end to this quagmire of shadow.

But as the cavern approached, Eleri stiffened. Every surface in the cave was a blade. Icicles stippled the ceiling, sharp and jagged. The rock walls gleamed with an odd shining mucus.

On the ground, enormous stalagmites thrust upward, slicing the dark. With each step that Eleri took, the lines of light and shadow shifted, dancing and slicing like a tyrannosaur's jaws.

"The Cavern of Teeth," he whispered.

Tortha's reply was stiff. "Let's get this over with."

But even as she stepped forward, her leg clanged against the base of a stalagmite. The sound echoed through the cavern—and overhead, a few of the icicles quavered.

Eleri stared at them, eyes wide. If those icicles fell, they would impale the exiles in a horrific spray of blood and bone. Would they fall? Would they . . . ?

Silence. The icicles steadied, retaining their tenuous grip on the ceiling. Even so, it took five long seconds for Eleri to find his voice. "You've crossed this cavern before, right? And none of the icicles fell?"

Tortha hesitated. "Not . . . exactly."

"What?"

"Our first scoutin' party went this way," she whispered.

"But the party I was in . . . we went a different way. It was our job to find a safer route. We could never get a full squadron through here, not without bringin' all them icicles down."

Eleri stared at her, horrified. "Then why are *we* going this way?"

"'Cause it leads to the weakest point in the tunnel system, and we've only got two fireblasts. Sorielle says two blasts won't bring down the main tunnel, so we've gotta find another way to start a collapse."

Eleri stared across the cavern, feeling sick.

Tortha's tone was tight. "On the far side of this cavern, there's a narrow stretch of tunnel near the exit. It runs right above the wider tunnel—the one the Prairie Alliance is gonna use. If we collapse the narrow tunnel, it should come down on the wider tunnel and smash both of 'em."

A wave of despair swept through Eleri's bones. So many things were wrong with this plan. "What if we collapse the top tunnel, but the bottom tunnel isn't even affected? All this could be for nothing!"

"Ain't got a choice, dirt muncher. We've only got two fireblasts, remember?"

"What happened to your 'alternative plan'?"

"This *is* the alternative plan."

"But we—"

"This is our best chance!" Tortha shook her head. "In fact, it's the *only* chance we've got."

His nerves frayed, Eleri decided to let the argument rest. His vision refused to focus. For a wild moment, he knew nothing but the glimmer of the cavern walls. But in the cold, a strange memory trickled into his skull.

When he was younger, in the dead of winter, it had snowed. The weight of the snow had snapped a few small twigs at the top of a conifer tree. The weight of those twigs— and the snow—had collapsed the twigs beneath. In turn, this pile of debris had smashed through a thicker branch, and then another, all the way down.

It was the same concept, wasn't it? Start with a small disaster up high and let it cascade, building destructive force as it fell.

Eleri weighed the fireblasts in his claws, desperately wishing that he had one more.

"All right, let's go."

The Cavern of Teeth glinted, raw and hungry. Eleri tip-toed forward. He slipped easily between the stalagmites, with plenty of space to maneuver. So long as he kept the fireblasts steady, he felt relatively safe. His clawsteps were light: a series of quiet scratches, unlikely to stir the icicles from their ceiling nests.

Tortha wasn't so lucky.

With every step, the triceratops had to squeeze between the stalagmites, aware that a single knock or scrape could bring a ceiling of blades crashing down. Sweat trickled between her horns as she crept across the cavern. After each tentative step, she threw a fearful look upward, as if expecting the icicles to shake and spill.

Another step, then another. Five, ten, twenty, thirty . . . They were a quarter of the way across the cavern, then a third of the way. Eleri's gaze fell on a vast shape, broken and lifeless in the shadows.

It was a dead triceratops.

Tortha gasped. "Flaming feathers—that must be the captain from our first scoutin' party! It looks like . . ."

She trailed off, sounding queasy. Even in the faint light, Eleri could make out the grim tale of the moonchaser's death. The ceiling above him was bare of icicles, as if they had crashed down to impale the dinosaur below. But the strange part wasn't his body, lying in the frozen cavern.

It was his skeleton.

The captain's bones had been picked clean.

"Warmbloods," Eleri whispered, stomach turning. It was the only possible answer. The individual creatures were small, but a horde of them could strip a carcass in days. "Must be a whole infestation in here."

Tortha didn't respond.

They struggled on, slicing a path between light and shadow. The stalagmites thickened, sprouting closer and closer together. It was as if they had moved from the scraggly edge of a forest into a proper thicket, bristling with deadly trees.

"I can't fit," Tortha whispered.

A faint choke crackled in her voice: a raw, broken note that sent a chill down Eleri's spine. She'd never betrayed such fear before.

Eleri glanced ahead, and his stomach knotted. The icicles ahead were longer and deeper, plunging toward the cavern floor. To squeeze beneath them, Tortha would have to drop to her knees and crawl. A single jolt would send those blades falling.

"I can't do it," she whispered. "I can't . . ."

"Yes, you can!"

But she shook her head. Even this movement was shaky and hesitant—as if Tortha feared that she might knock a stray icicle from its perch. "You go ahead," she whispered. "You've gotta do this, Eleri. You've gotta destroy the tunnel."

Eleri stared. It was too late for Tortha to retreat—with every minute that passed, the risk increased that the invasion would begin. There was no time to retrace their steps. Either Tortha moved forward with Eleri, or . . .

"I'm not going to leave you!"

"You've got to!" she said, her whisper a choked rasp "Hundreds of innocent civilians will die if you don't—"

"You'll die if you're trapped here!" Eleri hissed. "You think I'm gonna blow up the tunnel while you're stuck inside?"

She drew a shaky breath. "It's war. Sometimes you've gotta make sacrifices."

"Not this one." Eleri glared at her. "Not this time."

Silence.

Overhead, the icicles dripped. Frosty tears plinked onto the stalagmites, adding a quiet melody to the eerie stillness of the cavern. Eleri's breath congealed before him, casting clouds into the cold.

"Come on," Eleri whispered. "We'll do this together, all right? One step at a time."

"If I set those icicles fallin', you'll die too!"

"Together," Eleri repeated. "For better or worse, we're doing this together. I won't leave you here."

She glared at him—but even in the shadows, she read the resolve in his eyes. No point arguing. If they raised their voices, they'd bring the ceiling of blades crashing down.

"Together," she whispered.

CHAPTER TWENTY-FOUR

TELLING TALES

At the foot of the mountain, battle raged. Zyre hovered above the tunnel entrance, watching in horror as claw met claw, jaw met jaw . . .

Blood met blood.

Soldiers collapsed, disintegrating into shrieks as the fighting swept over them. Ankylosaurs charged into squadrons of stegoceras, swinging their tails like thunderclaps. Iguanodons launched themselves at triceratops, raking claws across horned heads and stampeding feet.

Sorielle and Lerithon stood before the tunnel's mouth, guarding it against attack. Time was running out. At any moment, the Prairie Alliance would order their forces through the tunnel—and yet, there was still no sound of an explosion.

"Come on, come on . . . ," Zyre muttered. "Hurry, Eleri!"

Lerithon stood still and stoic, but Sorielle was pacing. She rubbed her tailspikes in the dirt, shaking her head as she muttered quick calculations under her breath. Zyre had a vague idea that she was estimating times, or perhaps the impact of the explosion. Whatever it was, it didn't seem to ease Sorielle's stress levels.

"Gosh, this is taking an awfully long time!" Sorielle said, looking up with overwide eyes. "Do you think they're quite all right?"

"I hope so." Zyre wheeled to perch on a tree, right before the tunnel entrance. Her battered body throbbed from being attacked in the Forest of Smoke, and she welcomed any chance to rest her wings. "It must be hard to navigate those tunnels, right?"

"Maybe they took a wrong turn," Sorielle said, horrified.

Better than the alternative, Zyre thought, but she didn't say it aloud. The last thing she needed was a panicky Sorielle to barrel into the tunnel network after the others. Knowing their luck, the entire roof would come crashing down a moment later.

Lerithon gave a long, slow exhale. "Dark is the night that approaches."

"Yeah, that's generally what happens when the sun goes down," Zyre said. Then she followed the sauropod's gaze, and her insides knotted.

Beyond the conifer thicket, a squadron was approaching.

Zyre took to the sky, ignoring the pang in her bruised

wings as she soared to snatch a better look. No, it wasn't just one squadron. It was a full platoon of triceratops, followed by two herds of ankylosaurs. They had fought their way across the battlefield, and there could be no mistaking their final target.

They were coming to invade the tunnel.

The exiles couldn't fight them off. With Lerithon on their side, perhaps they could hold a single platoon at bay—for a minute or two, at least. Just enough to buy some time for Eleri and Tortha.

Right now, their only hope was trickery.

"Do you know them?" Zyre asked urgently. "Will they recognize you?"

Sorielle shook her head. "I . . ."

"Sorielle, *will they recognize you?*"

"No! I mean, no, I don't think so . . ."

"Good!" Zyre said. "All right, here's what you've got to do."

She rapidly outlined her plan, while Lerithon ducked behind the thicket of trees. She cursed Lerithon's slow gait as he lumbered into hiding—and as his tail flicked out of sight, the first rank of soldiers marched into view.

Zyre landed on a high branch in the canopy and peered through the foliage, her heart racing. Right now, everything was riding on Sorielle's ability to lie.

If she failed, they were all doomed.

In the Cavern of Teeth, the world glinted.

Eleri crept beneath the low-hanging icicles. Tortha crawled on awkward knees, struggling to keep her body low. Even raising her head slightly could kill them. If one of her horns brushed a blade of ice . . .

Eleri paused, waiting for Tortha to catch up. An agonized halt echoed each step: clench, breathe, release. Clench, breathe, release . . .

"Eleri," she whispered. "Can you tell a story?"

"What?"

"I need a distraction. Just . . . please. I need . . . please."

Eleri heard the pain in her rasp: the injury she'd dealt to her own stubborn pride. If the circumstances were any different, Eleri might have laughed. The soldier who was too tough for "fairy tales" was begging for a story.

But this wasn't the time for mockery.

This was the time for courage. Not his courage, but hers. And even as he opened his mouth, Eleri knew in his lungs and bones and heart that this was the most important story he'd ever told.

"This is the Tale of Astrilar the Wise, who lived in the Time of the Fallen Star. As the world burned, millions of dinosaurs died, their feathers aflame and their bones blazing. Yet Astrilar built a sanctuary for her herd, deep in the bones of the Fire Peak.

"One black night, the mountain threatened to fall. It shook and quaked, spewing ash and liquid rock. The herd cowered, certain that their end was nigh. But Astrilar's visions led her to the heart of the mountain, where she placed a mighty shard of the Fallen Star. This shard held the strength of a thousand tiny starflecks—and amidst chaos and calamity, its power held the Fire Peak upright. As the world burned, the warren endured.

"And so Astrilar the Wise kept her kin safe. She kept her kin alive. And when the ash had stopped falling, and the poison rain had faltered, she led them out into the new world that lay beyond."

Eleri spoke so quietly that he could barely hear his own words. He wasn't sure if Tortha could make out the details—but with icicles teetering overhead, she didn't complain.

"Of course, Astrilar was afraid. She stepped from her tunnel into the open, staring across lands that had been scorched and destroyed. The sky was dark and stained with clouds. A strange mist lay upon the land. But Astrilar knew that she must be strong. She must hide her fear, to keep her kindred safe.

"And so she said to them, 'Behold, our land and future! It may be scarred, as are we all. But somewhere, we shall find a home. Somewhere, we shall find a future.' And Astrilar led them out across the desert. She led them across the great plains, which would one day be known as the Deadlands.

"It was a terrible journey, for the air was poison and the Burning Dust struck hard. Many perished along the way: the very old, and the very young. When they found food or water, Astrilar insisted that the weakest have it, taking none for herself. When carnivores attacked her herd, she led the charge to fight them off—and to protect the most vulnerable.

"The elders said that she was mad. That she would lead them into endless desert, and they would perish and wither and die. But Astrilar was an Eye of the Forgotten, and she had seen a land of hope beyond the plain. She knew in her heart that she was traveling the right way. And so she pressed on, even though she was afraid."

Overhead, an icicle dripped.

"Finally, Astrilar found a great mountain. This was no peak of fire, like the place where her herd had sheltered. It was a mountain where trees still grew. A mountain of lakes and waterfalls, ridges and ravines. And so she said, 'This shall be our kingdom. This shall be our sanctuary.' With that, Astrilar the Wise became the first Queen of the Mountain Kingdom, and finally her herd was safe."

Even as the last words of the story fell from his tongue, Eleri's mouth dried out. His instincts prickled. They were two-thirds of the way across the cavern—and yet something felt very, very wrong. Tortha had fallen behind.

"What's wrong?" he whispered, turning.

Tortha stared at him, pressed down tight on her belly. Slowly, her gaze traveled upward, and Eleri followed it. His mouth suddenly filled with the sour tang of dread.

The ceiling was alive.

Warmbloods clung to rocks and ridges, brown fur bristling in the shine of the walls. The creatures bared their teeth and claws, eyes ripe with hunger as they surveyed the unex-pected prey below. How many were there? Ten? Twenty?

Their eyes gleamed.

"They're too small to attack us," Eleri whispered. "They only go for eggs, and maybe newborn hatchlings. They can't hurt us."

"They can't." Tortha's voice was hoarse. "But the ici-cles can."

With a surge of horror, Eleri understood. Several warm-bloods clawed at the ice, scrabbling to dislodge the blades. Icicles swayed and teetered, threatening to drop . . .

"Run!" he rasped.

The time for silence was over. The icicles would fall regardless—and right now, their only chance was speed. Eleri raced toward the next tunnel, claws tingling as he clutched the fireblasts. Tortha crashed along behind him, a wild erup-tion of sound.

Overhead, the icicles splintered.

Crash! Crash! Crash!

Outside, Zyre perched in her hiding place.

Sorielle stood alone before the tunnel mouth, a lone guard as the Prairie's invasion force approached. The com-manding triceratops stomped forward, glaring at Sorielle. "Who are you? What are you doing here?"

Sorielle blinked, rising and falling a little on her toes. But she drew a deep breath—and to Zyre's immense relief, she recited the words that Zyre had just prepared for her. "At your command, sir! I'm here on the orders of Lord Calyor of the Fern Lea."

The commander blinked. "What?"

"We've been asked to postpone, sir," Sorielle blurted. "An emergency measure, just for ten minutes or so. There's trouble at the far end of the tunnel, you see, and—"

"Nonsense!" the commander snarled. "I'm here on the orders of King Torive himself, and I don't take orders from sniveling hatchlings."

"But Lord Calyor said—"

"Last time I checked, a king outranks a lord." The commander stepped forward, taut with impatience. "Now get out of my way, or I'll *get* you out of my way. Got it?"

Blade met blade in a clanging battle as icicles smashed onto stalagmites. Tortha cried out, hurling herself between two rocky outcrops as an icicle barely missed her head.

"Go!" Eleri cried.

He jerked to a halt, slamming his claws into the ground to stop himself just as an enormous icicle shattered in front of him. If he'd stopped a second later, it would have skewered him.

Heart pounding, he ducked around the icicle. His claws tightened around the fireblasts, but he couldn't loosen his grip; terror had seized control of his body, and his limbs refused to obey him. All he could do was run, gasping and rasping and . . .

Crash! Crash!

Icicles rained around him: a deadly torrent of teeth. Tortha cried out, and Eleri flinched, recognizing the pain in her voice, but he couldn't stop to check her wounds. He *had* to get the fireblasts out of here, or they would die in smoke and flame.

Crash!

Eleri's body shook. His tail whipped back and forth to stabilize him, keeping his balance as he stumbled across the cavern.

Finally, he plunged into the tunnel beyond. It was dark and narrow, but streaks of fungus glimmered on the walls. Eleri whirled, turning to face Tortha as she barreled toward him, her face wild with pain and panic.

"Go, go!" she cried.

Eleri didn't hesitate. He ran straight down the tunnel as Tortha dashed after him, shaking and thudding as icicles fractured behind them. The collapse was out of control now: not just a few stray spikes, but the entire ceiling of ice. Warmbloods squealed, erupting into scurries as their world disintegrated, but Eleri didn't stop to think about them. All that mattered was the chaos behind him and the deadly weapons in his claws.

Faint moonlight shone ahead. It was dusk.

"Now!" Tortha cried. "Get behind me and do it, now!"

The tunnel was so narrow that Eleri could barely squeeze back past her. He felt something wet and hot smeared across her hide. Horrified, he realized that he'd scraped her wound—but this time, Tortha didn't even grunt to betray her pain. "Now, Eleri!"

Eleri hurled the fireblasts back along the tunnel. Tortha was already charging for the exit, her great body heaving as she squeezed along the narrow space. Eleri scuttled behind her, forced to slow down and match her speed.

The fireblasts hit the rocks.

CHAPTER TWENTY-FIVE

FLAMING FEATHERS

The mountain exploded.

It began with a low grumble, as if the peak were suffering indigestion. Then an enormous *bang!* slapped the air. Zyre almost fell from her perch outside, winded by the invisible punch that smashed its way down the tunnel. In the distance, a violent echo tore the dark: *crash, slash, bang, thud* . . .

The tunnel heaved. The mountainside creaked, thrashing and dying like a wounded soldier. A wall of dust rolled along the tunnel, churning like a wave onto shore. It crashed out around them with a fatalistic *whumph!* before the night slipped back into stillness.

All was silent.

"What was that?" the triceratops commander barked.

"That's the emergency, sir!" Sorielle babbled. "Sorry, got to get back to Lord Calyor, he's expecting a report . . ."

She bustled away into the trees, leaving the flabbergasted ranks of soldiers behind her. The commanding triceratops gave a sudden cry of fury, as if the significance of this demolition had just hit home. Without their secret tunnel, there would be no surprise attack. There would be no slaughter.

There would be no victory.

He snapped an order to his soldiers, and they retreated, marching back toward the battlefield. As soon as they were out of earshot, Zyre fluttered down to join Sorielle and Lerithon in the undergrowth.

"Did it work?" Sorielle asked, breathless with excitement. "We did it, we really did it—and no one was inside the tunnel when it blew! Is it all over, do you think?"

Zyre stared back toward the tunnel. Dust and rubble spilled from its mouth, encrusting the moonlit dirt like blood.

"That depends," she said quietly, "on whether Eleri and Tortha made it out alive."

A vicious roar smashed Eleri's ears—and suddenly, petals of violent red and yellow rippled outward, filling the tunnel with an otherworldly shine. Fire glowed, molten hot against a backdrop of crashing ice.

"Go!" Eleri screamed, but his voice was lost in the roar

of the explosion. Fire crackled up and down, backward and forward, consuming the tunnel with smoke and light. The smoke stung Eleri's eyes. Rocks shattered and smashed as the air itself seemed to broil. He coughed, choking on lungfuls of ash. Even twenty yards from the blast, Eleri felt as if his skin were roasting.

They ran. It wasn't elegant, neat, or even particularly speedy. It was a mad, frenzied stumble of cries and curses. Eleri's ears rang, throbbing as if the explosion were repeating itself again and again and again . . . Tortha's wound bled fiercely, splattering blood into Eleri's eyes as he followed her.

Behind them, the disaster unfurled: a roaring tide of rocks that shattered in their wake. The ceiling spat down boulders, fragments ricocheting from the walls. The world was a roar of heat, of light, of sound and shards and shattering . . .

But the tunnel floor was holding firm! Panic churned in Eleri's veins—if this plan failed, if the tunnel didn't collapse onto its counterpart below, this had all been for nothing.

"Come on . . . ," he choked.

In a shrieking crash, the floor of the tunnel splintered. It cascaded into the tunnel beneath, flooding the abyss with rubble. There was another almighty crack, followed by a rumble that shook up through Eleri's bones. Their plan had worked—the lower tunnel was giving way! But right now, all that mattered was reaching that tiny ray of moon-light . . .

They burst into the night.

Tortha spluttered for breath, her entire body heaving. Eleri shot out behind her as the last of the tunnel gave way, crumbling into smoke and debris.

Silence.

The only sound was the pebbles, skittering to fill the new cracks in the landscape. A gust brushed through some nearby trees, and Eleri's stomach rose into his throat.

"We did it!" he whispered. "We . . ."

He realized where they stood. The clearing had half collapsed, as if a section of the land beyond had given way. But as his vision refocused, Eleri's eyes widened. He was incredibly close to the Broken Ridge. In fact, this was the clearing where he'd first met Tortha—where the pterosaur had swooped on the Prairie scouts, and Eleri had shouted a warning. Now the clearing lay before them once more, stark and bare.

No, not bare.

Across the clearing, a group of soldiers stood staring. A guard patrol from the Mountain Kingdom: iguanodons, oryctodromeus, and stegoceras. In the quiet, their leader stepped forward.

He was a fearsome soldier, with a crown of thorns and starflecks. An oryctodromeus in his prime, his body a ripple of muscles and vicious claws. He glared at the intruders, tight with loathing as he took in the sight. A pair of exiles, standing before an obliterated hillside. Smoke and rubble, death and despair . . .

"Little brother," he whispered. "What have you done?"

It was Agostron.

CHAPTER TWENTY-SIX

THE NIGHT OF HALF MOON

Eleri stared at his brother. He stood frozen in the clearing, his heart hammering in shock. "I . . . I didn't mean . . ."

"You've fractured half the ridge!" Agostron cried, his voice suddenly a bellow. "You, an exile, have returned to this place against our laws. You have brought only destruction to our homeland."

"There was a secret tunnel!" Eleri blurted. "The Prairie Alliance was going to send their soldiers along the tunnel, they were going to—"

"Silence!" Agostron cried, stalking toward him. "Do not *dare* to speak to your prince in such a way."

Eleri tensed. "My prince?"

And suddenly, it all clicked. The crown of thorns on Agostron's brow. The fact that he led a squadron from multiple herds, like a general in the Mountain Kingdom's army. The way that the other soldiers deferred to him, keeping their heads low until Agostron gave his command.

"Our father?" Eleri whispered.

A brief flash of pain crossed Agostron's eyes. "Our father fell on the first day of the battle. In the end, he barely fought to save himself." His gaze sharpened, whittled by a fresh surge of hatred. "Your betrayal was the end of him, little brother."

Eleri's insides crumpled.

It wasn't a physical drop. He stayed on his feet, and he kept his claws aloft. But it felt as if his innards had collapsed, each bone and organ falling onto the one beneath it, just as the tunnels had crashed onto each other.

"Gone?" he whispered.

"Gone." Agostron gave a bitter hiss. "Gone, because of you. And now you dare to return? You dare to show your face here, to destroy even more of our herd's domain?" He spun to face his squadron. "This is a convicted exile and a Prairie spy! Do your duty."

Snarling in fury, the soldiers advanced.

Eleri barely had time to brace himself. He could never fight them all—and the loathing in their eyes made his gut coil. These were soldiers of the Mountain Kingdom. After all he had survived, would he die at the claws of his kinsmen?

He stumbled backward, raising his own claws in a futile call for peace . . .

Tortha hurled herself in front of him. "You'll have to go through me."

Eleri stared at her, startled. In a cold rush, he remembered another night in this clearing. The flash of a pterosaur's wings and a warning cry in the dark . . .

A debt incurred. A debt repaid.

No, it was more than that. He saw the truth in Tortha's glare, in the defensive prickle of her posture. She *wanted* to protect him. With a start, Eleri realized that he had one true kinsman in this clearing—and it was not Agostron.

But Tortha was injured. The icicle wound left her slow, and she seemed dizzy from blood loss. She whipped her great tail and shook her head, threatening the attackers with her horns. Most of the soldiers charged straight toward her, keen for their chance to bring down a Prairie triceratops.

But Agostron ignored her. He slipped around her, his claws held high, his attention fixed on Eleri.

"Listen to me!" Eleri cried as his brother advanced. "It isn't what you think, Agostron. Everything we know, everything we've been taught, it's all a lie . . ."

Agostron lunged, his claws extended. Eleri darted aside, barely escaping a vicious swipe across the face. "It's the carrion eaters! This whole war, it's all been a trick. The kings are traitors, working with the carnivores to—"

"Traitors?" Agostron snarled. "*You* are the traitor, Eleri.

You already took the side of our enemies once, and you tore our family apart."

"I'm not taking their side!" Eleri lurched to avoid another swipe. "There are no sides! You have to let me talk to the Mountain Court, to tell them the truth—this whole war is a setup, just to— "

Agostron's claws struck home.

Eleri fell, gasping, as pain exploded down his side. The wound was only shallow, but it left him reeling in shock. Agostron had done this. Agostron had tried to kill him.

The time for talking was over.

Eleri leaped at his brother, his own claws extended. He lacked strength, but speed was on his side. He remembered what Tortha had taught him—to fight like an insect, using agility to strike his opponent.

He ducked and darted, lunged and dove. He became a blurred whirlwind of claws and snarls, zipping around his brother's bulkier frame. Agostron roared, frustrated and furious—but no matter how hard he swiped, he could never catch Eleri.

"You killed our father!" the prince cried, grief and rage exploding through his roar. "Your betrayal left him broken, Eleri. Too broken to fight for his life!"

Eleri faltered.

The words struck more violently than a physical blow. And in that moment of hesitation, Agostron pounced.

The prince leaped onto Eleri, smashing him into the

rocky dirt. Dust exploded up around them as they hit the ground, rasping and snarling. But Agostron was on top, with weight and strength on his side. He crushed Eleri into the dirt, pinning him as he pressed his claws to his throat.

"Father didn't care about me," Eleri whispered. "He didn't care that I was exiled. He didn't even—"

"He loved you!" Agostron snarled, his voice crackling with furious grief. "You were always his favorite."

Eleri stared up at him, bewildered. He remembered his father's words, muttered when he thought Eleri was out of earshot. *Nothing like his brother, I'm afraid. A disappointment, that one . . .*

"No, that's not true!" Eleri said. "I heard him—he said I was a disappointment, that I was nothing like my brother . . ."

For a long moment, Agostron glared down at him. Then understanding seemed to hit, and he barked out a laugh, brackish as desert rain. "You thought he was talking about *you*?"

Eleri blinked.

"He was never disappointed in *you*, Eleri!" Agostron leaned in, his breath hot and bitter. "He was talking about *me*. He always wanted me to be more like you."

Eleri would have laughed in turn, if not for the risk of slicing his own throat on Agostron's claws. "You've gotta be joking! You're the big strong soldier, the heir to the herd. I'm just the runt."

"You were the storyteller." Agostron pressed his claws

down harder. "The explorer. The one who dreamed of a better way . . . just like our mother."

"But you—"

"I was never good enough!" Agostron roared. "No matter how hard I trained, no matter how many practice battles I won, I was never good enough for him. Just another walking brute. A pile of muscle to toss onto the battlefield."

The starflecks in his crown glinted, bright and bitter.

He exhaled. "But you? You were different, Eleri. You were his great hope. He thought that you would save us, you know. He thought you would travel, meet other herds, and find another way for us to live—a way without wars and battles and blood . . ." Agostron's breath caught. "Father was going to change the inheritance. He thought that you should be the next prince, not me."

Eleri stared at him, unable to speak. It couldn't be true. It couldn't be . . .

But his father's words rang in his ears, the night that Eleri had earned his exile. *Sometimes, Eleri, you are so like your mother . . .*

"Then you betrayed us," Agostron hissed. "And I realized it was my only chance to get rid of you. My only chance to save my future."

He pressed his claws tighter. "My windwhisper might have failed to dispose of you . . . but I won't make the same mistake."

Eleri froze. "*Your* windwhisper?"

Suddenly, it all made sense. The fact that Zyre had followed them for days, creeping in their wake across the Deadlands . . .

His breath broke. Eleri had trusted Zyre. He had believed her story. Hadn't she saved his life in the Forest of Smoke? He had convinced himself that she wanted to help the exiles, to end the war . . .

Agostron raised his claws, preparing to strike with a killing blow.

Eleri didn't stop to think. He kicked upward with his hind legs, lashing out at his brother from beneath—and struck Agostron smack-bang in the belly. The larger oryctodromeus was flung backward, staggering and winded.

"You little runt! I'll—"

Tortha charged.

The other soldiers had fled, scattering into the woods to avoid her horns. Tortha was mad with battle fever, snarling and stomping and gnashing her teeth—and like a rockslide, she hurtled toward Agostron.

Agostron lay there, winded and dizzy. He tried to clamber to his feet, but he was too slow. He would never make it in time, not before he was crushed . . .

"No!" Eleri roared, leaping forward.

He crashed into Agostron and knocked his brother aside, mere moments before Tortha slammed past. The air whipped around them. Tortha's legs missed the brothers by inches; her tail whipped past Eleri in a vicious whirl of lethal strength.

Tortha slammed to a halt, kicking up a tornado of dust. She spun, scraping her claws in the dirt, and stared at them.

Silence. Eleri looked at Agostron. His brother shook with fear, bracing himself for a killing blow.

"Go," Eleri said.

Agostron paused. For a moment, he seemed ready to leap back into battle—but then he glanced at Tortha, who stood heaving and glaring. He scrambled to his feet, his face strained and feathers askew. He ran, skittering into the brush. With a rasp, he vanished between the conifers.

Tortha stepped forward. She looked utterly drained, her sides heaving as blood trickled from her wound. "You let him go!" she panted. "He was tryin' to rip out your throat, Eleri."

"He's my brother," Eleri said.

Her eyes widened slightly. Her expression softened, and she gave a slow nod. A glimmer of understanding shone behind her gaze. "He'll be back," she said. "With reinforcements."

"I know."

Tortha turned downhill, her gaze tight with determination. "Well then, let's go."

CHAPTER TWENTY-SEVEN

BROKEN RIDGE, FALLING SKY

The Broken Ridge was crumbling, but intact. The explosion had weakened veins of rock, sending chunks of stone skittering into the abyss below. Eleri and Tortha stood on the Southern Lookout, ogling the damage.

"Flamin' feathers . . . ," Tortha muttered, wide-eyed. "Reckon your herd is all right?"

Eleri studied the cracks. "I . . . *think* so." He had been terrified that the warren might have collapsed, but the damage to the ridge was less severe than he'd feared.

The surprise of Agostron's news still burned in him—not just with shock, but with blinding grief. The Broken Ridge herd was Eleri's only link to his father, who had faith in him when all others saw only a failure. And it was where his mother had died, with her secret dreams still trapped inside her.

The warren lay on the far side of the ridge, set considerably back beneath the shelter of the peak. If the ridge was still intact, the warren was most likely untouched. The sleeping oryctodromeus might have felt a faint vibration, but there was little chance of collapses or cave-ins.

"I should go and check . . . ," he began.

"Don't even think it." Tortha tossed her head to gesture at the crumbling ridge. "If you try crossin' that, it'll come down under you."

She was right. Eleri swallowed hard. He was cut off from his herd—and besides, he was an exile. If the elders caught him here, they could legally kill him on sight.

But as he turned to Tortha, his gaze fell on the landscape behind her. His breath hitched.

"No . . . ," he whispered.

From the Lookout, he could see the battlefield below. The Half Moon bathed the world in light and shadow— and even from here, he could make out the shapes of warring soldiers. But it wasn't the battlefield that caught his gaze.

It was the Deadlands.

An army was massing at the border of the Deadlands, right at the edge of the Cold Canyon. Not the Prairie Alliance's army. Not the Mountain Kingdom's forces.

The carnivores.

It was too dark and distant to make out details, but Eleri

knew it in his gut. At least two hundred carrion eaters, gathering to feast after the tunnel attack. They lurked out of sight, down in the depths of a shallow gully where the battling armies couldn't see them.

As Eleri stared into the gully of predators, something prickled at the back of his mind. It was half an idea, playing at his consciousness, but it hadn't quite clicked into place . . .

With a cold flash, he remembered Lerithon's words. The Eye of the Forgotten had sensed an ancient memory of this place—and his herd had exiled him for it. *One's vision sang of blood, of death, of pain. Of a land nearby where the earth was angry and great stones fell to crush many souls . . .*

It had happened before. It could happen again.

"The Land of Falling Sky!" he breathed.

"What?"

"Look where they're standing!" Eleri waved an excited foreclaw. "We call that gully the Land of Falling Sky. The cliffs above are always crumbling—there are heaps of rockslides down onto the plain."

Tortha's eyes bulged. She didn't even need to speak. The plan struck them both at once, and they turned, scrambling back into the wilderness. The question was, could they set it off before the predators made a feast of Eleri's kin?

Eleri took the lead, darting along the mountainside paths. They descended into ravines and scrambled up onto peaks, following their undulating curves. Finally, chests heaving, they reached the cliffs above the Deadlands. These weren't the Exile Cliffs, where Eleri had farewelled his herd. These were the Cliffs of Falling Sky.

Far below, the carnivore army swelled. Squadrons trailed across the plains, heading to join their companions in the gully. Their bodies writhed: a mass of shadows, filling the gully with their jostling forms.

Eleri felt sick. The carnivores were here to gorge on death.

"Not if I can help it," Eleri muttered.

"What?" Tortha asked.

"Nothing. Let's do this."

Tortha scanned the clifftop, searching for the spark to cause maximum mayhem. Eleri studied the landscape with his oryctodromeus eyes, paying attention to the angles and positions of the rocks. He and his herdmates were burrowers—and although he had no interest in warren construction, he knew just enough to spot a structural flaw.

Time to put that knowledge to work.

"That boulder," he said, pointing with a foreclaw. "If we can knock it *that* way, onto that little ridge below, I think it'll bring the whole lot down."

"It looks pretty dang heavy . . ."

"I thought you were a big strong soldier. Should be easy enough for you, right?"

Tortha mock-glared at him.

They approached the boulder, which teetered promisingly at the edge of the drop. Tortha gave it an experimental nudge with her horn, but it refused to budge. She considered it for a long moment, then turned sideways and pressed the uninjured side of her torso against it. With an almighty grunt, she threw her weight against the rock and heaved.

Nothing happened.

Tortha swore and pushed again, grinding her heels in the dirt. The boulder gave the slightest creak—a wheeze of complaint—but it barely teetered half an inch before collapsing with a *humph!* back into its groove. "Flamin' feathers . . ."

Tortha braced, about to throw herself at the rock again—but Eleri raised a claw to stop her. "Wait!" he said. "You're losing too much blood."

Although she was throwing her uninjured side against the rock, the impact was still shaking her wound. It was bleeding heavily now, and Tortha looked dizzy on her feet. But there was no time to waste—the carnivores were marching forward, edging ever closer to the Mountain Kingdom.

"I can't . . ." Tortha huffed, raw with effort. "It's too heavy."

Eleri studied the base of the boulder, nestled in the dirt. With a violent pang, it reminded him of the warren's Speaking Stone, where his father had always stood to govern meetings of the herd. The image of his father swam in his mind, rippling like whispers in the dark.

Nothing like his brother . . .

Eleri shoved the memory aside, breath catching. He couldn't waste time grieving. Not yet.

Most of the clifftop was rock, but it was interwoven with

clay. A terrible spot for digging—but if he could moisten the clay, perhaps . . .

"Water!" he blurted, turning to Tortha. "Come on, follow me!"

He led her back into the trees, scrambling between conifer trunks and bristling ferns. The air grew damp as they plunged into deeper foliage, smashing through the undergrowth and heaving exhausted breaths.

"Where . . . ?" Tortha managed.

"This way!"

They burst from the trees onto a riverbank, rich with ferns. Eleri's stomach rumbled, teased by the sweet scent of river moss. High above, Astrilar's Loch crowned this part of the kingdom. This famous lake was where the hero's herd had finally settled—and where Astrilar's tale had ended. It was bordered by the Sleeping Falls, which had not flowed in generations. Only one waterfall still ran nearby, a trickling shower that gave the Tumbling Stream herd its name.

In the past, Eleri would never have trespassed in another herd's domain. It would be an insult to the Prince of the Tumbling Stream, and a grave embarrassment to Eleri's father. But his father was gone—Eleri sucked back another sharp breath—and the rules had changed.

The Tumbling Stream soldiers were down on the battlefield, and their civilians would be sheltering in caves behind the waterfall. The Carrion Kingdom's army was drawing closer by the minute—and at any moment, two hundred or more vicious carnivores would storm the Mountain Kingdom.

This was no time for inter-herd niceties.

On the riverbank, a clutch of small white flowers grew. Eleri recognized them as Healer Weeds, used by the herds of the Mountain Kingdom to treat their wounds. He ripped up several clawfuls, mashed them in his fists, and pressed them to Tortha's torso.

"We ain't got time . . . ," Tortha protested.

"I need you," Eleri said. "I can't stop that army alone."

Tortha groaned, gritting her teeth as the petals stung her wound. "This had better work, dirt muncher."

"Just trust me," Eleri said.

Farther along the riverbank, strange plants grew with enormous curved leaves. They jolted a memory in Eleri— the Tale of Reshora the Kind, a stegoceras who had used such leaves to carry water to her dying mother's nest. As the memory flared, Eleri's steps grew jerky. His father had told him the tale when he was just a hatchling, curled up sick with fever in his own nest . . .

"The leaves!" Eleri said. "We need water."

He used his claws to slice an enormous leaf from a plant, while Tortha used her teeth. Eleri filled the leaf with water and curled up its edges, holding it gingerly in his fore-claws. Tortha dragged her leaf along the ground with her mouth, spilling most of its contents—but it was better than nothing. They were running out of time.

They hurried back through the wilderness, following the path they had taken earlier. Tortha swore and abandoned her leaf when an upraised root spilled the rest of its water across the ground.

"Keep goin', I'll be back in a second!" she huffed.

Eleri kept struggling up the hill, carrying his bundle of water carefully, while Tortha bustled back toward the stream. She returned a few minutes later with bulging cheeks, her mouth full of water.

"Good idea!" Eleri rasped.

With her lips sealed, Tortha's only response was a nod.

Back at the clifftop, Tortha spewed her mouthful of water at the base of the boulder, moistening the clay. Eleri tipped out the contents of his leaf, spreading it around the edges of the rock. The carnivores were advancing below, and there was no time to retrieve another load of water. No matter what, this had to work.

With a sharp breath, he dug.

It was the hardest dirt he'd ever sliced into. Back at the warren, the earth was soft and malleable—but here, the clay was almost rock. Eleri tried to remember his lessons on digging: the best way to arch his back or angle his claws. The water helped, but his claws soon clogged with gelatinous muck. He scraped them off on the side of the rock, ignoring the slops and slurps of clay that fell away, and plunged his claws back beneath the boulder. His father's voice echoed in his mind. *Dig, dig, dig . . . One, two, three . . .*

Every swipe of his claws was an effort. His body stung with exhaustion, and his raw wounds burned. Still, Eleri pressed on. What choice did he have? The carnivores had killed his mother. His father too, in a way, by concocting this fraudulent war. Now they had come to devour the rest of his herd.

Eleri couldn't let it happen.

He *wouldn't* let it happen.

Finally, the boulder creaked. He'd carved out a deep hole at its base. Staggering backward, he offered Tortha a weary nod. "Work your magic, moonchaser."

Tortha gave him a tired grin. She looked slightly steadier, as if the Healer Weeds had eased the pain of her wound. Either that, or she was energized by the idea of crushing an army of carrion eaters under a cliff.

"Skedaddle, dirt muncher," she said. "Time to see how the professionals do it."

With an enormous bellow, she charged.

Tortha sprang upward at the moment of impact, throwing her body weight against the boulder. It rocked on the spot for a moment, before grumbling forward with a great roar. Tortha landed, scrambling to keep her footing as the boulder teetered on the cliff's edge. It rocked violently, threatening to stay in place. *One second. Two seconds. Three . . .*

The boulder toppled, crashing over the edge.

It fell in a series of heaving cracks, smashing its way down the cliff face. With a terrible groan, it slammed onto a narrow ridge below. Chunks of rock and broken trees clattered down the cliff, churning up more debris. Stones and boulders, tree trunks and pebbles . . . They all slid downward in a cavalcade of crashes.

The carrion eaters had just noticed the danger. A few cried out—and with shouts of alarm, they began to flee. The rockslide gathered speed, crashing toward them with ever-increasing heft and hustle.

"Flamin' feathers . . . ," Tortha whispered, eyes wide.

The rocks hit.

Far below, carnivores scattered. They roared, screaming in shock as rocks crashed around them. Most stood out of range of the rockslide, but their panic was rapidly creating a stampede. The army splintered into chaos, retreating from the cliffs toward the deeper Deadlands.

Fragments of stone shot into the air, smashing into some of the soldiers' heads and knocking them to the dirt. One raptor fell—and a moment later, three of its companions pounced on it, instinct driving them to gorge on fresh carrion.

Eleri stumbled back, unable to watch. Tortha hollered in triumph, and then quickly clamped down on her cry as Eleri jabbed her with a claw.

"Shh!" he hissed. "We're still exiles, remember?"

She turned, her face alight. "We did it!" she whispered, utterly elated. "We turned their plan right back on 'em, Eleri."

An odd nausea rose inside Eleri, as if his belly were threatening to crawl into his gullet. He could hear the cries and snarls from the plain below, as the soldiers feasted on their fallen comrades. He'd done this. He'd caused those deaths. Was he any better than the carrion eaters?

In a cold rush, he remembered Agostron's words. *You were different, Eleri. You were his great hope. He thought that you would save us . . . find another way for us to live—a way without wars and battles and blood . . .*

What would his parents say if they could see Eleri now? Just another warrior.

Just another killer.

But he had done it to save lives, hadn't he?

There was no easy answer.

"You're a soldier, Eleri of the Broken Ridge." Tortha's tone was fierce. "And today, you won this battle."

CHAPTER TWENTY-EIGHT
THE GENERAL

Eleri fled through ferns and brush, shrubs and shadow, his heart hammering as his wound throbbed. He tried to run lightly at first, but there was no point; Tortha smashed through the foliage with the ruckus of a dozen dinosaurs.

Gasping, they descended through the foothills into the Cold Canyon. Their march slowed as they ventured across an open expanse of rock at the base of the ravine, but saw no sign of pursuit. The soldiers, it seemed, were too busy on the battlefield to worry about two rogue exiles.

"Tortha! Eleri!" a delighted voice called, somewhere in the shadows ahead. "Over here!"

Sorielle rushed forward to greet them, bouncing on her toes in excitement. "We heard the enormous explosion! Did our plan work? Did you blow up the main tunnel?"

They nodded wearily.

"Oh, that's just wonderful!" Sorielle beamed. "I knew you could do it, I simply knew it. What a marvelous job you've done. Did you see the rockslide? Oh, it gave us such a fright! That was jolly good luck, wasn't it? Sent the carnivores running with their tails between their legs."

"From a broken sky the dark stars fall," Lerithon mused.

"That was us!" Tortha said proudly.

Sorielle gaped. "What?"

"We caused the rockslide," Eleri said.

Sorielle stared, eyes bulging. Then she bounced again, overcome by fresh excitement. "Oh my, that's so clever of you! I bet those carnivores will be absolutely fuming . . . Did you speak to your father, Eleri? Did you tell him how our kings have betrayed us?"

Eleri shook his head, mouth dry.

It hit him, suddenly, that their true plan had failed. Yes, they had stopped the tunnel invasion. Yes, they had sent the carnivores running. But they had not shared the truth with their herds—or united their kin against the Carrion Kingdom.

Agostron would never vouch for Eleri. In all likelihood, he would tell the other herd leaders that Eleri had sparked an explosion to attack the Broken Ridge, not to save it. In their eyes, Eleri was no hero of the Mountain Kingdom.

He was a traitor twice over.

Tortha and Sorielle had no leverage to speak to their

own herds—by destroying the tunnel, they had ruined the Prairie Alliance's plans. The exiles had cemented their status as outlaws, never to be trusted.

And what evidence did they have of a planned invasion? The Carrion Army had scattered, vanishing back into the Deadlands.

The others spent the next ten minutes in riotous conversation, trading their tales of success. Sorielle gasped when Tortha described the fight between the brothers—but Eleri's heart wasn't quite in it. He hung back, emotions tangling as he remembered Agostron's words. *He thought that you would save us . . . find another way . . .*

And not just his father. His mother too. If Agostron was right, she had secretly dreamed of ending the war.

Eleri forced the memory down. He couldn't think about it now. They were still in enemy territory, with their lives hanging by a thread. Later, he could reflect on Agostron's words. Later, he could come to terms with his father's loss—and in a way, his mother's too.

But for now, he fixed his attention on Zyre.

The anurognathid was silent. She perched on Lerithon's back, her expression impossible to read. Eleri stared at her, his foreclaws closing tight. This wasn't the time for confrontation. They had to get out of here, to flee, to escape . . . but the words bubbled out of him, inescapable as tar.

"My brother paid you."

His accusation hung in the air, sharp and stilted. Tortha

263

cut her story off midsentence, bewildered by this sudden shift in conversation. She turned to Eleri, tilting her head in a silent question.

Zyre stared at Eleri. She did not speak.

"He paid you to follow me," Eleri said. "To make sure I never came back."

Every muscle in the group tightened, and a low growl escaped Tortha. Eleri's words tasted bitter on his tongue, but his gaze didn't waver from the windwhisper's face.

Finally, Zyre raised her eyes. She swallowed, as if struggling for a response. When she finally found it, her confession was a waterfall of words, tumbling into the night. "I didn't know he was your brother. But whoever he was, he paid me to follow you, and to sell you to the carnivores."

Tortha started forward, bristling. "You filthy little—"

"Wait!" Eleri stepped in front of Tortha. "If anyone's going to deal with her, it should be me."

Tortha scuffed her claw in the dirt, taut with rage. But then she gave a shaky nod, stepping back and allowing Eleri forward.

Silence.

"How much?" Eleri wasn't sure that he wanted to know the answer, but he couldn't hold back the question. "How much was my life worth to Agostron?"

"Twenty starflecks."

Tortha gave a low whistle.

"You only had one starfleck," Eleri said. "Did my brother give it to you? An advance payment?"

Zyre gave a slow nod.

Eleri's throat tightened. "But then you gave it to me. In the Forest of Smoke, you gave it to me—and it saved my life. Why?"

"I couldn't do it," Zyre whispered. "I couldn't just let you die."

"Not even for twenty starflecks?"

"No. Not even for that."

"Why not?"

"You were trying to save us all."

Zyre's words hung between them, soft and flaking. They did not echo or boom throughout the canyon. They simply dangled, a whisper of the nightstruck wind. And as he stared at her, his chest heavy, Eleri knew that she was telling the truth.

"Forgive me," Zyre whispered. "I've helped you before, haven't I? Please, let me help you again."

Tortha gave a low hiss.

"Zyre," Eleri said slowly, "I can't just—"

"We should discuss this later." Sorielle shifted uneasily. "The carnivores are still out there, and I should think they'll be keen for revenge. We should escape before—"

Across the canyon, a clawstep crunched.

Eleri spun, his instincts tingling. Breath by breath, a pack of silhouettes skulked into view. They slipped from the shadows behind a group of trees and boulders, their bodies taking form as they slid into the moonlight.

A squadron of raptors. At their head stood a familiar figure: an enormous tyrannosaur, her teeth gleaming. Eleri's skin chilled as he recognized her: General Korvia, the monstrous beast who had chased Eleri from the oasis larder. Her muscles were the size of tree branches, with claws that could slice Eleri open like a tuft of sweetferns. From the glint in her eye, she would be delighted to do it.

"Keen for revenge?" General Korvia asked, a hungry twist at the corner of her mouth. "Oh, you have no idea."

"That's them!" one of the raptors blurted. "That's them, General—the ones who tricked us! The oryctodromeus and the triceratops."

Eleri blinked, staring at the speaker—and with a shock, he recognized him. It was Yirian, one of the raptors who had dragged him to their oasis larder. Beside him stood Thystril, his companion.

"Indeed?" General Korvia tilted her great head, studying the exiles thoughtfully. "So tonight is not the first time these brats have caused us trouble."

"Not in the slightest," Thystril said, his voice barely a hiss. "May we have the pleasure, General?"

General Korvia considered for a moment. Then she gave a slow nod, the corners of her mouth curving—and revealing a flash of vicious teeth. "They gave you the slip once before. I think it's only right that you redeem yourselves."

In unison, the raptors pounced.

With a churn of dust and gravel, Tortha roared her battle cry and hurtled forward. Zyre shot skyward with a shriek, skittering beyond the reach of claws. Sorielle was right beside Tortha, galloping in a roil of nervous energy, while Lerithon raised his great tail in preparation to sweep their attackers aside.

Their bodies met. Yirian and Thystril ran straight at Tortha, furious that the triceratops had tricked them. Four other raptors hurtled toward Lerithon, while Eleri seemed forgotten in the chaos.

He glanced around, desperate for a way to help his friends. Sorielle and Tortha reared back-to-back, crashing down with their great legs to fend off their attackers. Judging them safe for now, Eleri scrambled toward Lerithon. The starsweeper was bellowing, his legs bleeding as the raptors gouged his shins.

"No!" Eleri shouted. A raptor dug its claws into Lerithon's chest and clung on, climbing up the sauropod's side and scoring wounds into his skin. Its eyes were crazed as it scrambled upward, aiming for the base of the sauropod's throat . . .

Eleri leaped.

He hit the raptor from the side, sending it hurtling into Lerithon, as if smashing an insect against a rock. Eleri and the raptor both fell, limbs entangled as the raptor snapped and snarled. Eleri landed on top of the predator, who was temporarily stunned by the *thwack!* of the rocks beneath him. Eleri scrambled away, barely avoiding a lethal snap of teeth.

The moonlight vanished.

Eleri looked up, stomach churning, as a huge figure loomed above him. General Korvia stood tall and fierce enough to block the moon. She bent slowly, studying him, a vicious smirk between her teeth.

"What's your name, little earthsinger?" she hissed.

Eleri glared at her, defiant.

"If you don't tell me, I'll climb into the Mountain King-dom and find your herd." Korvia's voice was eerily slow. This wasn't a blustering threat. It was a calm, calculated statement of fact. "I'll crush their warren. I'll wait until they crawl out, kicking and screaming—and then I'll end them. One. By. One."

Silence. Eleri was vaguely aware of the fighting around him: the clangs and roars and shrieks. But his head rang with the horror of her threat. Korvia could do it. She could walk right up that mountain to the Broken Ridge, and nothing could stop her. Agostron and his little gang of bodyguards wouldn't stand a chance.

"Eleri," he said. "My name is Eleri."

". . . of the?"

"Of the Deadlands," he said quickly. "I'm an exile. We're all exiles. There's no one you can hurt to punish us."

The general studied him, her head twisting. Then she

gave a slow nod, as if she'd decided to believe him. "Well, Eleri of the Deadlands, you and your little friends have caused me a great deal of trouble tonight."

Eleri didn't respond.

"My soldiers are hungry, you see. So, so hungry. There has been discontent in the ranks. We promised them a feast tonight. A feast to end all feasts." She bent closer, her eyes narrow slits of fury. "Tonight was our chance to end the discontent. A chance to save our kingdom."

Eleri knew, at that moment, that his life was over. The fury in her eyes looked lethal, let alone the glint of her claws. But even so, he refused to cower. He would go down with his head held high—and he would fight back any way he could, even if it was only with words.

He was a storyteller, after all.

"Hey, at least a few of 'em got fed," he said. "Thanks to our rockslide, I mean. Shouldn't you be thanking us?"

A low, cold growl leaked between Korvia's teeth. "I will thank you, Eleri of the Deadlands, by giving you a taste of the pain that you have caused my army tonight."

"Nah, I'm good," Eleri said. "Always found ferns tastier than corpses, you see."

The tyrannosaur reared, her entire body tight with rage. She opened her great jaws, revealing a row of glistening teeth.

In that moment of fury, Eleri leaped.

It wasn't a particularly nimble leap. It was a mad, wild

tumble. But instead of scrambling backward, as Korvia had expected, he hurled himself forward—right beneath her enormous body. The tyrannosaur snarled, perplexed as she snapped at empty air.

Eleri struck.

He pounced upward, raking his claws across her lower belly. The tyrannosaur screamed, bending and swiping again in fury—but it was too late. Eleri ducked beneath her tail, darted out behind her, and dashed around to her side. Memories of Tortha's combat lesson rushed through his mind: *Be fast, be agile. Be as annoying as an insect, too fast and small to catch . . .*

He might be small, but he wasn't slow.

Korvia roared, stomping around to the side—but Eleri was already gone. He vaulted beneath her again, hurtled up, and slashed a fresh wound across her underbelly. The general staggered backward, almost crushing Eleri by accident.

Half a second later, Zyre struck.

The tiny anurognathid dove straight for Korvia's face. Her claws raked the general's left eye—and the tyrannosaur staggered again, screaming in agony. Blood poured from her eye socket and she reared backward, half-blinded.

By sheer luck, Eleri swerved to his left and escaped her wild stamping. "Come on!" he shouted, darting back toward his friends, who were still locked in combat with the raptors. "Lerithon's tunnel!"

It was the only choice. The place where Lerithon had

been exiled, cast from the Cold Canyon into the dark. It led to the labyrinth beneath the Deadlands—and eventually, to the underground river. Still, it was a terrible risk. If they lost their way in that pitch-black maze . . .

They ran.

The world was a blur of shouts and chaos. Eleri's friends barreled behind him like thunderclaps. Zyre zipped overhead, breathing a succession of panicky rasps, before she succumbed to the pain of her bruised wings and landed on Sorielle's back.

They hurtled into the dark maw of Lerithon's tunnel. The raptors shrieked behind them, skittering along in pursuit. Their injuries slowed them—but even so, they were gaining ground.

"Right!" Eleri choked out.

Their only hope was to lose the pursuit in the tunnels, leaving the raptors scattered through the underground labyrinth. They dodged and darted, choosing random paths whenever the tunnel forked. Tortha swore as she struggled on, hissing curses at her wounded side. Sorielle's breath came in wheezes, echoed by the weight of Lerithon's footfalls. Occasionally, a glowing streak of foliage would add a faint layer of gray to the black—but for the most part, they ran in darkness.

"Which way?" Tortha demanded, gasping for breath as they stumbled into another junction.

Surprisingly, it was Lerithon who stepped forward. His great neck curved down to face one of the tunnels, lit by the glow of a nearby frond. "Once, one found a grove of dreams within the dark . . ."

The phrase was oddly familiar. Eleri stared, struggling to remember where he'd heard it before. Not too long ago, Lerithon had said something very similar, but Eleri couldn't quite place the memory.

"You remember this place?" he said. "From when you first got exiled—before you joined us?"

Lerithon gave a pendulous nod. "From then . . . and from before. Many lives ago, before the bones of this land were scorched by mist and flame . . ." His face crinkled, hinting at a wistful smile. "Long ago, these tunnels sang. Ancient creatures lived and died here, sleeping in the shine."

"Ooh, you've had a vision of this tunnel?" Sorielle said hopefully. "From before the Time of the Fallen Star?"

"Great," Tortha muttered. "Sounds like reliable military intel."

But Lerithon was already moving, heaving his massive frame toward the tunnel he had chosen.

The path coiled, tangling like bracken. With every twist and fork, the number of clawsteps behind them dwindled. Seven raptors, six, five, four . . . Finally, just three sets of claws clattered behind them.

Three enemies.

In the dark, in close quarters, three raptors were enough to kill them. Perhaps not all of them, but the weaker members of their group. And with a cold twist in his belly, Eleri knew that he would be the easiest target.

Eleri staggered on, his muscles throbbing. They were done. Their bodies heaved, their wounds bled, and their lungs struggled to choke down the dark. And yet still they ran, until they neared a junction between tunnels. A cracked atrium of stone, with passages branching in different directions . . .

"Stop!" Lerithon cried.

His great voice echoed, ricocheting off the tunnel walls. Eleri jerked to a halt . . . and before him, a mass of thorny vines engulfed the junction. Some snaked across the tunnel roof like a spider's web, but most sprawled across the floor: a tangle of spikes, lit by a few rare luminescent blooms.

Eleri's heart jolted. With a horrific lurch, he recognized the plants. "Murkthorns!"

These rare vines grew in some of the deepest valleys of the Mountain Kingdom. Even so, Eleri had seen them only once before in his life. His knowledge of them came not from experience, but from a story.

Claws clenching, he remembered the origin of Lerithon's words. *Once, one found a grove of dreams within the dark* . . . The starsweeper had used that phrase before, halfway through the Tale of Yari the Strong.

According to the story, murkthorn spikes were poisonous— not enough to kill, but enough to plunge their victims into hours of feverish sleep. If the exiles had blundered into that grove of thorns, they'd have lost consciousness in minutes.

If Lerithon hadn't cried out . . .

"We can edge around the thorns," Sorielle whispered, her voice raw. "There's space to squeeze past, to reach the leftmost tunnel . . ."

But Eleri hesitated, staring at the murkthorn grove. This was danger . . . but it was also an opportunity. Perhaps it was the greatest opportunity they'd been handed tonight. If they were going to take a stand, this was their chance.

"Sorielle, Lerithon, keep going!" Eleri whispered. "Take the left tunnel, like you said. We need to keep up the sound of running, to draw them forward quickly."

Zyre fluttered down from Sorielle's back, barely visible in the glow of the murkthorn blooms.

"And what about us?" Tortha's voice was a nervous hiss. "We just sit 'round here and have a sing-along, do we?"

"No," Eleri said. "We set an ambush."

BLOOD IN THE WATER

It was too dark to see the others properly, but Eleri assumed they were nodding. At the very least, no one protested.

Sorielle drew an exhausted breath and ventured onward, edging around the outskirts of the murkthorn grove. Lerithon lumbered after her, careful to avoid any poisonous spikes. The pair moved slowly, guided by the shine of luminescent vines.

When Sorielle reached the leftmost tunnel, she slapped her tail against the rocky floor and walls as she ran, mimicking the sound of a larger herd fleeing into the dark. Lerithon stomped heavily, kicking up dust and stone as he vanished after her.

Once their two decoys were gone, Eleri sprang into action. Rearing on his hind legs, he swiped at a dark tendril of vine from the ceiling. He was careful to grip a bare patch of vine, without any stray thorns to pierce his skin. "Help me, Tortha!"

He didn't need to explain. She grabbed the other end of the vine with her teeth, heading back along the tunnel. Their chosen vine hosted only one luminescent bloom, which Eleri stripped away. Without it, their trap was invisible in the dark.

Together, he and Tortha drew the vine across the floor before the mass of murkthorns, standing at opposite edges of the grove.

"Hold it tight!" Eleri hissed.

He couldn't make out Tortha's expression, but from her insulted huff, it seemed a fair guess that she was glaring at him.

The trio of raptors sidled along the tunnel toward them. Eleri and Tortha remained dead still, as motionless as boulders. Zyre perched in darkness, waiting in silence for their ambush to unfold.

Scratch. Scratch. Scratch.

The raptors' claws dragged on the rocks. Somewhere ahead, Sorielle and Lerithon were making a decent commotion—and as their echoes slapped back into the junction cave, the raptors picked up their pace. They were gaining on their prey.

Scratch, scratch, scratch . . .

The first two raptors skittered forward, fast and ravenous, and hurtled straight into Eleri's trip wire. They hit the vine with a startling twang, crying out as murkthorns pierced their lower legs.

Eleri lost his grip, but it didn't matter. The thorns had pricked the raptors—and the damage was done. With a startled cry, the first raptor stumbled into the larger mass of murkthorns. Its cry became a gurgle as more thorns stabbed its skin and it slumped, sinking into unconsciousness. Half a moment later, the second followed, yowling and hissing as it collapsed to the tunnel floor. With each leg jabbed by multiple thorns, the killers should lie comatose for hours.

The third raptor hesitated. It glanced around, straining to assess the danger—and its gaze settled on Eleri.

They had come so close to a miraculous defeat of the raptors, but it appeared the exiles' luck had run out. The raptor's eyes were crazed, alight with rage and hunger as it prepared to leap . . .

Eleri braced himself for a storm of deadly claws and teeth.

But as it lunged, Zyre struck. The tiny anurognathid dive-bombed the raptor, aiming for its eyes with a wild shriek.

The raptor instinctively blinked, wrenching its head away. Eleri darted aside as Tortha's tail whipped backward, slapping the creature with all the force of a sapling in a storm. The raptor gave a strangled cry as it flew backward, flung against the tunnel wall. It hit the stones with a dull thump and slumped, unconscious.

"'Hold it tight'?" Tortha snapped. "What do you take me for, a total numbskull?"

"Not a total one, no . . ."

Tortha ground her teeth. This was no time for quibbling, but her tone made it quite clear she was half-tempted to shove Eleri into the murkthorn grove as well. "Come on, dirt muncher—let's go!"

Eleri didn't need telling twice. The other raptors might have been lost in the tunnels—but with a few unlucky twists and turns, their paths could cross again at any moment.

Eleri and Tortha slipped around the edge of the grove, following their friends into the leftmost tunnel. Zyre flitted behind them, her wings beating a percussive patter in the dark. It didn't take long for the three of them to catch up, since Lerithon's progress was slowed by the narrow passage.

"Are you all right?" Sorielle asked.

"We're fine!" Eleri's throat was tight. "Just keep going . . ."

Again, Lerithon took the lead. The exiles hurried on, pushing their bodies, near the brink of collapse. Every step ached. Every breath quaked. Yet still they ran, filling the tunnel with echoes as they fought to keep the air in their lungs.

"Hear that?" Tortha rasped. "Ahead . . ."

Eleri strained, but a wave of dizziness crashed over him. He shook his head, fighting to focus—and suddenly, he heard it too. A faint gurgle. A melody. A whisper . . .

Eleri's voice cracked. "The underground river!"

"A path to home may sing of souls," Lerithon said, his tone solemn. "Once before I have met this place."

"Do you know the way?" Sorielle asked eagerly. "Back to the Grotto?"

Lerithon considered this for a long moment before nodding his great head. "The stars have led one home before. In times of fear, one cannot forget how darkness lies."

"I'll take that as a 'yes,'" Eleri said.

He scrambled onto the riverside ridge—and with a series of exhausted huffs, the others plunged into the river. They strained against the current, lungs raw and limbs trembling. The tunnel forked. The river twisted.

Lerithon did not waver.

And through a maze of lightless water, the starsweeper led them home.

CHAPTER THIRTY

THE HERD

In the Grotto, the exiles slept.

The night passed. A day whispered by. Another night closed in, wrapping them in a bristle of sweetferns and lichen. Eleri woke only for his shifts on sentry duty—but there was no sign of pursuit.

For now, it seemed, they were safe.

On the second night, they stirred from their stupor. Eleri mashed fistfuls of healing herbs and slathered them across their wounds. Tortha was still weak, her torso slashed by the icicle, but the bleeding had stopped. After a long rest, she was able to stagger across to the river and take a drink—and even nibble at a few ferns.

"I'm so glad you're feeling better, Tori!" Sorielle said.

Tortha swallowed her mouthful of ferns and glared. "If you call me that one more time, *Sori*, I'll drag you up to the Carrion Kingdom as a peace offerin'."

As her threat lingered in the air, Eleri fought back a laugh of relief. They were going to be all right.

They spent the night in quiet conversation, sharing tales of their ordeal. It helped, somehow, to speak it aloud. To tell the others of his fear as he'd tiptoed across the Cavern of Teeth. His panic as the icicles had crashed around him.

His horror as his brother had raised his claws.

But he didn't speak of his grief. Not yet. That was one emotion he wasn't ready to share. As the night tightened and the others slipped into weary sleep, Eleri volunteered for sentry duty. He sat by the river, staring into its depths. It rippled, black and hungry. His mind roiled as he remembered his father, standing alone at the Mountain Court.

His father, voting to save him.

Agostron's cold words echoed in the back of his skull. *He thought that you would save us, you know . . . find another way for us to live . . .*

Eleri stared into the depths. His father was gone. His mother too, with her secret dreams of peace. But perhaps— just perhaps—Eleri hadn't been a disappointment after all. He hadn't ended the war, nor had he united the Mountain Kingdom with the Prairie Alliance. He hadn't exposed their kings' treachery. But by destroying the tunnel, he'd bought them time. He'd bought them hope. He'd used a story to inspire himself, bringing the legend of Astrilar the Wise to life once more.

And for now, perhaps that was all he could wish for. To honor his parents' wishes, he must be strong. He must fight to save the herd that had rejected him—not with muscle or strength, but with his mind.

And with his stories.

In the dark, a faint flutter cut the silence. Eleri turned, startled—but it was only Zyre, skittering across the cave. She had kept to herself since the battle, avoiding Tortha's wrath and Sorielle's disappointment. Now she perched beside Eleri like a defendant at the Mountain Court, waiting for judgment.

"You fought beside us," Eleri said.

"I was paid to kill you."

"But you didn't."

A long pause.

"No," Zyre said. "I didn't."

"Not much of a spy, really," Eleri said. "Aren't you supposed to put client loyalty above all else?"

"Profit isn't personal. That's what my parents always told me."

"And this?" Eleri gestured vaguely at the cave, where the rest of the exiles slumbered. "This place? These . . . allies? Is this personal for you?"

Zyre gave a jolting nod.

Eleri watched her for a long moment, his insides tight.

He thought of Agoston, paying this tiny spy to betray his location. To sell him to the carnivores. Zyre had agreed to do it, hadn't she? She had agreed to kill him, to fill her pouch with starflecks.

But she hadn't done it.

Zyre had saved them—not once, but many times. She had risked as much as any of them to end the war, and she had sacrificed more than most. And so Eleri gave a slow nod, turning his gaze back to the river.

"Me too," he said.

They sat in silence, watching the water weave its story through the dark.

As dawn broke, the exiles gathered at the Speaking Stone. It sat in the heart of the Grotto, casting silent shadows on the cave floor. Zyre perched at the edge of the group—as if she longed to join them but hadn't quite found the confidence.

Not yet, at least.

"What now?" Tortha asked finally. Her voice was a rasp, but stronger than before. Her old belligerence was creeping back in, lending her strength and purpose. "We've still gotta stop this war."

"We have to unite our kingdoms," Eleri said. "Together, we're stronger. Together, we can stand against the carnivores. Not soldiers of the Mountain Kingdom, or of the Prairie Alliance . . . but soldiers of Cretacea."

"But how?" Tortha demanded. "We've done all we can, and our herds are still fightin'. They're still dyin'."

"The Carrion Kingdom is still out there," Eleri said. "Their army might've scattered, but I'm sure they'll regroup. They've got the Fire Peak as their sanctuary, somewhere to hide away and lick their wounds. But we've got an advantage, don't we? They think their plans are secret, with them lurking out here in the Deadlands . . . but we're out here too."

Silence.

"We can spy on them." Eleri glanced at Zyre. "We can gather evidence—we'll find proof that they're planning to invade, and that our kings have betrayed us. If we do that, we can finally bring our herds together."

"The stars burn," Lerithon said quietly. "They are at war with the night: explosions of fire and ash and destruction. Still, their light may guide a weary traveler."

They all considered this.

"You're saying that something good can come out of this?" Eleri asked finally. "Even something destructive can lead to new hope?"

Lerithon bowed his head.

Silence curled around the group once again. Droplets trickled down the back wall, plunking a quiet little rhythm on the stones. Eleri looked at the river, staring once more into the black.

"Eleri," Sorielle said, "can you tell us a story?"

Eleri blinked. "What, right now?"

"Go on, dirt muncher," Tortha said. "Can't think of a better time."

Eleri stared, taken aback by her response. He cast his mind through the stories in his skull. He could recite countless sagas of Cretacean history, from the Tale of Scyliara the Lost to that of Jyrok the Cunning. But none of them seemed to fit the occasion. None of them depicted the dirt, the grime, the blood, the weariness . . .

The hope.

Eleri drew a deep breath. "This story is called the Tale of the Grotto Herd. It's the tale of a warrior, a spy, a genius, a traveler . . . and a storyteller." He paused. "A herd not based on species, or bloodline, or kingdom. A herd based on survival. On courage. On trust."

The river whispered. As dawn broke outside, trickles of light leaked into the cave, painting tiny stars on the riverbank.

And in the quiet, Eleri of the Grotto told his story.

ACKNOWLEDGMENTS

First, a huge thank-you to Tracey and the team at Adams Literary—this book might never have existed without your help and guidance. Thanks also to the Henry Holt team, including Claire Maby, Mia Moran, Carina Licon, Jackie Dever, Jessica White, Kelly Markus, and Ann Marie Wong. I am especially grateful to Brian Geffen, who threw his support behind this manuscript and led our little dino buddies on their journey to publication.

Many thanks to the Goosemoot crew, including Nic, Ellie, Liz, Kate, Eliza, Peta, and Ebony. I owe an extra special thanks to Amie and Lili, who both read early drafts of this book and offered such insightful feedback. After my hiatus from writing, you gave me the motivation I needed to get back on the horse (or rather, the dinosaur).

As always, thanks to my amazing parents for your love and support—and for being such excellent sounding boards for plot ideas!

Sending a giant hug to Jason for your love, patience, and encouragement. I remember babbling about my ideas for this story while we lined up outside the art gallery on one of our earliest dates. In the years since, my ideas became a book and our relationship became a marriage. I couldn't have done this without you.

Above all, thank you to my readers. I hope that you have fun joining me on this new adventure!

SKYE MELKI-WEGNER started writing as soon
as she could hold a pen. She was immediately drawn to fantasy,
and soon her notebooks overflowed with dragons, pixies, and
wizards. After graduating with an honors degree in law, she
traded in practicing law for writing fantasy novels. Her first
middle grade trilogy, The Deadlands, draws inspiration from
her time working in a museum (where some of her colleagues
were dinosaurs).